KILLING JOHNNY FRY

Devil in a Blue Dress
A Red Death
White Butterfly
Black Betty
RL's Dream
A Little Yellow Dog
Gone Fishin'
Always Outnumbered, Always Outgunned
Blue Light
Walkin' the Dog
Workin' on the Chain Gang
Fearless Jones
Futureland
Bad Boy Brawly Brown
Six Easy Pieces
What Next
Fear Itself
The Man in My Basement
Little Scarlet
47
Cinnamon Kiss
Life out of Context
The Wave
Fortunate Son
Fear of the Dark

Edited by Walter Mosley
Black Genius
The Best American Short Stories 2003
Maximum Fantastic Four

KILLING JOHNNY FRY
A SEXISTENTIAL NOVEL

WALTER MOSLEY

BLOOMSBURY

First published 2007

Copyright © 2007 by Walter Mosley

The moral right of the author has been asserted

Lyrics from 'Isis' by Bob Dylan copyright © 1975 by Ram's Horn Music.
All rights reserved. International copyright secured. Reprinted by permission.

Bloomsbury Publishing Plc, 36 Soho Square, London W1D 3QY

A CIP catalogue record is available from the British Library

ISBN 9780747586081

10 9 8 7 6 5 4 3 2 1

All papers used by Bloomsbury Publishing are natural, recyclable products
made from wood grown in well-managed forests. The manufacturing
processes conform to the environmental regulations of the county of origin.

Printed in the United States of America by Quebecor World Fairfield for you

I decided to kill Johnny Fry on a Wednesday, but it was a week before that I was given the reason. I'm almost embarrassed about my decision to take a life. It was so pedestrian really.

It all started on the day I had lunch with Lucy Carmichael at the Petit Pain Café on Amsterdam near 80th Street. Lucy wanted to show me her portfolio because she hoped that I could get her connected with Brad Mettleman, an art gallery agent who loved to take advantage of straw-haired, blue-eyed young women.

I had met Lucy at a conference of commercial French translators. She was there with her mother. Mrs. Helen Carmichael was a textile importer who needed someone to help her read correspondence from Francophone African nations. She couldn't pay even my low rates, but her daughter was beautiful, so I talked to her about university alternatives, taking sidelong glances at the lovely young woman.

After a while it came out that Lucy, the daughter, was just back from Darfur, where she had taken photographs of starving children. I let it drop that I had done work for Brad Mettleman.

"The photographers' agent?" Lucy said. "I met him one time. He visited my Art-as-a-Business class at NYU. I'd love to get in touch with him. You know it's important for an American audience to see what's happening to these people."

"I'd be happy to introduce you," I said.

I didn't mean it, but Lucy took my number and invited me to come with her and her parents to a gallery opening that night.

1

When we parted, Lucy kissed me on the cheek, right at the border of the corner of my mouth.

I knew that Brad would love her. She was slight but well formed, with blond hair that reminded you of a sunny day. Her blue eyes were severe and her face was stern, which, on a beautiful girl like her, gave the impression of passionate intensity.

I say that Brad took advantage of young women, but the women I'm thinking of never complained. Certainly I was having lunch with Lucy because she was fair-haired and quite lovely. She had a habit of putting her hand on your forearm and looking you in the eye whenever she talked to you.

While I was going through the photographs of young children of the Sudan, I was thinking about the kiss she'd leave me with as I put her in a cab to take her back home to the East Village or Dumbo or whatever artists' community she was living in.

"Politics and art are inseparable," the young woman was saying as I thumbed my way through the stiff sheets of suffering and death.

The large-eyed children looked to be at the end of their recuperative powers. I wondered how many of the Sudanese orphans were still alive. I wondered also why I didn't seem to care about their fates. It was, of course, awful what was happening in Darfur. Children were dying from being deprived of the most basic necessities. They were being displaced, slaughtered, enslaved, raped. But what got my heart going was the expectation of Lucy Carmichael's moist peck on the corner of my mouth.

"It's powerful work," I remember saying. "I'm sure Brad would be very excited about it."

I was also sure that he'd want more than a provocative kiss for representing her to one of the dozen galleries he worked with around Midtown.

"Do you think so?" Lucy asked, putting a hand on my bare wrist.

I looked down at the almost porcelain-white fingertips pressing against my dark brown skin.

When I think back on it, it was that touch, as much as anything else, that brought on Johnny Fry's death sentence. My tongue went completely dry, and no matter how much bottled mineral water I drank, I was still thirsty. That thirst and what I did to slake it were the first two nails in Mr. Fry's coffin.

My breathing became shallow but my heart was thumping hard. I leaned forward three inches. Lucy did not retreat. I had the definite feeling that she wouldn't have turned away from a kiss right then.

I was twice her age, minus a year, but she didn't move her hand or her face. She kept smiling and staring.

I exhaled through my nostrils, quite loudly it seemed to my ears, and all sorts of serious thoughts entered my mind. I had met Lucy's father at that gallery opening in NoLita. The short, balding, white man was a year younger than I. His daughter was coming to me for help and she had a young boyfriend named Billy who was living in Boston, working for a theater company there.

And then there was Joelle, my girlfriend—hell, we might as well have been married. I stayed at her place every weekend and we'd been together eight years—longer by far than both my marriages put together.

There was an understanding between Joelle and I that we'd be monogamous. We didn't have to get married or make some kind of material commitment. She made a good living as a freelance marketing expert for fashion and design companies, while I did all right translating from French and Spanish to English for small businesses, technical companies, and private parties.

"We have separate lives that are lived together," Joelle told her younger sister, August, when the latter complained about my intentions.

"He's a man and is therefore a dog," August told her older sister.

"I know him better than you," Joelle told me she'd said. "He's a good man and would never hurt me."

Lucy's hand remained on my wrist through that long train of thought. Her smile had not dimmed. I wanted to lean over that extra six inches and brush those young lips with my hungry mouth. I wanted to but I didn't.

I had already strained my agreement with Jo by telling her I was going to Philadelphia that noon when really my train didn't leave until five. Actually, my train reservation had been for noon, but I'd asked my travel agent to get me a first-class ticket, and she couldn't get first-class before the five o'clock train. By the time I realized I was leaving on the later train, I'd already told Joelle that I was slated to leave at midday. It was after that that Lucy called, following up on my promise to connect her with Brad. I had only made the offer so she'd stay near me. But I felt an obligation—and there was the possibility of that good-bye kiss.

I pulled my hand back and poured another glass full of sparkling water. I drank it down in one thirsty swig.

The blue eyes across from me sparkled, and Lucy's shoulder came forward an inch or so. *Too bad*, the gesture said. *Maybe next time.*

I walked her out to the curb and put her in a taxi. Just before she got in, I promised to call Brad. She kissed me on the lips quickly and then gave me a brilliant smile.

I stood there on the corner of 80th and Amsterdam watching the taxi wend its way westward through heavy traffic. I remember thinking that I could keep up with the cab on foot. I had to stop myself from following and waving at her.

4

When she was finally gone, I realized that I had to go to the bathroom—all that mineral water I downed while watching the curve of Lucy's violet blouse with the lime buttons.

I had the key to Joelle's apartment. The doormen knew me by sight. She was across the river, meeting with a boutique jeans distributor from Newark. I'd go upstairs, do my business, and then call her cell phone and ask her to guess where I was. That would assuage my guilt by letting her know I was still in town.

Robert, the day man, wasn't at his post at her building on 91st and Central Park West. I loped down the hallway toward the third bank of elevators and took car number sixteen to the twenty-third floor.

Joelle had inherited this apartment from her grandmother, who'd died twelve years before, when Jo was just twenty. It was a big place. The entrance area led to a hall that came upon a sunken living room, which had large windows that looked out over the park. I loved staying at Joelle's place.

I was happy that I hadn't made a move on Lucy.

They were so silent that I almost walked in on them. Jo was sitting on the top part of the back of the couch. Her black blouse was pulled up to her armpits, above her breasts, and her black pants were almost off—except for the bottom leg, which somehow clung to her left ankle. John Fry wore only a gray silk T-shirt. He was standing there between her legs teasing her sex with his erection.

She was staring into his eyes, her copper-brown hands gripping his pale white chest and left shoulder. He looked as if he were concentrating on something inside him. Maybe he was holding back. Maybe he was playing with her.

They kept at that game for some time.

I noticed that he was wearing a condom—a red one. For some reason the color made me angry. At times he'd enter her deeply.

These were the only moments that she made any sound. A kind of moan that came out as "oh" and, now and then, a "please don't."

I wondered, almost idly, if she would tell me later that she tried to stop him; that she'd told him no.

After a while I turned away because I couldn't seem to think while watching them.

Looking down the hall toward the door, I knew that I should go. There was no benefit in confronting them. John Fry was bigger than I was (in every way) and I had no weapon with which to hurt him. And, after all, Joelle was not my wife. We stayed together often, but it was her apartment.

I decided to leave.

I walked down the hallway toward the door.

I had made it through the front door and took the first three steps down the hall when Jo emitted a loud, pain-filled scream. I hurried back down the hall and into the apartment without thinking. It was almost as if I had forgotten what I'd seen before. All I could think was that my girlfriend, my lover, was in pain.

When I got back to the vantage point onto the living room, I realized my error. Jo was on her stomach on the floor and John Fry hovered over her, pressing down slowly with his hips. I could see the red shaft pressing deep and deeper into her rectum. He was whispering into her ear words that I heard only as a rumble. She was nodding vigorously, saying, "Yes, yes. Oh yes, Daddy."

Daddy.

I made it to the hall again. Again there was a shout of ecstasy. But this time I pushed the elevator button and took car number eighteen down to the first floor.

"Hello, Mr. Carmel," Robert, the doorman, said as I approached his desk.

There was a wary look in his eye. I could tell that he knew about

Johnny Fry and Jo. He was her doorman. Every Christmas she gave him a $200 tip. He wasn't going to burn that bridge. No, sir.

I took my wallet out of my pocket and said, "Funniest thing. I came by because I thought I left my wallet here, but halfway up in the elevator I looked in my briefcase and there it was. I never put it here, but I guess I did this time. Sorry I didn't check in, but you weren't here."

I didn't know how long the doorman had been away from his post, but it didn't matter. He wasn't going to tell Joelle about me if he didn't have to.

Our business was finished, but I loitered a moment more. Robert (I never knew his last name) had lighter skin than mine, and there was some crimson in the pigment. His eyes might have had a mild Asian cast and his accent was definitely not of the United States.

"You follow boxing?" I asked him, thinking that Jo was probably shouting upstairs and realizing with a mild shock that I had not closed the door to her apartment.

Would she and Johnny Fry laugh at the open door? Would they imagine her neighbors stopping to listen to her screams of ecstasy?

"No," Robert said. "I like football. You know, soccer."

"See you later," I said.

I walked out of the building, the Eliot, and headed south on Central Park West.

To my right were the monolithic residential apartment buildings and to the left was Central Park. I followed that path down to the Museum of Natural History. I went in there hoping to use the men's room. I bought a ticket, located the toilet, and then wandered around the exhibit of North American mammals.

The wolves running in the night were magnificent. At one time those taxidermied mannequins were powerful, bloodthirsty, and pure, living on the outskirts of mankind and his petty concerns. Gazing at those creatures, I felt a hollowness in my chest, a feeling akin to infatuation. Their freedom exhilarated me.

I spent some time wandering around the exhibits, jealous of the animals and their instinctual lives. Now and then a cluster of children would roll past laughing, gazing in awe, playing. I heard them, but my eyes witnessed their movements as if there was total silence in the room. It was the same silence I came upon when Jo stared Johnny Fry in the eyes as he entered her, moved away, and entered her again.

Two teenage girls were giving me furtive glances and giggling. One of them was heavyset, wearing a sea-green sweater. She had red-brown skin like Robert's, but her hair was blond. Her friend wore a pink tube top with no bra and little need of one. She was white but not Caucasian. She was whispering, giggling, staring at my crotch.

That's when I noticed that I'd gotten an erection thinking about Jo and Johnny.

I turned away, walked down a long corridor into the Hall of Fishes, and with an inelegant move, shifted myself around so that the hard-on wasn't so terribly obvious.

After that I left the museum and walked down past Columbus Circle, down Seventh Avenue with its delis, electronics shops, hotels, and tourist stores.

Somewhere between 50th Street and 42nd, I passed an adult video store. I walked past the door and then turned back. I went in and strolled up and down the aisles of DVD pornography. The films were arranged into various subjects. There were black, interracial, amateur, Asian, BDSM, anal, come shots, bi, animal, chicks with dicks, gay, lesbian, and then there was a broad area where it was straight, nonviolent, generally white sex. Just beyond the vanilla I found a DVD in the small Features section. This was a story starring a woman named Sisypha Seaman. It was a tale about a woman who was having an affair with some young stud and what happened when her husband found out.

I'd never bought a film like that before. It's not that I didn't want to, but I was always too ashamed to bring something like that up to the cashier. I was afraid that the clerk would be a woman and she'd sneer at me needing to see sex instead of finding my own girlfriend and having real love in my life. I had a girlfriend, but she wouldn't know that, and how could I tell her without sounding like a pathetic liar?

But I wasn't afraid that day, not at all. I carried the DVD case, titled *The Myth of Sisypha*, to the front of the store, where an East Indian man sat on high so that he could see what was going on down the aisles.

"Yes, sir," he said with a slight sing to his voice. "Is that all, sir?"

"Yes. That'll be all. How much?" I was beginning to get nervous. I worried someone would come in and see me, recognize me.

Instead of answering, the clerk picked up a microphone and shouted something, in Hindi I suppose. He read a number from the back of the DVD jacket and stared down the center aisle expectantly.

The glass case in front of the cash register was filled with pornographic eye candy. Banana-colored plastic dildos, canisters filled with condoms, a box of tubes containing anal sex lubricants. I wondered if Johnny bought his red condoms and lubricants in a store like this one.

While I was thinking, a young man, also East Indian, came running out of the back somewhere, in his hand a disc that had nothing printed or painted on it.

9

The young man was quite short and thin. He wore black cotton pants, black tennis shoes, and a white dress shirt buttoned all the way to his throat. He handed up the DVD to the man behind the elevated glass counter.

"R-321-66a," the young man said.

The elevated clerk entered numbers into the cash register and said, "Thirty-eight dollars and fifty-one cents, sir."

I paid in cash, with exact change.

The cashier snapped my purchase into the jacket, placed the jacket into a brown paper bag that he folded tightly around the DVD, then he taped the package shut, placed it into a flimsy plastic bag that had I LOVE NEW YORK printed on either side, and handed the bag down to me.

"Thank you."

"Thank you."

I came out of the door into the bright light of the sun. I looked around furtively to see if anyone had marked my exit from the sex store. But no one was looking at me: not the housewives or kids out from school, not the homeless man pandering for change or the French tourists reading their map of the city.

No one saw me with the triply wrapped *Myth of Sisypha* dangling from my left hand, the same hand that held my briefcase filled with the photographs of dying African children.

When I got down to 18th Street, I stopped at Dionysus's Bounty, a liquor store.

"Do you have cognac?" I asked the dour-faced cashier.

"What kind you want?" he asked with a sneer.

"What's good?"

"How much you spend?"

"Hundred dollars," I suggested, and he smiled. I suspected then that he owned the store.

He went into a back room and I stood there, forgetting momentarily about Jo and Johnny. But then a door or something in the back squealed, and I thought of Jo calling the white man with the red condom Daddy.

Daddy.

"This the best I got," the owner said. "One hundred eighty dollars, but it's eighty years old and smooth like a young girl's skin."

I paid in cash.

Telling the man I didn't need a bag, I placed my briefcase on his counter and opened it. I put the I LOVE NEW YORK bag in a flap and was about to put the bottle in when the liquor store man put out a hand to stop me.

I thought that he was going to say something about the DVD, but instead he pointed to one of Lucy's photographs, which was partially exposed, poking out from the blue folder that held it.

I pulled out the topmost portrait. It was of a very dark-skinned child, maybe eight years old. She was exceptionally thin and her forehead was covered with sores. Fat flies fed on the dripping wounds.

"What is this?" the man asked.

It was only then that I looked at him closely. He was white, European no doubt, with white hair that was thinning down the middle of his head, revealing a pink and freckled scalp. He might have been sixty and at one time he had been powerful; I could tell by the muscles in his forearms and the size of his softening hands.

"Sudanese girl," I said. "There's a war going on over there. Thousands dying."

"Long time ago?" he asked, maybe a little hopefully.

"No. Now. Today," I told him.

"People can do this to each other?" he said. "They are monsters."

11

Nodding, I put the picture back in its folder and closed the case. I left the store wondering who he was condemning.

It was a long walk to my apartment in Tribeca. When I crossed Canal at Washington, I remembered how Joelle had told me that we lived the perfect distance from each other.

"This way we can never take each other for granted," she'd said, a wisp of her straightened hair bisecting a light brown eye. "We have to work to get to each other."

Maybe she was seeing Johnny Fry way back then. But no. John Fry came later. She met him for the first time at a party given by Brad Mettleman at his place in Brooklyn Heights. It was what Brad called a garden party. I was invited because I'd translated a series of letters that Brad had received from Spain and Paris over the last year. He'd said that I helped him stay on top of the competition. I brought Jo to the party because I brought her everywhere. She told me when we first got together that she didn't need to be married or even to live with someone, but she wanted to feel included.

Johnny was there. I had seen him before. He hung around Brad, and for a while there, I ran into him quite often. He had been the personal trainer for one of Brad's photographers, a Tino Martinez, at Crunch Gym. Johnny was an aspiring musician, and Tino's father was a music producer in Argentina. The elder Martinez got Johnny in touch with a Chicago music label that produced pop jazz. And even though Johnny was more of a classical guitarist, the label, Sun and Moon Records, had made noises about cutting his first album. The deal fell through, as I remembered, and now Johnny was trying his hand at importing folk art.

At that party he was pestering Jo to help him with marketing his as-yet-unproduced album.

"I gave him my card just to shut him up," she'd told me after he'd wandered off to bother someone else.

Was that when it began? I remembered that she'd complained of a headache and wanted to go home alone. How long ago? Six months, no more. Did he bring her red condoms and lubricant that first night?

Completely out of character for me, I swung my fist into the brick wall to my left. An elderly woman walking a boxer that was too big for her to control said, "Oh my."

The dog started barking at me, but the pain in my fingers was louder. I grabbed my fist and went down to my knees while the elderly woman, clad in a cranberry housedress, struggled and pleaded with her dog.

"Axel! Stop!" she shouted. "Heel! Axel!"

I finally got to my feet and jogged the last two blocks home. The entrance was just a door in a brick wall like the one I had attacked. I hunkered down against the wall and for the next five minutes I concentrated on opening my injured fist. The middle fingers were beginning to swell, and the pain radiated up to the middle of my forearm. Every fraction of an inch hurt more than the last. When I finally got the hand open, I was afraid to close it again. But I did it. After ten minutes I had opened and closed my fist three times.

Nothing was broken—I was pretty sure of that. But my hand would be useless for a while.

I laughed at myself as I tried with my left hand to get the keys out of my right-side pants pocket. After managing that feat, I was fumbling around trying to get the key into the lock when the door came open.

It was Sasha Bennett, the thirty-something law student from the fifth floor.

"Hi, Cordell," she said, smiling quizzically. "What's wrong?"

"I was walking and I fell," I said. "I put out my fist, don't ask me why, and now I can't even unlock the door."

13

I laughed, but she didn't smile in return. I must have looked half-mad out there. The grin on my face probably seemed like a lunatic's scowl.

"Let me help you," she said, reaching for the briefcase.

Sasha's father was from somewhere in Eastern Europe. Those people were dark-skinned and Asiatic. Her mother came from Indiana. Sasha's face was very wide at the cheekbones, and her almond-shaped eyes were darker than brown. We'd had coffee together a couple of times. She once invited me to come with her and some friends to a summer rental on Fire Island, but I told her my girlfriend wouldn't understand.

I followed her up the narrow stairway. She wore tight-fitting gray slacks and a yellow blouse. Even through the pain I admired her generous rolling gait.

The walls, metal stairs, and ceiling were all painted medium gray. The clanging of our shoes on the metal found a resonance with the pain in my hand.

"Give me your keys," she said when we got to my third-floor door.

Our building had once been the business office for a food distribution warehouse, now also defunct, across the street. It was tall and slender. When it was turned into apartments, there was only enough room for one unit per floor.

I handed over my keychain, saying, "The one with the blue rim is for the bottom lock. The red one is for the top."

"What about the middle?" she asked.

"Never lock it."

For some reason that made her smile, then laugh.

After working the keys in their respective locks, she pushed, but the door didn't budge.

"You sure the middle one isn't locked?"

"It sticks," I said, wincing at the pain in my hand. "You got to push hard."

Grunting, she applied her shoulder and the door gave way with a cry that would from that day forward always remind me of Joelle and Johnny.

Sasha put my briefcase down on the small walnut table that sat in the little foyer. I shambled past her, going to open the drapes that covered the westward-facing windows. The great thing about my apartment is the light. The living room has a window that looks out on the Hudson to the west, and my bedroom window faces the east. I get it coming and going: sunup and sunset.

"You want a drink?" I asked Sasha.

She cocked her head as if I had said something odd.

"I bought this really old cognac and I'd like to try it."

"Why don't you invite your girlfriend over?" she asked.

"I'd rather drink it with you."

That look again.

"I have to, to study," she said. "If I have anything to drink, the whole night'll be shot."

I walked over to her then and kissed her on the lips.

"Thank you for saving me, Sasha."

"Okay." She took half a step backward.

"Maybe we could have that drink some other time," I suggested.

"Yeah." Her smile warming. "I'd like that."

After she left I took three ibuprofen tablets, choking them down with three two-finger shots of cognac. I was sweating and cold, and my hand ached, but if you asked me, I would have said that I was feeling no pain.

My one indulgence is my television. It's a sixty-inch plasma screen with DVD, TiVo, full cable connection, CD player, computer

15

connection, and satellite radio. It's set up against the windowless wall of my living room, and more nights than not I fall asleep on my futon couch watching a movie or late-night cartoons meant for adult audiences.

After the painkiller began to kick in, I closed the drapes and put *The Myth of Sisypha* into the DVD player.

I hadn't seen many pornos. The only time I'd ever sat through one was at the rare stag party I attended. What I remembered was lots of genitalia, garish makeup, and disinterested men and women going through the motions. But this one seemed different.

In this film a bronze-hued black woman, Sisypha, and her husband, Mel, a rather paunchy white man, started out sitting at a dinner table. The meal had been served and they were eating. There were no opening credits, no sound track other than the noises that people make. The effect was that you felt that the cameras were spying on actual people just living their lives.

The couple talked about their day and seemed to be very close. At one point Mel asked Sisypha if she was unhappy because they hadn't been able to conceive. Her response was that they loved each other and that was the most important thing.

Later on, lying in the bed, they kissed goodnight and embraced as if they were about to make love, but then the scene switched to the morning.

At this point I began to wonder whether a mistake had been made at the sex shop. Maybe they gave me the wrong disc. Maybe there were R-rated versions of their triple-X-rated movies. Maybe I had gotten one of these by mistake. I thought that I'd have to take it back. But the story was still interesting to me. It was a lot like my story with Joelle. She always said that she loved me, that she was satisfied with our situation. She was still young enough to have children but said that she wasn't interested.

The next morning Mel left for work, and Sisypha went about her day. Sometime in the afternoon, a workman knocked at the front door. He was young and Mediterranean, muscular in his overalls and T-shirt. His aquiline nose and perpetual sneer gave the impression of an ugly nature, but Sisypha seemed to like him.

"Hi, Ari," she said. "Have you come about the pipes?"

"Yes, miss," he said in a definite Greek accent.

By now I knew what would happen. They'd kiss once or twice, the scene would flip away and then come back to find them lying naked under the blankets. I was about to turn it off when the worker tore off her skirt, got down on his knees, and began teasing her clitoris with the tip of his very large and pointed tongue.

Sisypha's breathing was laced with her orgasm. The way her legs twitched and her eyes gorged themselves on the vision of Ari's tongue proved that she was either a consummate actor or that she really loved having sex with this man. Her passion was at least as convincing as Jo's when Johnny Fry entered her rectum.

The sex between Sisypha and Ari escalated over the minutes. His erection was long, hard, and crooked. It bent downward but then turned up again toward the head. She rode him, rubbed his cock between her well-formed, light-brown breasts, took half of his enormous member down her throat. All the while Sisypha moaned and Ari grunted like a big dog warning off an intruder.

In all this time there wasn't the obligatory come shot: the man ejaculating on the woman's breasts or ass. But Ari was getting more and more excited. His hands were shaking, his eyes were pleading for something. Sisypha began smiling at him.

"Do you want me to make you come?" she asked.

"Yes." The word tore from his throat.

She grabbed his erection, sneered, and then slapped it hard. He screamed in pain.

17

"Still?" she asked.

"Yes," he replied in a subdued tone.

She slapped the erection again, this time with even more force. "Still?"

I unzipped my pants with my left hand, and the thick, squat erection sprang forth.

"Please," Ari begged.

"Sisypha, what is this?" someone said.

For a moment I believed that it was Ari trying to reassert his dominance. But the camera shifted, and I could see Mel standing at the door, carrying his briefcase, wearing his wrinkled suit.

Mel was a stocky guy with a receding hairline and a slightly protruding belly. He was white with gray eyes. We looked nothing alike, but certainly I saw him filling my role in this fiction.

Mel began yelling and gesticulating wildly. He kept saying that he was going to call the police, which of course made very little sense since no crime had been committed. Sisypha tried to stop him, but he pushed her down and picked up the phone. At that point Ari slapped Mel, knocking him to the floor. And, with his penis still more than half erect, he used a conveniently placed roll of electric tape to lash Mel to a chair. Before Mel was aware enough to scream, Ari used the tape to cover his mouth.

Sisypha tried to calm Mel, but he still struggled against his bonds, making muffled screams.

Then Ari placed a stool before the one Mel was tied to and sat, pulling Sisypha onto his lap. He positioned her so that she was facing her husband and entered her with his enormous erection.

I decided now that Sisypha was indeed an exceptional actor. Every time that Ari thrust into her, she gasped and responded with a groan of pleasure. But at the same time she would look into her husband's eyes with shame just as convincing. Finally Ari lost

18

control and fucked her with abandon. She couldn't keep from having a powerful, uncontrolled orgasm. When Ari was ready to come, he made her get down on her knees to lick the thick white fluid as it flowed down the hard, snakelike veins on his erection.

I tried to stroke my own erection, but my hand hurt too much, and so I couldn't bring myself to orgasm even though I wanted to in the worst way. My breath was coming fast, and when I looked into Mel's pleading eyes, I wanted to cry along with him. After all, wasn't I in the same position as he? Forced as I was to see my lover groaning and writhing in the embrace of another man?

When Ari had experienced his last spasm of ecstasy, Sisypha fell away from him and begged Mel to forgive her. She hadn't meant to hurt him; she would never have exposed him to her wanton nature on purpose.

But Ari got between them and sneered at her entreaties.

"He likes it, Sissy," Ari said. "Here, look." And with that he ripped the buttons on Mel's pants.

A stubby erection poked out.

"See," Ari said. "He likes it. He's excited to see you get fucked by my big cock. He wants you to get down on your knees and do to him what you did to me."

Sisypha gazed into Mel's eyes. His stare was frightened and unsure. Tentatively Sisypha got down on her knees before him. As she began sucking and stroking the stubby erection, he stared at her with a tender gaze and bucked his hips to show her how good it felt.

I poured myself another glass of cognac, drank it down, and poured another. I was Mel. I was Mel. Impotent, restrained, submissive.

But at least he was loved by her. At least she had come back to him.

19

Then Ari got down on his knees behind Sisypha. When he entered her, she let out a passionate groan that made me try again to stroke my erection with my injured hand. But the pain was too great. I couldn't pleasure myself and so I watched helplessly while the big Greek stud hammered away at Sisypha. She twisted and pressed back toward him. Now and then she'd raise her lips from her captive husband's erection and yell, "Fuck me! Fuck me harder!"

Tears were streaming from my eyes. My erection strained so hard that the tight skin shone brightly in the plasma glow, like dark glass.

Then the big Greek stood up from behind the dark-haired girl. His erection was so hard that it tilted upward despite its crookedness, great length, and girth. It was literally dripping from the excited juices of his lover. Ari stood over the woman dangling the erection in Mel's face.

"You smell her pussy on my cock?" he asked the man. "Does that get you excited?"

Mel tried to move his head away but at the same time Sisypha started whimpering and working her hand and tongue very fast. Mel couldn't help himself; he had to come while Ari waved his erection in front of his face. And even though there were tears in his eyes, I could tell that Mel was having a very powerful sexual experience.

In that moment I imagined his life. He woke up every day and took a bus to work. He came home and laughed at the same stories, watched the same TV shows, had sex once a week in the same positions, congratulated himself for being liberal and liberated when actually he wasn't any different from any anchovy sealed into a flat tin with a dozen others just like him. His wife loved him the way she'd love a six-year-old boy, smiling at his innocence while he pretended to be a man.

Ari was still laughing at Mel's weakness when Sisypha jumped up and pushed him away. Her anger was palpable and a little scary. The big man knew that he'd crossed a line and so he put his clothes on.

"You know my number when you need a real man," he said, buttoning his shirt and going out the door.

I was so relieved to see him go that I actually sighed. I poured another shot of cognac and drank it down in one gagging swallow.

My erection was waning.

I expected to see Sisypha untie her husband, for them to realize that they loved each other and then to make love.

Or maybe, I thought, the camera would now follow Ari to some other hotbed of sex at his home or some club.

I wasn't concerned because even though I had been unable to have an orgasm I felt spent, as if I had some kind of transcendental experience. I had seen many brilliant movies in my time, but nothing ever moved me as much as that first scene of *The Myth of Sisypha*. Not *The Bicycle Thief* or *The World of Apu* or *Tokyo Story*. No movie ever talked directly to me before. No movie had ever pulled the heart out of my chest and laid it beating at my feet.

I was finished with this film. Mere sex could not move me as much as Mel's demolition at the hands of his wife and her lover.

But the next scene had nothing to do with sex. Sisypha pulled the stool even closer so that she was sitting only inches from her husband. For a long time she stared into his eyes. I noticed that the right side of Mel's face was red and slightly raised, as if Ari had really struck him.

"If I take the tape from your mouth, will you scream?" she asked him.

He nodded, and I wondered if he understood the question.

"You will scream?" she asked again to make sure.

21

He nodded again.

"If I untie you, will you try to hurt me?" she asked then.

After a moment's hesitation he nodded, a bit sadly.

"Do you love me, Melvin?"

Nod.

"Do you hate me too?"

Nod.

"What can we do?"

Melvin hung his head and shook it slowly. Whereupon Sisypha got up and walked from the room. Mel looked after her and for a long time there was no action at all, just Mel looking at the doorway through which his wife had gone.

And then Sisypha appeared at the door carrying a small baby-blue suitcase. She knelt down in front of him and closed up his pants, a loving gesture.

"I'll call Yvette and tell her to come untie you," she said. "I'll get in touch in a few days to see what you're thinking."

That was it for me. I started crying and couldn't stop. I fell from the futon onto the floor and sobbed. Mel's impotence struck a chord at my center. He didn't want to hurt his wife but he would hurt her. He didn't want to scream but he had no choice. The decision was not his to make. Sisypha was the one in charge, the one making decisions. Through her passion, through her clear eyes, she made her choices and followed them.

I punched the ALL OFF button on my universal remote. The room went black, and I stayed down on the floor. Somewhere in between bleats, I drifted off into sleep.

Even though my excitement had gone unslaked, I dreamt about violence instead of sex. I was Mel, and when Sisypha asked me if I would hurt her, I shook my head and stared out with innocent eyes. But when she cut off the tape, I grabbed her by the throat and squeezed with every ounce of my strength. I could feel my fingers popping and the muscles in my shoulders straining. I exerted so much force that I was panting, but I wouldn't stop. I intended to choke the life out of Sisypha. She would stop breathing for all time.

But no matter how much I pressed, she just looked back at me, surprised and distressed at my lie.

"I'm sorry," she said to me. "But I needed more than you were willing to give."

"I loved you," I cried.

"You still love me," she said with empathy that I detested. "Even if you could kill me, that wouldn't stop you from loving me."

I stood up in a rage and shouted, "I'm leaving you!"

"You can't leave me," she said. "Not unless I let you leave. But as long as I want you, you will be tied down in that chair, and I can have as many men as I want and you will be silent. And you will like what I do."

I wanted to say no; in my mind I did say it. But the words I spoke were entreaties. "Please," I begged. "Please don't leave me. Don't take your love from me."

"You belong to me" was her reply. "I'll never let you go and I won't leave . . . this time."

"Thank you," I said, hating myself for the weakness I showed.

The floor must have been cold, or maybe it was the liquor, maybe it slowed my circulation or something, because then I was floating in the polar seas amid giant icebergs that were crashing into each other. The sounds of the shattering mountains of ice frightened me more than anything. Every time one glacier rammed into another, I shuddered and rolled myself into a ball so that I could sink below the waves and be safe from the exploding debris.

But I had to surface in order to breathe. The cold air hurt my lungs, and the crashing got louder and louder, until finally I woke up, shivering.

I thought my dream was coming from some loud, late-night TV show but then I realized that it was the telephone ringing in the darkness. I tried to get up but I'd forgotten about my injured hand. I grabbed at the coffee table, pulled away in pain, and fell forward, hitting my chin on the hard corner. The phone stopped ringing just before the answering machine would have picked up.

I may have passed out for a moment or maybe I was just drifting back into sleep. Then the phone was ringing again. The digital clock on the cable box read 3:12. I got to my feet using my unsteady left hand for leverage. I banged my shins on the coffee table and kicked over the cognac bottle. The phone went silent, again before the machine would have picked up. It had started ringing for the third time when I finally got to it.

"Hello?" I said in a simpleton's voice. "Who is it?"

"It's me, L," a woman said.

I knew that I knew the voice and, knowing that I couldn't place it, I knew I was drunk.

"It's late," I said more in explanation than complaint. "After three."

"I called the Roundtree Inn," she said, and I realized that it was Joelle on the line. "But they said that you hadn't checked in."

"Philadelphia," I said, remembering that I was supposed to go down on the five o'clock train. I had a meeting at eight in the morning with an agent for a consortium of Spanish businessmen that needed translators in New York. My agent had gotten me the gig. It meant a whole new world for me if I made the right impression.

"What's wrong, Cordell?" Jo asked, almost as if she loved me.

As if, I thought, and then I wondered why I thought that. Then

I remembered her and Johnny Fry on the couch and on the floor. And wasn't I tied to a chair?

"Cordell?"

"I was going to the train station," I said. "In the afternoon . . ."

"I thought you were on a noon train?"

"They didn't have first-class, and I wanted to write on the way down, on my laptop. Anyway, I was leaving my house and suddenly I got weak, dizzy. I tried to turn around, to go back home, and I fell."

"Are you all right?" she asked fearfully.

"Yeah. Yeah. I just hurt my hand, but when I got in, I realized that I had a fever. Real high. One oh two. I guess I've been sleeping since then. Sleeping."

"Do you need me to come over?" she asked, a little half-heartedly, I thought.

"No, honey. I took some Tylenol and I had a bottle of vodka." I had taken ibuprofen and cognac. That phone conversation was the beginning of many lies I was to tell.

"Since when?"

"What?"

"Since when do you have a bottle of liquor in your house?"

"Oh. I bought that a while ago. You know, uh, one day I walked home from up in your neighborhood. I passed this little liquor store. They had all this Russian vodka in the window and I decided to buy . . . some."

"Are you drunk?"

"No. Not at all. I was just dead asleep."

"Maybe you should go to the doctor, L. Maybe you're really sick."

"I don't think so," I said. "I mean, I feel cool now. Just weak after the fever. I'll be, I'll be fine in the morning. Get up early and hoof it down to Philly for my meeting."

"So you're okay?" she asked. "I was so worried when you hadn't checked in. I thought you were just late and I fell asleep. But when I woke up, just a little while ago, you still weren't registered."

"Nothing to worry about," I said, feeling almost normal. "I'm sorry I didn't call. After putting ice on my hand and taking those Tylenol, I just fell right out."

"You sound funny," Joelle, my lover of eight years, said. "Are you sure that you're okay?"

"Great. Are we still getting together this weekend?"

"Of course we are. Don't we stay together every weekend?"

"I just . . . well, I just didn't want to take anything for granted."

"You can't take me for granted, L," she said sweetly. "I'm your girlfriend. Why would you even think such a thing?"

"It's just waking up from such a sound sleep, I guess."

For a while then, the line was silent. The darkness began to form into shapes that were foreign to me. I knew that if it were daytime, I'd understand the shadows and spaces, but at night, slightly inebriated, it was as if I were in another person's space.

"L?" Jo asked.

"Yes, honey?"

"Do you ever drop by during the day?"

Yes. And yesterday I was up there watching you get fucked in the ass by Johnny Fry and his big red condom.

"If I did, you'd know it," I said. "Either we'd see each other or I'd leave you a note."

"Oh."

"How come, honey?" I asked innocently. "Would you like me to call before I come over?"

"No. Of course not. It's just that . . ."

"What?"

26

"When I got back from my meeting in New Jersey, I found the door open."

"Huh. That's odd. Could you have left it open?"

"Yeah. I kinda had my hands full when I left, but you'd have thought someone would have seen it and closed it for me."

I wondered if she was trying to make fun of me. For an instant I hated her—fully and completely. Then it passed. She was just worried, and I . . . well I couldn't bring myself to mention her infidelity. It just wouldn't come out of my mouth.

"I better get to bed," I said.

"Call me when you get down to Philadelphia?" she asked. "You know I want to know where you are."

"Sure thing. Bye."

I meant to get up early and take a taxi to Penn Station, but I didn't set an alarm or anything, and I was pretty drunk. When I woke up it was dark and I thought I had made it in time, but it was just that the shades blocked out the midday sun. It was 11:30 in the morning. I had already missed my meeting.

When I went into the living room, I realized that one of the pillows from the futon had fallen on the phone; when it rang in the morning, the ringer had been muffled, and I hadn't heard it from my bedroom.

There were four messages on the answering machine. All of them were from Jerry Singleton, my main translation agent.

"Cordell," the first message started. "I got a call from Norberto down in Philly. He says that you're late for the meeting. What's going on?"

By the fourth message he was threatening to cut me off, saying that I wasn't the best or the cheapest translator he could find. He told me to call him before the end of the day or he'd make sure that I never worked for anyone in New York or anywhere else.

He was so angry that it made sense in an odd way that my hand had swollen to almost twice its normal size. The knuckles were spread painfully apart, and that reminded me of Jo and Johnny Fry; him spreading her rectum with his wide erection.

For a while I tried to imagine making coffee or breakfast, but soon I realized that neither was possible with my injury. There was a small diner two blocks away that served breakfast all day long.

I was already dressed and so I just went out the door, forgoing the usual lockup. As I started down the stairs, I heard a door on an upper floor open.

By the time I was halfway down the block, she called after me, "Cordell."

Sasha was wearing a purple dress that was mid-thigh in length and matched her purple and white polka-dot high heels. The bodice showed her generous cleavage, and she was wearing makeup.

"Wow," I said.

"What?" she asked as she came up to me.

"You're gorgeous. Down to the shoes."

It was the right thing to say. She took my arm and pulled me along.

"Where are you going?" she asked.

"Ultimately to the doctor," I said, holding up my bloated hand for her inspection.

"Oh my God," she said. "That's terrible. You should go right away. I'll come with if you want."

"I'd rather you had breakfast with me," I said. "I was going over to Dino's for some food."

She smiled and hugged my biceps with her wrist and breast.

As we walked, I tried to remember if I had kissed her the night before.

28

The young Latina waitress took us to a booth in the window. She set down our menus and we told her that we were ready to order.

I usually have Egg Beaters with turkey sausage and decaffeinated coffee, but that noon I ordered Dino's special chocolate chip pancakes with maple-cured bacon, and a beer.

Sasha ordered chicken soup with matzo balls and talked about her younger brother, who was coming for a visit all the way from California for the weekend.

"Enoch is a genius," she said nonchalantly. "Everybody has been telling us that since he was two. He gets As on everything and aces all his tests. He's thirty and has never held a job or gotten a degree, but still my father says that I should be more like him."

"A genius?" I asked and she laughed and touched my good hand.

"Have you ever found out that somebody you were with was with somebody else?" I asked without expecting to.

Sasha looked at me with her large dark eyes. She took a deep breath and that lovely cleavage rose.

"You mean somebody told you about it other than her?"

"I mean I walked into her apartment and saw him sticking his dick in her ass." I had no idea that the words were going to come out of my mouth. Immediately I felt ashamed.

"I'm sorry," I said. "I didn't mean . . ."

"What are you sorry about?" Sasha asked taking my left hand in both of hers. "It's her that should be sorry. What did she say?"

"She didn't see me and I, I left."

"Are you going to call her?"

"She called me last night. I wanted to say something but I couldn't. I just couldn't." I felt like crying. I held my breath to keep the tears at bay.

"That's so fucked up," Sasha said. "I mean, she probably didn't mean for you to see it but . . . how long have you guys been together?"

"Eight years, just about." I released the breath and the sorrow moved off.

"She should have told you. But now you have to face her. You have to tell her that you know."

"Has that ever happened to you?" I asked.

Sasha let go of my hand and sat back against the orange Naugahyde bolster. She looked down into her soup for half a minute or more.

"When I was fifteen, I had this eighteen-year-old boyfriend," she said. "Ray Templeton. He had jet-black hair and a big, strong chest. He'd dropped out of high school a long time before to work in a garage. It was his dream to one day become a NASCAR racer. I was really in love with him, even though my parents told me that he was too old and a loser.

"One day I was going to surprise him. I had knitted him a sweater and I wanted to bring it to his garage. So I went home to change and when I got in the house, I heard my mother crying out 'Oh God, Oh God, Oh God'—like that. I thought she was in there with my father and I was totally disgusted, but then I heard him groan, and I realized it was Ray in there with my mom."

"What did you do?"

"I went in and screamed at them. I yelled and threw a lamp down. Ray jumped out of the bed to calm me down, but I just got madder, 'cause he had a full erection. Finally my mom started begging me to forgive her, and I ran off. I ran out the front door and around the side of the house because I didn't want anyone to see me crying.

"I was sitting out there for a while and then I heard my mother shouting 'Oh God, Oh God' again. For a while I thought I'd just wait until they finished, but they just went on and on fucking for fucking hours."

The hardness of her face made Sasha look like a totally different woman. She was taking in deep breaths, and her ears reddened.

"So what did you do?" I asked.

"I left. I went to see my friend Marie and asked could I stay there for the night. My parents didn't know any of my friends, and so I just waited until the next day and then I went to my father's office and told him why I wasn't home."

"Damn," I said. "Damn. So what happened then?"

"He divorced her. Moved out the next day. First we rented an apartment, and then I went to live with cousins in Brooklyn, and Enoch went with my father."

"What did your mother say?"

"I never talked to her again. She went down to North Carolina with Ray for a while. I knew that because his sister told me. But then he played the same shit on my mom and she went out to Los Angeles to work in makeup for Hollywood. Every once in a while she tries to get in touch, but I won't talk to her. She's a cunt and I hate her."

And she did—I could tell.

I was amazed by the amount of destruction that Sasha laid out around her. Her father's life and her brother's as well as her mother's.

I thought about Sasha running out and her mother, who probably hadn't ever had sex like that before, unwilling or maybe unable to turn away from the teenage mechanic.

"Do you hate me now?" she asked.

That made me laugh, and laughing felt good.

"No," I said. "How could I hate you? You haven't done anything to me. You haven't tried to hurt me."

31

"I like you," she said with real feeling in her words. "The only reason I haven't come knocking on your door is because you said about your girlfriend and you seemed to want to be with only her."

"Wow. Really?"

"Why wouldn't I?" Sasha asked. "You have those big beautiful lips and those long fingers. Anyway, I like a man who you know wants to be looking at you but then he gets kinda shy."

For a moment or two I forgot how to breathe.

"I'd like to see you too," I said. "But can you give me a few days to work this shit out in my head?"

"Sure. My brother's gonna visit anyway. Maybe we could go out for dinner or something next week."

She took my injured hand in both of hers very gently, moving the tips of her fingers around the swollen knuckles.

"That would be nice," I said.

I must have looked down because she touched my chin so that I'd look back into her dark eyes.

Slowly she began to increase the pressure of her caress. Outside people were walking. In the booth next to us an old couple was arguing about something having to do with a cousin. My hand, especially between the knuckles, began to throb with pain.

"Do you like pain, Cordell?" she asked, staring into my eyes.

My hand was hurting, but I didn't pull away.

"Does this hurt?" she asked me.

"Yes," I whispered.

"You can trust me." She squeezed harder.

My shoulders rose in response.

"All you have to do is pull away," she said, a demure smile on her lips.

I closed my eyes and let my head nod slightly. My breath

became a staccatolike huffing, and my neck shortened like a penis in the cold.

Suddenly Sasha let go of my hand. I opened my eyes to see her still gazing at me.

"Why didn't you yell at them?" she asked me.

"I don't know."

"Go on," she said, dismissing me. "Go to the doctor, and next week we'll see what else you like."

"I'll pay," I said.

"No. I'll get this one," she responded. There was no room for argument in her tone.

When I stood up from the table, I stumbled, almost fell. Outside I looked back into the restaurant and saw Sasha waving at me, smiling like she always did.

Walking down the street, I realized that I was afraid of my neighbor. She had gripped my injured hand with a good deal of force. She was trying to hurt me, daring me to pull away.

After a few blocks I realized that I was jogging down the street.

Dr. Charles Tremain had been my physician for more than twenty years. I had gone to him for fevers, headaches, and sporadic checkups. This wasn't the first time I'd just dropped by the office on 69th Street between Madison and Lexington avenues. His receptionist, Maya, smiled when she saw me, and then reacted in shock when I showed her my hand.

She put me in a private room right away. There the new young nurse from Ghana, Aleeda Nossa, told me to take off my clothes and put on a pale-green paper robe that lay on the examination table.

"But I'm just here for my hand," I explained.

"Dr. Tremain wants you to take off your clothes," she replied.

33

She was a lovely young woman with exceptionally dark, almost blue-black skin and large almond-shaped eyes. Maybe twenty-five, maybe thirty. Her figure was extraordinarily full, but she was not at all big or heavy.

"Mr. Carmel," she said expecting me to disrobe.

"Can I have some privacy?" I asked.

She smiled fetchingly and sashayed out the door.

I quickly disrobed and put on the pastel paper gown. From the doctor's window I could see rooftops for three or four blocks. There were small gardens and barbecues, tables and chairs set out for the uptown summer residents. Two men, stripped down to their waists, were building a fence between two abutting roofs. A small dog leashed to a doorknob was leaping up and down, probably barking at them.

There was an anatomy book on a small table in the corner of the small room. I picked it up, but before I could open it, Aleeda returned with an electric thermometer. She touched my shoulder and placed the tip of the gauge gently in my ear.

"Ninety-eight point four," she said after no more than ten seconds had passed. "Close enough."

"It's my hand giving me grief," I told her, holding it up for her to see.

She caressed my wrist so softly that I hardly felt it. Her eyes grew large and worried.

"Oh my," she said and my heart thrilled.

With her fingertips she traced my swollen knuckles as Sasha had done. Then she looked at me and asked, "What happened?"

"Fell."

We stared into each others' eyes a moment, and then she looked down.

"Mr. Carmel," she said, as if I had somehow insulted her.

I hadn't realized until I looked that I had a full erection pressing up against the paper. It wasn't only hard, but there was also a growing wet spot at the place where the head was raising the flimsy gown.

"I'm so sorry," I said turning to the side.

Aleeda heard the pain in my apology. She touched my neck and said, "That's okay. It happens sometimes. It's good at your age to be able to achieve such a thing."

"Maybe you shouldn't touch me, though," I said, "I mean, men my age don't usually get touched by women as beautiful as you."

She grinned and removed her hand.

"The doctor will be in in a moment," she said, and left again.

I spent the next little while trying to think my erection away. But it was just as if that was its natural state.

Dr. Tremain was a short and stocky white man who gave off an aura of physical and emotional strength. He was mostly bald with gray hair around the sides and he wore silver-rimmed glasses.

"That a gun in your nightie?" he asked.

"I can't explain it, Doctor," I said. "Aleeda looked at my wrist, and it stood up like a soldier."

"How old are you now, Cordell?"

"Forty-five."

"Then I'd say you're cured."

"My hand's even bigger."

He studied the swollen mitt, pressing it here and there and asking me how it felt.

"Nothing broken," he said after a while.

"Shouldn't you x-ray it?"

"Nah. Soft-tissue damage is all. Does it hurt?"

"Now and then it throbs," I said. My erection was still going strong.

35

"I'll give you some Percocet samples I have. And also an anti-inflammatory. That should get the swelling down pretty quickly. If it's still giving you trouble after the weekend, come on back."

He looked down at my stubborn cock and laughed.

"And cover that thing up," he said. "It makes me feel like an old man."

I walked home again. It took two hours.

Somewhere along the way, my erection eased up. It was still excited, larger than usual, but at least it wasn't pressing against my pants. On the way I bought a rib-eye steak at the Gourmet Garage on Seventh Avenue—that and some brussels sprouts.

The temperature was somewhere in the nineties. I was extremely tired by the time I got home. I broiled the steak, chopped up the sprouts, and sautéed them in butter. I ate the whole meal and drank two glasses of cognac before remembering *The Myth of Sisypha*.

Sisypha's friend Yvette came to release Mel. She was a petite, demure, white woman who was embarrassed by Mel's impotence. She didn't say a word to him, just cut his bonds and left.

He turned off all the lights in his house, then sat by the window looking up at a half-moon. When the night turned to dawn, Mel picked up his briefcase and stumbled out the door.

From there we saw him at work and then home again, sitting in darkness and staring at the waxing moon. Then he was at work again, and then at home.

The next morning, as he walked out the door, the phone rang. He stopped but didn't go toward the phone. It rang a dozen times and then stopped. Mel stood there staring at the phone, and soon it began to ring again. Still he didn't move to answer it.

36

The fourth time the ringing started, I believed that I would go crazy with the tension.

This time Mel picked up the receiver but didn't say anything. For maybe thirty seconds he held the phone to his ear, staring out with a blank expression on his face.

Then Sisypha's throaty voice was heard.

"I know it's you," she said. "I know you have to go to work. Go on. But after, come home and shower and wait. I'll send someone. Do everything he tells you."

The film showed Mel in his cubicle again. A woman in a rose-colored dress came to sit in his visitor's chair. She asked him if anything was wrong. In a surprisingly normal voice, he said, "No, Angela. Why would you think that?"

"You haven't spoken a word to anyone and you've worn the same clothes for four days straight," she said. "They're all wrinkled and . . . a little ripe."

"My wife had to go visit her mother," he lied. "She sprained an ankle or something and needed Sissy to do chores and some, some cooking."

"I hope she's okay," Angela said.

"Oh yes," he assured her. "She's coming home tonight. This was the only clean suit I had, but now everything's going back to normal. Sissy's a great housekeeper and a wonderful wife."

Angela smiled and Mel did too. But when she rose and turned away, Mel's face became somber and blank again. Angela glanced at him and frowned, but he didn't notice.

That evening Mel came home and showered as he had been asked to do. He was sitting in the chair by the window wearing his suit pants and dress shirt. The front door was open. After a meditative moment of silence, an effeminate young redheaded man came in. He was wearing ochre-colored hot pants and a violet silk blouse. Under his arm he carried a canvas tarp wrapped around a long and slender bundle.

The younger man approached the elder. After a moment or two, Mel looked up. He took a deep breath but said nothing.

The young man put the tarp on the floor and rolled it out. Inside were six metal poles, all of which were almost a yard and a half in length.

The young man went to the sofa and pulled it out into a bed. "Lie down on your back," he said.

After a moment's hesitation, Mel complied. The young man took up one of the poles. I noticed that there was a manacle attached to either end. He locked the manacles around both of Mel's wrists while he lay passively. Then the man repeated the process with Mel's ankles. I then saw that the nearly catatonic husband was wearing his socks and shoes.

The redhead took two of the four poles he had left and screwed them together, making one long pole. He repeated this process with the two remaining poles. These longer poles had bolts in them that attached to holes drilled toward the manacle ends of the arm and leg restraints. When everything was attached, Mel was splayed out on a rectangular rack. He couldn't move very much, but then again, he wasn't trying to move.

The youth walked to the threshold, stopped for a moment to look at the chained man. He then turned off the light and left without closing the door.

With speeded-up photography, the twilight turned to night.

The light snapped on, and Sisypha was standing there.

She'd been pretty before, sexy and well formed, but now, wearing a very short white dress and no makeup, she was exquisite. Her golden-brown skin nearly shimmered in the fluorescent lighting.

She took off her red high heels at the entrance, leaving them outside. Then she shut the door with a slam and walked to the side of the bed.

Seating herself demurely, she said, "Hi, honey."

There was a great deal of pain in Mel's wordless stare.

"I'm so sorry," she said. She placed a hand on his chest and stared into his aggrieved eyes.

After a while she stood up and walked off toward a door. The camera followed her into a large, well-appointed kitchen.

She turned on a light, opened a drawer, and took out a large butcher's knife. She tested the edge and then took out a sharpening stone to hone it further. When she was satisfied with the sharpness of the blade, she walked back into the room with the knife held nonchalantly at her side.

Upon seeing the knife, Mel opened his eyes wide.

"Sisypha," he said fearfully.

She brought a finger to her lips and shushed.

"What are you going to do with that knife?" he asked, ignoring her command.

"Do you need to be gagged again?" she asked softly.

"Put the knife away," Mel said, almost shouting.

Sisypha laid the knife at his side and took a bundled-up pair of white socks and a roll of electric tape from her purse. She set the purse next to Mel's head and then took out a black metal clip. This she put on his nose, closing off the nostrils. When Mel opened his mouth, she shoved the socks in, put a span of electric tape over his lips, and then removed the clip.

By this time Mel was struggling mightily against his bonds. He was trying to scream, but the gag worked perfectly.

I began to wonder if Mel was not an actor at all. Maybe, I thought, he'd seen Sisypha in other films and met her somewhere—

by happenstance. When he complimented her work, she told him that she'd like do a film with him. He was happy, excited, but then, when the shooting started, he found that he was a prisoner of the filmmakers. Maybe he thought that they were making a snuff film and he was about to be slaughtered.

Maybe they were.

Satisfied that Mel couldn't scream, Sisypha took up her twelve-inch blade again. She lifted the cuff of the left pant leg and shoved the knife underneath, ripping violently through the fabric up past his pale knee.

Mel jumped and gave a muffled shriek.

"If you move, I might cut you by mistake," she warned. There was a kind of breathy, sneering satisfaction in her tone.

Mel went still, and she smiled.

"That's better," she said.

This time she tore through his suit pants all the way to the belt. Mel went stiff trying not to move.

With a feral grimace Sisypha began hacking away at the thick leather of the belt while Mel whimpered, trying to keep still.

Once the belt was severed she moved to his white shirt and then back down to his briefs. Whatever she cut, she did with frightening force.

When Mel's front was totally nude, you could see a cut on his right side and one on his upper-left thigh. He wasn't bleeding much, but I was sure that this was no rehearsed scene.

Now Sisypha pulled off her white dress. She was naked underneath. Her breasts stood up without help or plastic surgery. Her copper nipples were so large that they sagged slightly. She lay down next to her husband, cupping her hand around his shrunken sex.

"Will you behave if I take off your gag?" she asked.

40

He nodded.

She worked the tape off as gently as she could and then pulled the socks from his mouth.

"Let me go, honey," Mel said.

She did not reply but kept moving her hand up and down on his flaccid penis.

"Please let me go," he said.

"It's starting to get hard," she told him.

"I don't want to, Sissy," he said. "I want you to let me go. I promise, I promise I won't hurt you."

"And I promise that I won't hurt you . . . too much," she said.

Now she was pulling on his cock vigorously, and it in turn was straining upward.

"Please," he said.

She looked from the erection to his face and said, "Do you need me to gag you again, baby?"

"No. No."

"Because I expect to fuck this cock and to do all kinds of other things to you and the only begging I want to hear is for more."

Mel seemed about to say something, but he swallowed the words.

"What did you say?" Sisypha asked, in a mild but threatening tone.

"Okay," he whispered.

"Okay what?"

"Okay. I want more."

Sisypha got up on her knees, continuing to stroke his erection. She kissed it, now and then smiling and cooing at its urgency.

There was just enough slack in Mel's bonds that he could bend his knees enough to buck upward toward her mouth.

"That's right, baby," she said. "Push. Push."

41

Mel's reticence turned to excitement. A wry smile came into his face.

"Did you see how big Ari's cock was?" she asked.

"Yes. Yes, I did."

"The first time he fucked me, I thought he was going to tear me open. I asked him to stop but he, he just kept plowing that big thing right into me . . . All the way to the balls. Every time he did that, I could feel them bump up against my ass."

At this point Mel started emitting a low moan.

"I begged him, but he wouldn't stop. I slapped him, and he slapped me back, not even missing a beat. And then we started to do it for real. I started begging him to fuck me harder. And he did."

"Oh my God," Mel uttered, going faster himself. "Oh my God."

"Are you about to come?" Sisypha asked him with great anticipation.

"Yes, yes, yes," Mel cried.

I was panting along with him. My only sorrow was that my swollen hand still couldn't wrap around my own erection.

All of a sudden Sisypha reared back and slapped Mel's stubby hard-on. He gasped, and she grinned broadly.

"I'm not letting you come yet, baby" she said impishly. "Every time you're about to, I'm gonna thump it good."

This did not stop Mel from thrusting and pushing with his hips.

"I don't know if that's gonna stop it, baby," he said.

She thwacked his erection again, and again he gasped in pain. The camera moved in for a close-up, and you could see that one side of his cock was reddened and a little more swollen than the other.

"I'm going to sit on it for a second," she told him. "It might sting at first."

Then she straddled him and lowered slowly. His face twisted up so that you knew she was right about the stinging.

She leaned very close to his face and whispered, "Don't you dare come."

"I think I might be having a heart attack," he said.

"Could you think of a better way to go?" she asked, grinning and moving up and down.

This general activity went on for some time. Sometimes she'd straddle him. At other times she stroked him with her hand and talked to him about all the depraved things she'd done with the big Greek. Every time he seemed about to have an orgasm, she slapped his hard cock, and he yelped.

Now and then she'd sidle up next to him, playing gently with his sex and whispering apologies.

"I'm sorry I have to do this, Mel. But I don't want to lose you and this is the only way I know to make sure that you're mine."

At one point she stood up and pulled the frame toward the bottom edge of the bed until Mel's butt was almost hanging off the side.

"I'll be right back," she said before walking out of the room.

While she was gone, Mel just lay there, teetering at the edge of the bed. He was breathing hard and looking around, a lost soul on a sea of sensuality.

When Sisypha returned, she was wearing a crystal-clear rubber-like phallus. The straps holding the dildo in place around her hips were also clear, making the sex toy seem almost like a natural appendage.

It was very long and thick—even more so than the Greek's naturally generous endowment.

"What's that?" Mel asked, his eyes once again wide with fear.

Sisypha stood over him, letting the big thing hang down over his face.

"It's my cock," she said, stroking the thing sensually. "My big dick."

"What, what, why do you have it?"

"I'm gonna fuck your ass with this thing."

"No."

"Yes."

From her purse she brought out a small plastic tube and a medicine bottle. She squirted some salve from the tube onto the tip of the clear, flesh-textured phallus. Then she took a capsule from the plastic bottle and held it under Mel's nose. There was a small popping sound and Mel's head went backward as if he smelled something very pungent.

"What was that?" he cried, his voice unnaturally high.

"Amyl nitrite," Sisypha said.

She was already walking toward the end of the bed. She got in under the bottom bar and between his legs and with one hand lifted the frame so that his butt was suspended over the plastic cock. Then, in one deft move, she plunged nearly the whole length of the dildo into her husband.

"Oh my God!" Mel said, while taking in a great gulp of air. "Oh no. What is that?"

"The nitrite relaxes the muscles long enough to get it in," she said. "It'll hurt after a few minutes, but by then I'll already be there."

Then Sisypha moved her fake erection in and out, slowly. There was a smile on her lips as she watched it move into him. After a minute or two, Mel began to call out in pain.

"It hurts," he cried and Sisypha plunged deeper.

"Please stop," he yelled and she swayed her hips from side to side to open him up more.

She fucked him hard and fast while he strained against the manacles and cried out loud.

44

At one point she withdrew completely. This also seemed to cause Mel pain. I thought that it was over and let out a sigh of relief. I had lost my erection, not because I was outraged by the act but because I felt that Mel was no actor and he was really being tortured.

Instead of stopping, Sisypha pushed the frame off the side of the bed and then lowered it so that Mel was lying on his stomach on the carpeted floor.

"No more," Mel pleaded. "It hurts too much."

Sisypha did not seem to hear him. She got another capsule and broke it under her husband's nose. Then she plunged into him and fucked him with real abandon. His yells were a bit more pleasurable, and when she finally came, grinding down violently with her hips, Mel seemed to be pushing back, trying to accommodate her thrusts. Sisypha, for her part, grunted loudly. The camera caught her face in a moment of grim and sneering satisfaction.

She stood up and took a deep breath.

The dildo was stained with feces and some blood. She took it off and dropped it on the floor. Then she pulled on her white dress and walked out of the house without another word to her husband.

He lay motionless and silent on the floor, on his belly, next to the sofa bed.

For over a minute the camera showed Mel lying there bound and spread-eagled. Then the youth came in again. He unhooked the long poles and disassembled them. He freed Mel's feet and hands.

Nude except for his socks and shoes, the brutalized man rolled into a ball while the youth wrapped up his traveling rack and left, again without closing the door.

I turned off the TV then. For a moment I considered taking out the disc and breaking it. But there was a glass of cognac in front of me and, I thought, I'd need two hands to break the DVD.

I went through the bathroom and kitchen to the bedroom, undressed, and then went to the shower. After that, I lay down on my bed with the light still on and fell asleep on my back, something I almost never do.

Three hours later, I woke up on a wave of nausea. Jumping from the bed, I tried to make it to the toilet, but I fell to my knees, vomiting on the floor at the foot of my bed. I sat there on my hands and knees, waiting for the moment when my strength would return and I could get the mop from the kitchen. But then I threw up again. I hadn't eaten very much in the last two days, and so the third bout was just dry heaves, but these seemed to weaken me even more. There was a cold sweat across my face, and I wondered if I really was sick this time.

I hate throwing up, but the few moments afterward are nearly sublime, when the retching is over and it feels like a reprieve.

That's how I was feeling when the phone began to ring.

There was no way that I was going to rise. No way. The only reason I didn't slump down on the floor was that I'd have to lie in my own vomit if I did.

The phone rang eight times and then the answering machine engaged. The speaker was two rooms away, but still I could make out Joelle's sweet voice. I sat back on my haunches and thought about standing. Then I raised my elbows onto the mattress behind me and pushed.

I literally stumbled from the bedroom through the kitchen and into the bathroom. When I fell into the living room, Jo was saying, ". . . okay. Good-bye."

I dropped down into a half-lotus position next to the phone, picked up the receiver, and punched in her number.

46

She answered on the first ring, "Hello?"

"What time is it?" I groaned.

"It's two fifteen. Where have you been, L?"

"For the past ten minutes I've been throwing up," I said. "Before that, in the daytime, I was in a daze, wandering all over the city."

"I thought you were going to Philadelphia?"

"I know. I meant to go, but then I woke up at eleven thirty."

"What's wrong with you, L?" Joelle asked.

You are, I said in my mind. *You fucking fucking Johnny Fry on the floor of your apartment. You looking into his eyes as if he were the first man to ever touch you.*

My thoughts were one thing but my voice said, "I think I'm missing you."

"What?"

"I've had you on my mind for days," I said with feeling. "All I can think about is you and sex."

"Sex?"

"You sound like there's something strange about that," I said.

"No. It's just that you haven't talked like that for . . . ever."

"But that's how I feel. I went to see Dr. Tremain, and when he asked me how you are, I got an erection."

Jo laughed with a little shout of glee.

"What did he say?" she asked.

"Was I glad to see him?"

"Did it go down?"

"No. It lasted an hour."

"An hour!"

"You know how it is," I said. "When I put my pants on, the dick was still hard and it rubbed against the material. Every time it did that, I thought about you, and every time I did that, it got harder."

47

"Is that what happens?" she asked.

"Yeah. Haven't you ever heard a guy talking about it before?"

"No," she said. "You know I haven't known but three men, sexually."

Four, I wanted to say.

"I have an erection right now," I said, and it was true. Her lies and mine blended together to make me very excited. My breath was coming fast.

"You have to wait until tomorrow night," she said with a sly smile in her tone. "We'll stay in just in case you get too excited and have to do something."

I got dizzy. Here Jo was lying through her teeth, and all I wanted was to get in her bed and rut. My breathing got all crazy. One moment I couldn't take a deep inhalation, and the next, I was panting.

"Are you okay, L?" Jo asked.

"I need you so bad, I'm aching."

"Really?"

I nodded and sighed, but the word *yes* got swallowed.

"Promise me you won't masturbate until we see each other tomorrow," she said.

I think it was the first time she ever used the word "masturbate" talking to me.

"Okay," I said in a voice half an octave higher than usual. "But why?"

"I want all of it," she said, and I nearly passed out. "Every drop."

"I have to go, Jo," I said. "If I talk to you any more about sex, I won't even have to jack off."

It was like two completely different people talking to each other. We might have been Mel and Sisypha, Dick and Jane.

"Okay," she said. "You go to bed and rest."

48

The moment she hung up, the spell was broken. My erection eased, and I got the mop from the kitchen. After cleaning up the bedroom floor, I returned to the living room.

I went back over the previous scene in *The Myth of Sisypha*, concentrating on Sisypha while she worked her clear phallus on Mel. Her face was strained like a true lover's while she gripped his thighs tightly to get the best leverage on her thrust. His cries only served to make her more passionate. And there was something toward the end that I had missed: when Sisypha had Mel on his belly on the floor, just before she achieved her orgasm, she pulled his hair back so that their faces were touching.

"Kiss me," she said in a sexually hoarse voice.

He did.

In that moment I could see that he had given in completely to her. He didn't want to be tied down there being battered by her giant dildo, but he gave in to her desire. Her need had become his will.

After that I went off to bed.

Lying there on my back, I could hear my heart rumbling like far-off thunder. I remembered Sisypha telling Mel that if he had a heart attack, it would be a good way to die. That made me laugh, and in the middle of my chortling, I fell off into sleep.

I didn't wake up until two in the afternoon.

I climbed out of bed more certain and sure of myself than I had ever been, ever. I opened all the windows of my house, inviting the breeze off the Hudson to blow through my catacomb-like rooms. I made coffee and checked my answering machine. Twenty-one messages. Sixteen were from Jerry Singleton. He cursed me and told me that he was no longer my agent. He promised to destroy my career. I erased his threats and they were gone from my life.

There were four entries made by Joelle, calls she had made before she finally got me. She was worried—more so in each successive recording. She really sounded like I was her one and only love. I tried to recapture the sexual intensity I had about her in the night, but it was gone.

There was one message from Sasha Bennett.

"It was great to have lunch with you," she said. "And I'm really looking forward to getting together for dinner next week. I'm sorry if I hurt your hand. It was just a feeling I got, you know? But I'm not really like that. Well . . . bye."

I erased everything. It felt good to have a clean slate.

I logged on to AOL and went into my banking account.

I had saved $58,000 in the past two decades, $2,500 a year plus interest. There were also two $10,000 T-bills and $8,600 in my checking account.

My rent was $1,350 and my expenses were no more than $1,000 a month, probably less. I didn't buy clothes often, nor did I take many vacations or own a car. I could live for at least two years without making a dime. That felt very good.

I picked up the phone and punched in a number.

"Hello?" the inappropriate new receptionist said into the receiver.

"Brad there?"

"One moment," she said, putting me on hold. Almost immediately she got back on and asked, "Who may I say is calling?"

"L," I said.

"Mr. L?"

"Just tell him L."

On hold again I succumbed to a giddy bout of laughing. I hadn't laughed like that since I was a teenager. I was still chuckling when Brad got on the line.

"Cordell?" he asked. "That you?"

"How you doin', Brad?"

"I'm fine, but you got my secretary all pissed off."

"Why?"

"Because you were rude, she said."

"What's her name."

"Linda Chou."

"J-O-E?"

"C-H-O-U."

While jotting down the name, I said, "Listen, Brad, you know Lucy Carmichael?"

"No."

"She was a student at NYU when you lectured there once. She's a photographer."

"Yeah? What she look like?"

"I quit my job as a translator," I said. "I think I want to start repping artists."

"Quit? I thought you were freelance?" Brad asked.

"I am. I, I was. But I just don't wanna do it anymore. So I thought I'd try my hand at being an art agent."

"And this Lucy Carmichael's going to be your first client?"

"Yes sir. She's got these photographs of children in the Sudan that are excruciating. I'm sure one of your Midtown galleries will jump at them. Will you help me out?"

"I don't know what to say, L. You sound crazy."

"No," I said. "Not at all. I'm just tired of these fuckin' small businesses and my agent and arguing over my fee."

"You don't think I have to fight about money?"

"Are you gonna help me, Brad?" I asked my oldest New York acquaintance.

"So you're giving up translating just like that?" he asked.

51

"I've been thinking about it a long time," I said. "It's just that I realized that I have to do it. I saw these pictures and I said to myself, it's time to get motivated."

I was sitting on the sofa in my living room. The sun was streaming in and the wind was blowing over me. The DVD was on again, but the volume was set to mute. Sisypha was meeting with Mel at a café in the daytime. While they talked, a tall, very beautiful black woman walked up to the table.

"I'll tell you what," Brad was saying. "If you promise to keep translating for me, I'll see what I can do."

"Sure," I said. "No problem."

"Okay," Brad said. "I'll get Linda to fax over the information on a few galleries that might be interested in that kind of work."

Sisypha knew the black woman. She stood up to kiss her on the lips. The woman shook hands with Mel and sat down.

"Thanks a lot, Brad," I said as I turned off the DVD player. "I really need this."

"What you need is a headshrinker," he said.

"Talk to you later," I said.

Sitting there at the threshold of a new life, I inhaled deeply and felt a pain down the core of my chest; a pain that was physical but also in my heart.

"May I speak to Lucy Carmichael, please?" I asked a woman who'd answered the phone at Teletronics, one of the dozens of new cell phone providers.

"Whom may I say is calling?"

"Cordell Carmel."

"Hold on."

While waiting, I practiced flexing my right hand. The anti-inflammatory was doing a good job on the swelling. I could get my fingers down far enough to make my hand seem somewhat like a bear's paw. There was still some pain, but it only served to make me feel hopeful, somehow.

"Hello?"

"Lucy?"

"Mr. Carmel."

"L. Everybody calls me L."

"I didn't expect to hear from you for a while," she said.

I explained that I had spoken to Brad and that he said he was too busy to take on anyone for at least a year. Lucy thanked me in a downcast tone. Then I told her that he suggested I try to represent her work.

"I told him that your work was too important to ignore. He said if I felt that strongly, he'd introduce me to the right gallery owners, which would give me an edge."

"Really?" she asked.

"Yes. He's faxing me today about the gallery owners. Maybe you could come over tomorrow evening and we could go over the approach we'll take."

"No kidding?"

"I think your work is very important," I said, feeling every syllable. It was important; important for me to make a living.

"What time should I come?"

"I have a pretty busy day," I said. "What about eight?"

"My boyfriend's supposed to come down this weekend," she said, and then paused. "But I'll tell him that something's come up. This is so great."

I nodded and then said yes.

"See you tomorrow night," I said.

"Bye."

After that I ordered six yellow roses to be delivered to Linda

53

Chou at Brad Mettleman's office. On the note I had them say, *I'm sorry if I was rude. Cordell Carmel.*

I left my house at three and went to my favorite little Italian bistro on the Avenue of the Americas near Houston. I sat outside in the hot sun eating fresh mozzarella, eggplant, avocado, and fried calamari. I had hours to kill.

I usually showed up at Joelle's house around seven. She liked to work on Friday mornings and straighten up in the afternoon.

I was in no hurry. I realized at some point during the day that our relationship was over. I wasn't upset about it. I didn't even plan to tell her that I knew about her and Johnny Fry.

Everything was new. I'd quit my job, had two women I could at least pursue, and I had at least two years in which I didn't have to earn a dime.

I laughed out loud. Johnny Fry's big red dick had set me free.

I didn't feel a thing for Joelle anymore. I didn't even want to see her, but I figured that I should go to her house and tell her so. I'd tell her the truth: *I just don't love you anymore.* That's all I had to say.

"A glass of red wine, please," I said to the waiter, a young would-be actor named Jean-Paul.

He smiled at me, and I smiled back. It was a new life. I was free for the first time that I could remember. I sat there watching women go by dressed in the scanty clothing they put on for the summer heat. I was thinking about Sisypha. She could be any woman walking down the street, and no one would ever guess what she was like or what she was doing at home. You'd look at her and think, *There goes a nice-looking woman. Wedding ring. Probably has two kids and no orgasms.*

I decided that one day I'd meet Sisypha and ask her something that would catch her attention.

I grabbed a cab at 6:20. The Pakistani cabbie took me to Joelle's building on Central Park West. Jorge, a middle-aged, half-bald Dominican man, was at the front desk. He waved me by without announcing me.

I dreaded the elevator car reaching her floor. It wasn't that I felt bad about having seen her and Johnny; it was that I didn't want her anymore. I didn't want to see her or talk to her or to pretend to care.

When the elevator stopped and the doors opened, I waited a moment, took a deep breath, and then stepped out into the hall. I was planning to break up with her before we ate. I'd sit down in the living room, and when she offered me a drink, I'd say, "I have something to talk to you about, Jo." I wouldn't call her honey or sweetheart or darling—never again.

She opened the door and smiled. Her copper-brown skin and dark hair were glowing, literally. She had on a knee-length brown skirt and a green T-shirt that hugged her slender figure. When I looked at her, I felt nothing. I mean, I noticed that she was glowing, of course, but that held no attraction for me.

The thought that Johnny Fry had been there in the afternoon crossed my mind.

She opened her arms to welcome me, and I reached down and pulled the T-shirt up over her breasts, as it had been with Johnny two days before.

"L!" she yelped.

Her nipples were both hard and plump, darker brown than her copper mounds. I took one in my mouth and sucked it hard and then licked the other one. A satisfied hum came up in my throat.

55

"L!"

I wrapped my arms together just below her butt and raised her so that I could rub my face against her breasts.

"Oh my God!"

I brought the flat of my bruised hand up under her skirt from behind, curling the fingers firmly against her vagina. She moaned then.

"Close the door," she gasped.

I kicked the door shut and pushed Jo to the floor right there in the entrance hall.

"Let's go to the bedroom," she panted.

"No," I said as I pulled off her panties.

She was working my zipper down.

She got my erection out and stood up with it firmly in her grasp. She pulled hard and I followed. She brought me to the couch and sat on the back rest, guiding me inside her. I was so excited that I didn't realize at first that she was positioning me in exactly the same place that Johnny Fry had stood. I worried for a moment that I'd lose my excitement, but then a passion overtook me, and I began to buck in and out of her as hard as I could. I didn't feel anything. I was numb. All I could hear was Jo shouting, "Oh! Oh! Oh!" and the slapping of our flesh in staccato rhythm.

When I came, I was bucking so hard that I came out of her. She grabbed my cock, keeping up the rhythm by pulling back and forth.

"Keep coming," she told me, and I did. "Don't stop."

Even after I stopped ejaculating, my thing was still hard and I was moving back and forth. Jo pulled me to the other side of the couch and got down on her stomach. She put her hand in her mouth and then slathered her anus with her own saliva.

"Fuck my ass, Daddy," she cried. "Fuck my ass with that big hard dick."

Daddy.

I grabbed her arms and held them out so that she was pinioned a little like Mel was in the film. Then I plunged into her. She cried out and grunted in just the same way she had with Johnny Fry. She bucked up against me and cried, "Deeper." And when I pressed harder, she called out in pain as she had done with her other lover.

I ground away at her, and she writhed under me. In my mind I was in *The Myth of Sisypha*, and in Jo's mind I was Johnny Fry cuckolding myself.

When I came, it was like my whole being went into orgasm. There was no local feeling, just an overall ecstasy.

Afterward we lay there quivering. I imagined that Jo's passion came from getting me to behave just as her lover had done. I was shivering from an emotion I'd not experienced before, at least not since adulthood. It was a loathing deep in my heart. It was hatred so profound that I couldn't even locate what or who it was that I despised.

Was it me I hated, for playing such a fool? Or was it Jo, for making me jump through hoops like a goddamned dog? Maybe, like with my orgasm, it was everything that I hated: the moon and stars, gods and maggots.

"You're still hard," Jo said.

I was lying on my back in the sunlit room. My erection was standing straight up. And even though the only feeling I had was revulsion, I reached for Joelle's arm.

She rolled away from me, laughing.

"You can't come in me again until you wash off," she said. "I could get infected if you don't."

I grabbed her arm and dragged her to the bathroom. Yanking a towel off the rack, I said, "Wash it off fast."

Giggling, Jo used soap and cold water. I relished the bracing chill

57

over my balls and down my inner thighs. The cold renewed me and staved off the revulsion in my mind.

"My God," she said.

"What?"

"I thought if I put cold water on it, it might go down and give me a break."

"Does that work with your other boyfriends?"

"I don't have any other boyfriends," she said playfully.

I pulled her from the bathroom to the bed, propped up the back side of her knees with my arms, and plunged into her pussy this time. She gasped and stared into my eyes.

"Have you ever let another man fuck your ass?" I asked her.

"Never," she said shaking her head and staring me in the eye.

"Not even once with your first boyfriend, Paulo?"

"Not ever. Only you. Only you. Only you."

Every time she said it, I pressed into her as far as I could, and she gasped, keeping her eyes anchored to mine.

"You love me?" I asked, my voice cracking a little.

She put her hands on both sides of my face and said, "There's you and only you."

And then for a while I lost my mind.

We were on the bed and then on the floor. At one point she ran away from me, but I caught up with her in the kitchen and made her wash dishes in the sink while I fucked her from behind.

I remember moments of that evening, but there's no continuity; only snatches of sex here and there. I was crying. Jo was crying out. I was hurting. She was digging her nails into my thighs.

And then it was very late at night. We were both in the bed. The covers were off, and I was cold. Jo was asleep under the sheet. I was relieved that my erection had finally diminished. My testicles ached, as did my jaw and calves.

Lying there in the early hours, I went over what had happened. Jo had made me act out her lover's moves. When she looked into my eyes, she was telling *him* that she loved *him*. And I couldn't stop myself. It didn't matter that all I felt was hatred. It didn't matter that I wanted to leave her.

She had me by the balls, and as much as I hated her and me and Johnny Fry, I needed to be with her more.

I laid there on my back, waiting (for what I don't know), while she slept and night moved across the city. I couldn't get up and leave like I wanted to. I couldn't wake her and tell her that it was through. I was miserable and obsessed, in love with something I didn't understand.

While I was lying there, I remembered a line from Bob Dylan's song "Isis": "Isis, oh, Isis, you mystical child. / What drives me to you is what drives me insane."

The moment those words came into my head, I began to laugh. I laughed so hard that I got out of bed and went to the living room so as not to wake Jo. There I rolled on the floor, giggling and chortling. Mr. Dylan had given me a key. Maybe I didn't know how to open the door yet but I knew there was a way to understand.

The next morning found me bathed in sunlight through Joelle's big windows. I was rolled up into a fetal position with a thin loose-knit shawl draped over me. I remember breathing deeply and then realizing that the window was open.

She was sitting in her favorite chair reading a book. She wore a short pink slip, and her mane of brown hair was tousled.

"Good morning," she said, sunlight glistening all around her.

"Hi."

"Why are you sleeping out here?"

"I woke up and, and I was restless so I came out here not to bother you."

When I stood up, she said, "Oh, no, no, no."

I looked down and saw that I was stiff as a diving board.

"Honey, I'm raw," she said, ". . . everywhere. I can't. At least not till tonight."

"I think I just have to go take a piss," I said even though that was only half of it.

I went to the toilet and then got my pants off the hall floor. I put them on to hide the erection and then went back to the sun-drenched room.

"I won't be bothering you tonight either," I said, taking a seat on the sofa across from her.

"Why not?"

"I have a lotta work to do. The last few days I've really slacked off."

"Let me see your hand," she said reaching out.

Her touch was light and very exciting to me. It made me want to forget about Johnny Fry, but I couldn't.

"Boy," Joelle said. "You fell right on the knuckles."

"It's much better now. Two days ago I couldn't close my fist."

She kissed all four knuckles and said, "I love you."

"Don't say that."

"Why not?"

"Because if you say it, I'll be on top of you again. I can't help it. I feel so strong about you."

"What is it, L? How come all of a sudden you're so, so sexy?"

"I don't want to lose you," I said, and I had to hold back from crying.

"Oh." Jo came across to the sofa, put her arms around my head, and kissed me. "Baby, I'm not going anywhere."

"But don't you get bored?" I asked. "I mean we've only been having sex about once a week and I don't even remember the last time we went on vacation."

"That doesn't matter," she said. "Is that what you're worried about? You think some big stud's gonna take me away from you?"

"Don't men . . ." I stalled. "Don't men come on to you all the time?"

"No." At least she didn't look me in the eye when she said it.

But her lying didn't make me mad, it made me desperate. All I wanted was to peel off that slip and hammer my hard thing home. The feeling was so strong that I bit my lip. My neck was quivering.

Joelle put her hand against my forehead.

"Are you still sick?" she asked.

"Naw. Uh-uh. I'm just a black man besotted with a woman."

"Do black men get smitten differently than white guys do?" she asked flirtatiously.

"I don't know," I said thinking of Johnny Fry whispering his base desires while he took her on the floor, his huge erection much deeper into her than I could ever go.

"Why are you looking at me like that?" she asked, her shoulders coming up defensively.

"I want you."

There were maybe three moments of agonizing tension, and then Joelle jumped up.

"Let's go to brunch at the art museum," she said. "Come on. Let's get dressed and go."

Outside, the stress released. It was beautiful, not a summer day at all. More like late spring or early fall. The light through the trees in Central Park was dappled and dancing. The breezes had a hint of a chill to them.

61

Joelle's mood lightened when mine did. We talked about a line of silk T-shirts that one of her clients wanted to market. She thought that he should have them placed near jewelry that complimented the fabric.

I didn't understand, and she spent half our walk through the park explaining what women thought when they considered buying any garment.

"It's like when a woman is considering a boyfriend," she said.

"What does that mean?"

"There are a lot of aesthetic issues a girl has when she wants to hook up," she said.

"Like what?"

"Well," she said. "You know most sisters want a black man. Some younger African-American women will settle for a white guy who can think black if he has to."

Like Johnny Fry, I thought.

"And then there's how tall he is compared to her . . . in heels," she said. "And there's how he smells."

"You mean no funk?"

"That depends. Some girls like a guy who smells like a guy. Others want sweet or spicy, and still others want no scent at all. Those women don't really like men too much but they feel they have to have one . . . for appearances."

"Like a necklace with one of your T-shirts," I said.

"Exactly."

"What do you want, Jo?" I asked.

We were somewhere near the middle of the park. She put her arm around my waist.

"I'm happy with what I have," she said. And then she whispered, "Is it still hard?"

"Yes, ma'am."

She let her weight loll to the right and pulled me toward a thick clump of trees and bushes next to a stone bridge.

The leafage partially hid us, but someone could see . . . if they were looking.

"I know how to make it go down," she told me.

"How?"

"Take it out."

To her surprise, and mine, I unzipped, allowing my hard-on to jut out from my pants.

"Oh God," she whispered. "It looks even bigger than last night."

I remembered Sisypha slapping her lovers' hard things and wondered if even that would daunt my obsession.

Jo was wearing a tan skirt and a multicolored striped T-shirt that didn't make it down to her navel. She looked around quickly and then hiked the skirt up and turned her back to me while pulling her panties to the side.

"Are you ready?" she said.

Before she could finish the three words I was in her. She moaned loudly, "Oh God yes."

I almost lost my erection then. I was sure that someone would have heard that. I imagined being arrested for lewd behavior in a public place. But then another thought came to me: Johnny Fry and Joelle had stood in this very same spot. He had pulled her into this semisecluded space and fucked her while people walked over the bridge and on the path less than five feet away.

When I realized this, I began humping her, grunting like Sisypha had with Mel. Just when I was about to come, I spun her around and pushed her to her knees. She took the head of my cock into her mouth and my whole world turned into a grin. I was at the verge of ejaculation when I looked up and saw three Asians, a young man and two young women, on the path staring at me. I smiled at them and then experienced a violent teeth-grinding orgasm. My eyes opened wide, and my mouth could barely contain the smile. The three pedestrians stared at me in wonderment.

Jo was tugging at my pulsing erection, squeezing it and licking the come as quickly as it sprouted from the head.

After she was finished, she looked up at me and smiled, then grinned.

She stood up, pulling down her skirt, and took me by the hand. We walked past the giggling Asian girls and their friend. Jo gave them all a toothy smile.

We didn't talk anymore until we got to the museum.

Jo's uncle, Bernard Petty, was a landlord in the Bronx and Brooklyn. He owned more than fifty buildings and other properties, making him one of the few black businessmen in New York who was worth more than $100 million. Every year Bernard bought a patron-level membership at the Metropolitan Museum of Art in Jo's name.

There were lots of benefits to the membership. The trustees' dining room for instance, which was for members only, and a lounge for high-level patrons to relax in. You never had to pay an admission fee, and every show was on display for members when the museum was closed on the Monday before the official opening.

Jo took us up to the dining room, and we were greeted and put in a window seat that looked out over the park.

While I sat there going over the menu, Jo stared at me.

"What?" I asked.

"Who are you?"

"Cordell Carmel, translator."

"No. Cordell would have never done what you did in the park just now. Cordell would have giggled and made a joke and pushed me back on the path. Even if he could have kept it hard enough to start something, he wouldn't have finished it, not like you did with those people watching."

"So you think I'm not me?"

Jo's eyes widened to take me in. Then she shook her head and turned her attention to the menu.

I rested my head in my hands because I was dizzy again. All of that sex and cuckolding and uncontrolled passion was taking a toll on me—a toll I would have gladly paid every day of the week.

"Hi," a man said.

I looked up, and there stood Johnny Fry. He was wearing faded jeans and a white T-shirt tight across his broad, if pale, chest. He had brown leather sandals on his feet and lightly tinted yellow sunglasses propped up on top of his blond head. Next to the white man stood a coal-black woman with wild hair and nearly Caucasian features.

"John," Joelle said a little bewildered.

"Hey, Joelle, L. How you guys doin'? This is Bettye. She's from Senegal."

"Hello," the beauty said putting more emphasis than any American would on that "o."

"What are you doing here?" Jo asked.

"My family has a membership, and Bettye wanted to see the Egyptian art. What are you guys doing?"

"Having a little brunch after sex in the park," I said.

Bettye's eyes widened, but a shadow crossed Johnny's face. I knew I was right, I knew he'd had sex with her in the park too, I just wanted to be sure.

"He's kidding," Jo said, but there was an impish look to her.

Maybe, I thought, Johnny felt he owned Joelle sexually. Maybe he was jealous of his lover's boyfriend. All of a sudden I was enjoying myself.

"Why don't you guys join us?" I said.

"Oh I don't know," Jo and Johnny said as one.

"Come on." I stood up and took Bettye by the arm. I guided her to the chair next to me and gestured for Johnny to sit beside Jo.

The move was slick, I must say.

"Well okay," Johnny said. He pulled out the chair next to Jo and sat.

She looked very uncomfortable. It was no longer a surprise to me that I felt aroused by her discomfort.

"You look beautiful, Joelle," I said. "I love you."

That burnished her coppery skin.

"Oh. That's so sweet," Bettye said.

"Are you living in New York?" I asked the dark-skinned Senegalese woman.

"Teaching at NYU," she said, nodding with a certain amount of reserve.

"What do you teach?"

"Physics."

"Oh?"

"Does that surprise you?" she asked with a playful smile. Her white teeth were made even more brilliant by the blackness of her skin.

"I guess I never think of women in physics."

"I was trained in Cuba," she said. "In Cuba girls excel at math and science, not the boys."

I realized at that moment that I was losing my mind. I had just had semipublic sex in the park. I was sitting across from the man having an affair with my lover. And I was staring into his date's eyes with longing because in Cuba the women outstrip the boys in science.

66

"Honey?" Jo said.

"Yeah?"

"You're staring."

"I'm just amazed that girls excel in physics in Cuba, because it's always been reported in America that boys' brains are more set up for that kind of work."

"Oh no," Bettye said with wide-eyed assurance. "It is not true. It is only that men in your country do not want women to be smarter than them."

"It's not that they're smarter," Johnny Fry said with a smirk. "It's that girls have a different intelligence. Girls are good at, um, I don't know, uh, art."

"Oh," Bettye said with great emphasis. "And is that why so many of the physicists in Cuba are women?"

"Must have to do with communism limiting how boys feel about themselves." Johnny Fry was quite handsome. When he smiled, you could see how women would want to make allowances for his chauvinism.

"You're a fool if you think that," Bettye said, giving him no slack at all.

"I'm just kidding, honey," he said. "You know me, I can't even do long division."

When he called Bettye "honey," Jo stiffened a bit.

"What's your last name, Bettye?" I asked then.

"Odayatta," she said. "And yours?"

"Carmel. Cordell Carmel."

"It is like poetry, your name."

"Thank you."

"So, Bettye," Jo said. "How long have you been here in New York?"

"A year."

"And when did you and John meet?"

Bettye turned to him, the question in her eye.

"About three months ago," she said. "Yes."

"Waiter," Johnny said. "Excuse me."

A man of the Far East, maybe Sri Lanka, maybe Tibet, came over to the table.

"Yes, sir?"

"We'd like to order," Johnny told him.

"Oh no," Bettye said, fluttering her hands. "I'm not ready."

The young brown man bowed slightly and moved away.

"Johnny and I were to go away this weekend," Bettye was saying to stiff-faced Jo. "To Sag Harbor. But then I realized that I have a dinner with the university president tonight."

"So, John," I said. "What business are you into now?"

"Um, what?"

"Are you in a new business? Brad told me that you were thinking of some kind of import thing."

"Oh yes," Bettye said brightly. "John is going to be importing Senegalese carvings. The people of the village I'm from are the best at making them."

"Wow," I said. "So you guys are going into business together."

"Yes," Bettye said.

"You ready to order yet?" Johnny asked no one in particular.

For the rest of the lunch, Joelle and Johnny were almost completely mum. Bettye talked about how nice Johnny was to her. On her birthday he bought her a silver mesh necklace from Tiffany's.

"Jo has a necklace just like that," I said. "I think you got yours from Tiffany's too, didn't you, honey?"

"Yes."

"Yeah. Amazing that you guys both have the same thing. Isn't it, John?" I asked.

"Some coincidence," he agreed.

I had a great time seeing the lovers squirm.

I told Bettye that last week I would have been jealous of her romance with Johnny, "But now I've fallen in love with Joelle all over again. I can't get enough of her."

"We should go," Jo said then. "I have a headache."

On the walk across the park, we were mostly silent. Joelle was deep in thought, and I knew why. Even though she had a steady, long-term boyfriend, her erotic and romantic identity was tied to Johnny Fry. He wasn't supposed to have another girlfriend.

I could imagine how their conversations went.

"Do you still sleep with him?" Johnny would ask.

"It's nothing," she'd say. "Once a week on a Saturday night or Sunday morning. He sticks it in and then he's finished. It's nothing like what we have."

Maybe she told him that his was bigger and better and that he was a real man where I was just a hapless sort of guy.

"But maybe he has a girlfriend," Johnny might ask. "Do you think he's safe?"

"He hasn't been with anybody else," she would have told him.

I was sure this was true. Suddenly I was enraged *and* aroused. The juxtaposition of emotion and sensation threw my gait off. My feet crossed, and I fell down in the middle of the asphalt path.

"L," Jo yelped.

I had held my hurt hand close to my chest and so fell on my right shoulder. I wasn't hurt. I wasn't even thinking about falling. It was Joelle telling Johnny that I was a meek brother who wouldn't have even thought of being with another woman while she was drinking down his come in a city park.

"Are you okay?" she asked me.

"I don't know," I said.

She took my arm and tried to pull me up, but I stayed heavy on the ground.

"Are you all right?" a tall white man asked me.

He wasn't young, sixty or so, but he was a weight lifter. The blue wifebeater he wore was pulled tight across his chiseled chest muscles. He gripped my left biceps, and suddenly I was airborne. Then I was standing.

"Thank you," I said.

"No problem," the man said. He walked on, proud that his endless hours of repetitions had turned out to have some worthwhile purpose.

"Are you okay, L?" Joelle asked me. There was concern, even a rare show of worry, in her eyes.

She hooked her arm around my waist and supported me the rest of the way home. Her brooding and somber mood turned to anxiety for me.

In the apartment she helped me to the couch and took off my shoes. She made lemonade and kept checking me for fever.

"You should go to the doctor," she said more than once.

"I told you, I was just there. He said I'm fine."

"But why did you fall?"

"I haven't had that much sex in . . . ever, like you said," I told her. "I'm just light-headed over you."

But even while I said these words, I was thinking about her belittling my manhood to the white man Johnny Fry.

"You should stay here tonight," she told me.

"I can't."

70

"Why not?"

"The guy I stood up in Philly is in town. He has an all-day conference and needs to see me about that job."

"See him tomorrow," Jo said.

"I tried that. He has meetings all day."

"Can't you stay?" She had that pleading tone in her voice that I never turned down.

"I can't," I said.

Surprise and a little suspicion etched its way into Jo's face. I'm sure she was about to try her plea again, but just then the phone rang.

Jo went off into the kitchen, casually closing the door as she went.

The moment the door was shut, I jumped up and pressed my ear to the crack.

"Hello?" Jo said. "Oh, it's you. I can't talk now. . . No . . . I don't care what you do . . . No. Not tonight . . . You have a girlfriend . . . Yes. In the park . . . Uh-huh. Yeah . . . He's my man and I'm with him . . . No . . . I have to go . . . I have to go . . . Call me next week . . . Friday . . . No, Friday . . . Good-bye."

She hung up the phone with a loud bang.

By the time she was coming back through the door, I was on the couch again, looking bored.

"Who was that?"

"Johnny Fry."

"How did he have your number?"

"You remember I gave him my card at Brad Mettleman's party. He called me a few times when he still thought that he was going to cut an album."

"What did he want this time?"

"He wants me to help him market those Senegalese wood carvings."

71

"Oh. Are you going to?"

"No. He's a con man. I'd probably never even get paid."

I stood up then. "I better be going."

"Please stay the night," she begged. "Please."

"I have to meet this guy."

"Then come over after the meeting."

"It might be a working meeting, Jo. It could go very late."

"Will you call me?"

"Sure. Definitely," I said. "And if it's early enough, I'll drop by . . . I mean, if you don't mind."

"Of course not," she said. "You know you can come here any time you want."

I left Joelle's house at about 3:00 that afternoon. The day was still beautiful, and so I walked again.

People up and down the street smiled at me, said hello. There was a stiff breeze blowing and I felt relieved that Jo had broken up with Johnny Fry. Because that was surely what happened on the phone. She wouldn't talk to him until Friday, all the way at the end of the week.

I stopped at the Gourmet Garage and bought smoked whitefish and a prepared vegetable salad. Down the street from there I bought a bottle of white Burgundy from the Cellar.

There was a list of galleries that exhibited photography in the fax machine when I got home, that and a handwritten note from Linda Chou:

Dear Mr. Cordell Carmel,

I received the roses you sent. They're beautiful. You really didn't have to, but I'm glad you did. Please call me if you have any problems with these gallery owners. I'm really the

72

one who talks to them most of the time and I'd be glad to give any assistance you might need.

Sincerely,

Linda Chou

There was hunger in her words. Before that early evening I might not have understood Linda Chou's hankering. But now I'd seen it in Jo and Johnny, in Bettye and myself.

I realized that I had gone through my whole life starving and I never even knew it. I was angry at Jo and Johnny, but the real source of pain for me was that I had never known how empty and unfulfilled my life was. The sum total of my forty-five years was little more than the atmosphere within a hollow husk of a shucked snakeskin.

My woman was unsatisfied by me.

My work could have been done by almost anyone with high school French and Spanish.

My passion could be contained in a span of a few minutes a week.

And all this time I was completely unaware of my penury.

At 8:06 the buzzer sounded.

"Hello?" I said pressing the SPEAK button. Then I pressed LISTEN. Just that little bit of pressure shot lances of pain through my injured hand.

"It's Lucy."

"Third floor," I said.

I held the DOOR button longer than necessary because the pain it caused felt right, even good. It reminded me of Sasha and of Jo having her ass reamed wide, begging for more; it made me shiver with sexual excitement.

I didn't expect to have any amorous dealings with Lucy, especially now that Jo had dropped Johnny. But she was young and beautiful, and I had been starving for love even though I hadn't known it.

"Hi," she said, coming in the door.

She wore a diaphanous turquoise blouse with a white tube top underneath and a short-short pleated white skirt. She kissed me at the corner of my mouth and smiled.

"You look great," I said.

"Thanks. And thank you so much for trying to help me. It means a lot that you believe in the work and also about the children."

"Well let's get to it," I said. "I want to go through all the photographs again, and this time I want the back story on each one. I want to know these children and this world just as if I'd been there."

"What happened to your hand?" she asked.

"I fell," I said.

"Are you okay? Is anything broken?"

"No. It's nothing. Let's look at the photographs."

Lucy knew every name, remembered every town and village where she'd photographed. She knew the diseases that the children had suffered and how their parents had died. She knew the foods they ate and how much tainted water they received each day.

"You really immersed yourself in their lives," I said.

"People are dying," she replied. "I have to get their stories out there."

"What about magazines?" I asked.

"They buy a photograph or two, but no one wants to put much of this kind of suffering in their periodicals. And the few that do, their readers are already aware. I want to get these pictures into the hands of people who will be shocked and then want to help."

"And I plan to help you do just that."

It was well after eleven when I'd finished taking my notes. The stories about the dying nation of Sudan were deeply disturbing to me, much more so than the first time I'd seen Lucy's work. But, on the other hand, I was keenly aware that the suffering eased my own sexual discomfort. My worries were nothing compared to what these starving children were going through.

"I have some smoked whitefish and a salad in the refrigerator," I offered after we'd gone through her entire portfolio.

"Great," Lucy said. "I haven't eaten since breakfast."

I put the whole meal on a wooden platter and broke out the bottle of wine. We sat side by side on the living room couch, eating and drinking.

Lucy was very good company for someone so young. She asked about translation and the specific kind of work I did.

"Mostly manuals and articles," I said. "Even if I do a book, it's never fiction or even interesting nonfiction. Sometimes I translate correspondence for people like Brad. Pretty straightforward stuff."

"But I bet you find some knotty problems here and there," she said. "Words that have double meanings and things you don't understand."

"I guess so. But nothing I do is nearly as interesting or passionate as you," I said sincerely. "I mean, listening to you talk about the places you've been actually shames me. What are you, twenty-five?"

"Twenty-three."

"I'm forty-five, older than your father, and I haven't even been to Africa on a vacation. I don't think I've ever tried to save even one life."

75

"Maybe now you will," she said.

She reached over and pressed my hand.

Her elbow touched the ON button for my DVD, and *The Myth of Sisypha* came to life on the dormant screen. It was the innocuous scene where the black woman had just joined Mel and Sisypha at the café.

"Oh, excuse me," Lucy said. "Let me turn it off."

She picked up the remote but hit the FAST-FORWARD key instead of STOP.

Suddenly a black man appeared, and then they were in a sitting room somewhere, and the man was leaning back on a couch while the black woman was stroking his enormous erection.

"Oh my God," Lucy said.

I took the remote from her and turned the whole system, including the screen, off.

"Wow," Lucy said.

"I'm so sorry," I said. "I was having problems and I was walking home and I went past one of those sex stores and I went in . . . on a whim."

"I've always wanted to get one of those," Lucy said. "I never saw one before."

"Why not?"

"Those places creep me out."

"You could get your boyfriend to buy you one."

"Billy's sweet," she said. "But he's very straight about sex. He calls himself a feminist, and I love him for it, but I don't think that watching people having sex is necessarily misogynist."

The way she caught my eye, her statement seemed more like a suggestion.

"Well," I said. "I could go back to that store and buy you something, and the next time we meet I could, uh, give it to you."

76

"Could we watch some of this one?" Lucy suggested.

Instantly my heart felt as if it were trying to squeeze out every last drop of blood it held.

No was on my tongue. She was a child. I'd feel like I was child molester. I had a girlfriend . . .

I turned on the disc and reversed to the place where the black man came to the table in the café. Lucy jumped up to turn off the lamp. Then she sidled up next to me and poured us both a glass of Burgundy.

"This is Stewart," the black woman was saying, "a friend of mine. Is it okay if he joins us?"

"Sure it is, Julie," Sisypha said. "Maybe we should go up now."

"Hi," Stewart said to Mel.

The two men shook hands. They were both the same height, five eight or so, but Stewart was thin and dark where Mel was chunky and pale.

They walked out of the restaurant and across the street. In continuous reportage the camera followed them into a doorway and up some stairs.

Then the scene changed, and they were coming into an apartment. Julie shucked off her dress as soon as she came in the door. She had a beautiful dark body.

Her skin was the color of extra-dark blueberries.

"Take off your pants," Sisypha said to Mel.

Lucy grasped my finger.

When Mel refused, his three companions descended upon him. They were very patient, almost gentle, as they took off all of his clothes, talking to him as concerned adults would to a small child.

"That's it," Sisypha said as she pulled off his T-shirt.

"That didn't hurt, now did it?" Julie asked after she'd peeled off his pants and boxer shorts.

77

Julie and Stewart went to the sofa and began making out.

"I want to go," Mel said to Sisypha, who was holding him away from his clothes.

"Let's just watch for five minutes," Sisypha whispered. "After that, if you want to, we can leave."

Mel was confused. He wanted something from his wife and he was amazed upon seeing Stewart's massive thing.

Julie was on her knees before the long, hardening erection. As she licked and pulled on it, it got thicker and straighter.

Lucy was squeezing my finger and breathing loudly through her nose.

Mel became aroused and put his arm rather clumsily around his wife's neck.

As Stewart entered Julie from behind, I leaned over to kiss Lucy's neck. She kissed me full on the lips, and I stuck my tongue in her mouth.

"We can't do it," she told me between kisses. "I promised my boyfriend I wouldn't."

Julie groaned like a man through my subwoofer.

For a while I lost the thread of the film. I had worked off Lucy's gossamer blouse and pulled down her tube top. Her breasts sagged, but the thick, pink nipples were hard and upstanding. When I sucked one, a little fluid came out and into my mouth.

Lucy groaned like Julie and I looked up to see Stewart pressing his big thing into her anus.

"Look," I said to Lucy.

Her response was to take my erection out of my pants. She formed her thumb and forefinger into a snug ring for the head of my cock. She lifted that ring up and down keeping it on the head. It tickled and drove me crazy.

"Deeper," Julie cried.

78

"Don't touch it," Sisypha told Mel. She was pulling his hand away from his erection. "Just watch and let the excitement build."

I started bucking up and down about then.

"Do you want to come?" Lucy asked me.

"No."

She pinched the big underside vein on my penis, and I yelped in pain.

"That's what I have to do with Billy all the time," she said. "He always comes too fast."

She made her fingers into a ring again while Stewart spread the cheeks of Julie's buttocks apart and she screamed. He was putting his entire thing into her and then pulling it fully out. He did that again and again, slowly.

"Have you ever done that?" Lucy asked.

I nodded because if I spoke, I knew even her pinches wouldn't stop me.

Stewart pulled his thing out of Julie and said, "Come over here," to Sisypha.

The young woman got down on her knees before him as Joelle had done with me. Almost immediately the man came in great gobs over her face, into her hair, and on the floor behind her.

When he was finished, he put on his pants and shoes. Wiping her face off with her sweater, Sisypha linked her arm with Stewart and said to Mel, "We're going back to Stewart's place. You stay here with Julie."

"But . . ."

"Don't question, honey. Do what I tell you to do."

A look came into Mel's face. It was same expression he had when he finally submitted to her dildo.

My own erection subsided. I was still excited, but somehow I identified with Mel so closely that I felt like I was also supposed to obey her.

I turned off the DVD player, leaving us bathed in the blue light of the plasma screen.

"My God," Lucy said. "I've never seen anything like that. She was so strong. And he loved her so much."

Love?

"Did I hurt you?" Lucy asked me.

"No. Why?"

"You lost your erection."

"Will you stay with me tonight?" I replied.

"I can't fuck you," she said, shaking her head in the most fetching manner. She was still holding on to my cock and kissing me.

"That's okay. I just want to . . . you know."

"Come?" she suggested, an impish smile on her swollen lips.

"If you promise to wait until the morning," she said.

"Like Mel?"

"Yeah." She grinned and kissed me.

At that moment the blue light went out. Lucy and I stumbled through the dark apartment to my bed. We lay side by side and every now and then she'd reach out to make sure I was hard.

In darkness she told me about her life in Westport, Connecticut, and her family. Her stories were bland, and I'd begin to nod off now and then. But whenever I did, she'd give me a feathery touch, and I'd awaken.

Finally, however, I fell asleep.

I dreamt about the lunch with Johnny Fry, Bettye, and Jo. Instead of the cloaked suspicions of our real lunch, we were all talking honestly, expressing how we really felt about each other.

"I'm heartbroken because you love him," I said to Jo.

"I don't love him but I need him," she replied.

80

"I'm just the better man," Johnny added.

It was that moment, in the dream, that I began to hate Johnny Fry.

"I got a bigger dick," he said.

"And he knows how to use it," Bettye said with a vehement nod.

"And he's not afraid of living life," Joelle said. "He takes control and doesn't worry about what somebody might think."

I was the somebody she referred to, overthinking every situation.

Fury overtook me. My body was thrumming with rage. I felt myself shaking. I felt the whole world quaking. And then I woke up—fucking. Lucy was straddling me, her face, only inches from mine, contorted with orgasm. She was saying something I couldn't understand, lifting one hip and then the other and then coming down hard, her ass slapping against my pelvis.

"It's . . . so . . . fucking . . . thick . . ." she was saying. And then she frowned and twisted her lips as if some metamorphosis was transforming her very being.

I wanted to ask her if it was okay to be doing it, but instead I came so powerfully that even though my eyes were open, I still couldn't see a thing. Her haunches were pounding down machine-like against me. She was shouting something in my ear.

It was a perfectly clear and potent sexual experience. I gripped her arms, shaking her, because I was shuddering from the power of the orgasm. It was like some kind of spell. Sounds came out of my mouth that made no sense. I'm pretty sure that I ejaculated again, but that was the least of my feeling. My left calf went into a charley horse, but I didn't even respond to that.

If you had asked me at that moment what was happening, I would have told you that my whole life's aim was to be in that room, under that woman, not knowing the difference between pleasure and pain.

Finally the ache in my calf became overwhelming. I hopped up and walked around to work it out. When the pain abated, Lucy sat up and took my half-hard cock deeply into her mouth and ran her tongue over my balls.

"My God that's good," she said.

"What happened?" I asked her.

"We did it."

"But the lights were off . . . and, and, and I was asleep."

When Lucy smiled, everything, everything I had been feeling, fell together. She was laughing at me the way someone who cared would laugh. She saw my insecurity but wasn't fazed by it.

"I woke up about a half an hour ago," she said. "I guess I was feeling a little guilty about Billy and decided to go. I turned on the light to find my clothes. You were lying on your side but I could see that you still had an erection. For some reason I thought that was sweet. So then I started to feel guilty about walking out without telling you. I whispered in your ear, and you turned on your back but didn't wake up. Then I thought I'd pull on your hard-on and that would get you, but all you did was to start to move with my hand.

"I'm really sorry. It's never happened before, but you were just lying there and all I had to do was get on top."

She pulled on my arm, and I sat there beside her.

"So listen," she said. "I had a complete STD test before I got together with Billy. He did too. We're both fine." She sighed. "Do I have to tell him about this?"

"I haven't had an STD test in six years," I said. "But I haven't had sex with anyone but my girlfriend in nine years. So I guess it's okay."

"What about her?" Lucy asked.

I was thinking about Johnny Fry's red condom.

"She's safe. Nothing to worry about," I said.

Lucy sighed and then squeezed my arm. "I think you came twice."

"That second time I felt like I was having an epileptic fit. I thought I was gonna die."

"I never felt anybody come so hard," she said. "It's like you held me so tight that it made me feel that I was you."

A feeling of desperation entered through my shoulders. I worried that this would be the last time I'd ever have with Lucy or anyone like her. I didn't want her to leave. I didn't want to return to the emptiness that had been my life.

I suppose the despair showed in my face.

"What?" Lucy asked with a smile. "What's wrong?"

I took her by the shoulders and turned her around so that from the waist up she was on the bed and her knees were on the floor. Then I got down on my knees behind her.

"What?" she asked again.

Lucy had rounded buttocks that were young and quite firm.

I kissed the crack and ran my tongue from the top to the bottom, letting it waggle a moment in the few pale public hairs that protruded.

"Ooo, that's nice," she said.

Then with my thumbs I spread the cheeks apart.

"What are you doing, L?" It was the first time she called me that.

Her anus was small and pink with just a touch of gray at the aperture. I ran my tongue around the puckered eye and she gasped.

"Oh my God."

I pressed the tip of my tongue at the center and she reached back to touch my shoulder.

It was that touch that stayed with me for hours. Lucy's fingers caressing my shoulder, holding me in place, telling me, wordlessly, to stay right there.

Then she moved her hand, got a firm grip on her right buttock, and pulled it almost violently so that her anus opened an eighth of an inch.

I had only intended to kiss her lightly, hoping that I was the first to kiss her in this way. I wanted to be her first in something. I wanted to be something in her eyes.

But I was a little shy about putting my tongue inside her. I held back.

"Kiss it," she hissed. "Stick your tongue in me."

I still held back.

But then she moaned in anticipation and I realized that even me holding back was having sex with her; that I was in some emotional way already inside her. I pressed my tongue down and lunged with my head so that I felt her rectum give. I kept kissing her like that, my whole face between her buttocks. She was pressing back against my mouth, rolling from side to side.

"Oh yeah, baby. That's what I need," she moaned. "I need you. I want you."

I pulled back for a moment, and she shook her head against the bed, saying, "Don't stop. Don't stop. Please don't."

I went back to kissing her anus and pressing my face into her posterior. After long minutes of her moaning and goading me on, she crawled fully onto the bed and grabbed me by the arms. She was trying to move me. At first I didn't understand what she wanted but then I realized that she wanted to position us in the "69" position, only with her turned around with her back to me. That way she could turn her head to the side to perform fellatio on me while I could give my attention to her backside.

That lasted a little while, but she was so excited that I was infected by her passion. I came again. She didn't stop kissing my erection, though, and after a few moments it started to tickle, and I rolled away on my back.

She turned over and smiled at me.

"That was great," she said. "Nobody ever did that to me before."

"I never did it to anybody before," I said.

"Really? It felt so good. Why did you even think about it?"

"I want to be special to you, Lucy."

Lucy got a leg over me and straddled my belly. She let her bright hair fall down around my face, making a glistening blond tent of hair. The come on her breath smelled like mung bean sprouts.

"Are you satisfied?" she asked.

"Very."

"You're the best lover I've ever been with," she said. "I never even knew I could feel like that."

I didn't know if she was lying or just trying to make me feel good.

"Will you stay the night?" I asked.

"Will you hold me?"

"Of course."

"Billy never holds me after sex."

I wrapped my arms around her, and she slid down to my side.

Lucy and I made love in the morning before we got out of bed, and again in the shower, and once more in the living room when she was fully dressed and saying good-bye. The last two times I was too spent to come. My sex was aching, but I would have fucked until I bled if she hadn't pulled away and put on her clothes.

I asked her what she was feeling, and she said, "I don't know.

85

I've never done anything like this. But I guess we have to learn how to get around it. I mean, we can't be doing this all the time if we're going to stay with our lovers."

"No," I said. "I guess not."

I kissed her good-bye and told her that I intended to spend the whole week talking to gallery owners about her photographs.

After Lucy left, I decided to rein myself in. It was too much, what I was doing. Between the DVD, seeing Jo and Johnny, and Lucy (not to mention my supposed upcoming date with Sasha), I was way off track.

Even worse than all that, I had pissed off my agent and I hadn't even called anyone else for a real job, the job I was qualified to do.

I wasn't an art agent. I wasn't the kind of guy who threw everything over and then started out doing something completely new.

I wasn't a Don Juan or a Casanova.

It had only been a few days, and my life was nearly a ruin.

My first thought was to call Joelle and discuss what had happened with her. Joelle was the only person I was really close to. My father was dead, my mother was nearly in her second childhood, and both my siblings, brother and sister, didn't like me very much.

Joelle was the only one I could talk to. But when I thought about calling her, I remembered her grunting to the syncopation of Johnny Fry's thrusting hips. I thought of her looking into my eyes and saying, *there's only you.*

But I did pick up the phone.

I did punch in her number.

"Hello?"

"Hi, Jo."

"I thought you were going to call me last night, L?"

"I told you," I said. "The guy from Philly came. He didn't leave until nearly one. I thought you'd be asleep."

"It's almost two now. Where have you been all morning?"

"I just finished the first draft of the translation," I said.

"What was it?"

"A booklet that goes with a hundred-year-old bottle of balsamic vinegar. It's about the family that makes the shit. They need the first draft by Tuesday, and I still have to go over the edits."

"Vinegar?"

"Yeah. Ain't that some shit?"

"Are you going to come over?" she asked sweetly.

"Either I'm gonna sleep and then wake up to work or I'm going to work until I drop. Either way I won't be much company."

"I don't care," she said. "You could just come over and come to bed with me."

It was so nice the way she said it, so inviting and friendly. But when I wasn't with Jo, I had little feeling for her. There was no chemistry on the phone this time. And if I thought about her lies and deceptions, I felt like slamming my fist into another wall.

"You could go out with one of your other friends," I suggested. "You haven't seen Ralph Moreland in a while."

"I'm not interested in anyone but you, Cordell Carmel."

"Really?"

"Of course. Why do you keep asking me that?"

"I don't know. We haven't seen much of each other for over a year. Just weekends. Not much sex to speak of."

"Not much sex? What do you call Friday night and yesterday in the park?"

"I think it was just because I was scared."

"Scared of what?"

87

"Losing you," I said, realizing that somehow it was really true. I had already lost her without knowing it and now I was going through the feelings of trepidation leading up to that loss, as if I was playing catch-up with time.

"I'm not going anywhere," Jo said. "I'm here for you and I want you here with me."

"How about tomorrow?" I offered.

Jo hated spending weekdays with me. Her work so took up her life that she always said that she needed her weekdays alone *to garner her resources*. I hadn't spent a nonholiday weekday with her in over six years.

"Okay," she said without hesitation. "What time will you be here?"

"What time do want me?"

"Afternoon?"

"You sure you don't have to work?" I asked.

"I have an appointment but I can change it," she said. "You're what's important, L, not some job."

I brought my hand to my face and smelled the light, lemony scent of Lucy's incense-oil perfume. This served to make me feel guilty. Then I remembered Johnny Fry and I was angry again. That was when I began to understand the connection between emotion and sensuality. It came to me that somewhere between seeing Jo and Johnny rutting on that sunlit floor and now, I had come alive. And life hurt.

"Yeah," I said. "Three o'clock. I'll be there."

"You sound like you want to get off."

"I don't want to," I lied, "but I have to," and lied again.

Classical mathematics don't work with affairs of the heart. My sleeping with Lucy and flirting with Sasha and Linda Chou didn't even out what Joelle had done with Johnny Fry. I could never forgive her based upon those equations. I would never feel that things were harmonious between us.

I didn't want to go to her place, but I wanted her to want me to go. I didn't want her to have slept with Johnny, but whenever I saw her and I thought about them together, I wanted to have sex.

The confusion was too much. I left my house and wandered toward the Eastside. I made it north to about Houston and then east to West Broadway. There were thousands of people out in the street on that Sunday afternoon. Women wearing next to nothing and men pretending not to gawk. People sold silver jewelry, hand-bound blank books, paintings, pottery, and old records there on the street. I went farther east, past Elizabeth Street, past Chrystie.

I got tired after a while and stopped to sit on a blue fire hydrant in front of a tiny Peruvian restaurant. The hydrant sat next to a telephone pole. All over the wooden post there were stapled dozens of sheets of paper. People were looking for roommates, apartment shares, rooms. Some were leaving town and selling off their belongings. One woman had lost a male poodle named Boro. A lavender page promised you could lose thirty pounds in thirty days, free of cost. And there were nine white sheets with the photograph of a young black woman xeroxed on them.

HAVE YOU SEEN ANGELINE? the poster said, and then it gave a phone number and promised a reward of $150. It was the smallness of the reward that made me pay attention to the poster. Angeline must have come from poor folks who could hardly afford to pay a reward. I felt sorry for them and for the girl, even though she might be happier on her own. I was. At least I had been before I met Jo. My first wife, Minda, was a painter. She did portraits on the boardwalk at Coney Island. We got married on a whim and divorced on the rocks. We were nine months into the marriage when she told me that she'd rather share her bed with broken glass.

89

"What do I do wrong?" I asked her.

"You don't do anything." she said. "You don't even fart."

My second marriage was even shorter. Her name was Yvette and her father was a career soldier. He told me on our wedding day that if I broke his baby's heart, he'd run me down and kill me.

Remembering Minda's complaint, I decided to make a stand against my new wife's father. I told him that he should never drink from an open bottle in my presence because if he did, I will have likely put poison in it.

When Yvette heard what I'd said, she yelled at me and called me the devil. I said that he had threatened me first.

"That's okay," Yvette said. "A bride's father is supposed to say those kinds of things."

We went on the honeymoon but never had sex again.

She took me to court for alimony. The judge laughed, and the annulment was invoked.

There was an orange sheet underneath three pictures of Angeline. The only words I could make out were . . . A FRIEND.

For quite a while I tried to think of what the other words might say. But no matter what I came up with, I couldn't think of what they were selling, looking for, or giving away. Finally I went over to the pole and removed the three pictures and their worries about young Angeline that covered the orange sheet. I didn't feel too bad about it. There were six more posters of Angeline on that pole alone, and I had seen others all around the Village.

The orange Xerox said:

DIAL A FRIEND
Everybody needs a friend,
someone they can talk to,

someone who will listen without
judging them. If you are
lonely and there's no one
to hear your pain then call
1–888–627–1189. 35¢ a minute.
(This is not a sex line.)

It seemed to me an original idea. I thought of how many people
out in the world needed a friend sometimes and couldn't find one.
I wondered who it was that they got to man those lines. They
obviously used credit cards.

I tore off the number and put it in my wallet.

I went into the Peruvian restaurant and ordered seviche. They
served it with white bread and butter. The meal was $12 plus taxes
and tip.

After that, I wandered around for hours. While I walked, I
passed hundreds of people. Not one of them did I recognize—and
no one knew me.

I didn't get to my door until nine that night. I hadn't done a thing all
day. It was the fourth time in a week I was aware of doing absolutely
no work. Before that period, I hadn't gone a day without working in
years. Before then, I spent some hours every day either looking for
work or translating for practice or for a client. But now whole days
went by and I did nothing but wallow in misery or follow my dick.

By the time I got to my building, I was feeling hopeless. I was
looking for my key when someone shouted.

"Mr. Carmel."

It was Sasha, walking arm in arm with a young man. The man
was tall and dressed in a gray suit. His yellow shirttail was hanging
out, and his sensual lips were plastered with an inebriated grin.

"This is my brother Enoch," Sasha said as they approached.

"Hi." He put out his left hand for me to shake. That was probably because his right arm was around his sister's shoulder and if he let go he would have fallen.

"Help me bring him upstairs?" Sasha asked.

"Sure," I said. Keeping my grip on his left hand, I hefted his arm up and over my shoulder.

"I love my sister, no matter what anybody says," Enoch lectured as we went up the slender metal staircase. "She's the most beautiful, wonderful, friendly woman. And she's built like the old-time movie stars, like a real woman. I love the old-time movies. Wallace Beery and Ronald Coleman; Myrna Loy and Faye Wray. That was back when they knew how people felt in their hearts. Isn't that right, Sassy?"

"Sure, Inch. Sure," his sister said.

I had the feeling that they went through this scenario many times. A sad and lost younger brother coming to his older sister to cry in his beer over a life he always wanted and never had.

He went limp a flight below Sasha's door. We had to drag him the rest of the way, his heels knocking at each step.

I held him up while Sasha turned the key in the lock.

I dragged him across the threshold into the dark apartment. When she turned on the light, I was surprised.

Our apartments had exactly the same layout, but all the walls of Sasha's place had been removed. There were six pillars in a large room. The bedroom, kitchen, and living room all blended into one. Only the bathroom had a door and walls.

I dropped Enoch on his back on the futon couch.

He smiled at Sasha, holding out his arms to her.

"Kiss," he said like a small boy talking to his mother.

She gave him a loud, smacking kiss on the lips and then settled on the floor at his feet to take off his shoes.

"I can take care of him now," she told me.

"Okay," I said.

When I went through the door, she called after me, "Remember, we're going to have dinner soon."

I had hoped that she'd forgotten. I was overwhelmed with women and sexuality by then. But I nodded and waved, then I shut the door.

Down in my apartment I starting reading a novel that had been on my shelf for years. It was called *The Night Man*; it was a nonmystical story about a pedestrian vampire—a man who never went out in the light, who loved the darkness and lived in its domain exclusively. He eschewed the sun and everything that daylight brought. It was a tragic love story of prosaic proportions. The main character, Juvenal Nyx, meets a woman who is a being of light. He meets her on a bridge, where she intends to kill herself because of the loss of her child. Her husband blames her for being careless, and she has taken the responsibility even though it is questionable whether or not this self-abnegation is justified.

It was the first novel I had read in many months. So much of my time had been taken up with translations of manuals, business forms, and legal documents that when I was through working, all I wanted to do was watch TV.

But not that night.

I was actually afraid to turn on my television. My obsession with *The Myth of Sisypha* was sure to make me turn to that DVD sooner or later, and I wanted to cool down, to wean myself off of this painful preoccupation with punitive sex.

The love story in *The Night Man*, though a little melodramatic, held my interest for hours. It must have been past one when the knocking came on my door.

It wasn't a regular knock. Three taps and then a bang, then a thud or two, followed by something like the fast rapping of a metal pencil or, more probably, a ring.

I didn't want to answer. I knew who it was—at least, I thought I did. In my mind I felt intimate with the logic that led up to that knock: Sasha's brother had fallen asleep, and she was reminded of me because we met at the door. She wanted to come down and fuck me until the sun came up. That's what I believed.

Thinking back on it now, it seems like such an arrogant assumption. I wasn't a sex god. Women didn't throw themselves at me. I was just a middle-aged guy going through the regular traumas of my generation and species.

But even though it made no sense, I was absolutely sure that Sasha was on the other side of that door.

At first I thought that I could pretend that I was asleep or maybe out. I just wouldn't answer, and she'd go away.

But the deranged knocking continued, and I became a little disgusted with myself. Why shouldn't I be able to answer my own door? So what if she wanted to come down and seduce me? I didn't have to go along with it. I could tell her that I was back with my girlfriend and sex with her just wasn't what I was interested in right then.

So I went to the door and pulled it open without even asking who it was. Seeing Enoch Bennett standing there was a real surprise. All he wore was his gray suit pants with suspenders hanging down on either side, and one black shoe with no sock underneath, on his left foot.

His expression was blank at first, but when he looked at me, he began to blubber. He fell forward and I grabbed him, holding on

94

like some boxer finding that his only respite is in the arms of his opponent.

"What's wrong?" I asked him.

He tried to respond but all that came out were urgent, grief-stricken sounds that meant to be words.

I helped him to the futon couch and lowered him into a sitting position. He fell on his side immediately, bawling for all he was worth. When I sat down next to him, he grabbed my hands and pressed his face against them.

As he cried, I began to fear that something terrible had happened upstairs. Sasha had destroyed Enoch's life when he was just a boy by forcing their parents apart. Maybe in his drunken stupor he'd taken his revenge by murdering his sister. Certainly his sadness was something more than normal. And why would he have come down to a total stranger's apartment?

I scanned his hands and wrinkled trousers for blood but saw nothing. There were a few wet spots on his pants but the cloth's dark gray hue hid any other color.

"What happened?" I asked when his tears subsided a bit.

Breathing in quick, swimmerlike inhalations, Enoch sat up.

"I haven't seen Sasha in years," the young man said, his sensual lips trembling, ready to return to despair. "My therapist told me that it was time to confront her. To, to, to tell her how I feel about . . ."

"About what?"

"At first it was okay. She seemed happy to see me. I talked to her about it, and she, and she apologized to me. She said it was because of my mother, how much she had hurt her.

"It was just like my therapist said. We talked and, and, and then sometimes I would get angry and yell at her and tell her that I hated her sometimes."

I was sure now that Sasha lay dead upstairs. I wondered when I should call the police. Enoch was a little bigger, probably stronger, and definitely younger than I. I didn't want to get into a physical struggle with him.

It was then that I thought about the half bottle of cognac that I had left.

"Would you like a drink?" I asked, rising as I did so. If I could get him a little drunker, I could use a chair to wedge him in the toilet and then call 911.

But Enoch grabbed me by the wrist and held on tight.

"We got drunk in celebration," he said. "We went barhopping, and then, and then I was upstairs. My fingers were inside her and she was . . . she had her mouth on me. I pushed her away and told her no, not again. But all she did was hold her arms out to me. She didn't say a word, but I knew what she was thinking. She was thinking that I wanted her more than anything. And I did. I jumped on top of her. And, and, and when I woke up, she was lying there next to me, and room smelled like sex."

This revelation left me bemused. In my mind, a moment before, a murder had been committed. Now it was simply a case of adult incest; a brother and sister having sex in a secluded room because of too much drink. Maybe some jury somewhere would have found them guilty—given them prison time. Maybe there were countries where they would have been executed for their crime. Maybe I would have reacted to the confession of the bereft youth if the past few days had not been so filled with sex and depravity. But now I felt only relief. Sasha was upstairs sleeping it off, and Enoch was crying on my couch.

"Have a drink," I told him. "A drink will make you feel better, and in the morning it'll all be further away."

He began crying again, but when I poured him half a water glass of cognac, he downed it in three gulps. I poured him another. He only made it halfway through before he slumped down unconscious on the futon.

He wasn't lying on his back, so I didn't worry that he would die in his sleep. I draped a blanket over his shoulders, went back to my room, turned off the light, and lay down in darkness.

The sleep I hoped for refused to come. In the gloom I saw forms like huge drifting icebergs all around me. I knew that I was in my own bed and that there was no threat, but still I felt dread. I was jobless, and my lover used me like some lifeless mannequin. I'd had sex with a girl who was a child only a few years before and I was obsessed with a woman on a DVD.

It was true. I was thinking about Sisypha and her motivations a good part of each day. Why had she tortured her husband with such deep love in her voice and eyes? What lesson did she need him to learn? Why had Sasha seduced her brother? Why had Joelle made me go through the same motions that Johnny Fry had taken with her?

My limbs began to quiver in the bed. My forearms and feet trembled like small animals shivering in a thunderstorm. At that moment I had no sex. It had been taken from me, and all that was left was the certainty that some kind of tragedy was heading in my direction: my death. Somehow I knew was going to die soon. Someone was going to kill me, or maybe I'd kill myself.

The fear of death sat me up in the bed.

I reached out for the phone, thinking, without thinking, that I'd call Joelle. She had always helped me when I was afraid. She was very logical and reasonable when I called her with my irrational fears.

Once there was a white guy who moved into the building across the street from me. From the first day he seemed to be staring at me and I got it in my head that his intentions were murderous. He was some kind of serial killer who hated middle-aged black men who lived in the midst of the white world. I knew it was crazy, but every time I saw him, he'd give me that evil stare, and my heart thundered and I knew for a fact that he was going to kill me slowly with a knife, a big knife.

When I finally told Jo about my fears, she came down to my place and sat outside with me until the guy, Felix Longerman, came out of his front door. She went right up to him, engaged him in a brief conversation, and then dragged him across the street to me.

"This is Felix," she told me. "He works for Viking, in translations."

It turned out that some eleven years before, Felix and I had worked on a project together, and every time he saw me, he thought I looked familiar. I hadn't recognized him because he'd had a beard in those days.

My fears were so silly and yet they felt so real.

But that night, with the phone in my hand, I knew that Joelle couldn't help me. No one could. Brad Mettleman would laugh. Lucy would say that she was in the same position that Jo was.

I dialed a number.

There was no ring, just three clicks and then a voice saying, "Enter code or wait for first operator." There was silence for a few seconds and then the sound of a phone ringing.

"Hello?" someone answered on the second ring.

"Is this, ah, um, a friend?" I asked.

"Yes it is. How can I help you?"

"Uh . . . don't we have to do business first? Don't you want my credit card or something?"

"It's not necessary. Your number shows up on their records and the charge appears on your phone bill."

"Oh. Wow. It's that easy?"

"Yes, very easy. Now, what do you want to talk about?"

"I'm lost," I said, and the gloom seemed to recede. The pressure I had felt in my chest lightened. I took a deep breath and sat up straighter.

"What's your name?" the woman asked.

"Cordell."

"Nice to meet you, Cordell. My name is Cynthia."

"Hi, Cynthia. I have to tell you that even just talking to somebody makes me feel better."

"Where are you right now, Cordell?"

"I'm in my apartment, in my bed."

"Are you alone?"

"Pretty much. There's this guy sleeping on the couch in my living room."

"Who is that?"

"His name is Enoch Bennett," I said, and then I went into the whole story, everything that had happened except for my obsession with *The Myth of Sisypha*. That seemed a little too much like sex for sex's sake, and the ad for the dial-a-friend line had definitely said that this was not a sex line.

"Have you told Joelle that you saw her yet?" Cynthia asked.

"No."

"Why not?"

"I want to," I said. "But every time I see her, I get obsessed, sexually. All I want is to be with her, to make her mine."

"But she cheated on you."

"She's my only friend," I said. "I guess that's obvious, because I'm calling you. Not that there's anything wrong with you, but you can see that I don't have anyone to talk to. Joelle has been the only person I've been really close to in eight years."

"Don't you have any family?" Cynthia asked.

"No. I mean, yes. I have a brother, a sister, and a mother."

99

"Can't you talk to one of them?"

That made me smile.

"Cordell?" Cynthia asked. "Are you there?"

"I was just thinking that you aren't doing very good business trying to talk me into calling my family."

"This is a friend line," she said. Her voice was very calming. "I'm here to help you, not to get you to spend money."

"Excuse me if I doubt that," I told her.

"That's okay," she said. "I understand. Most people who call here, especially the men, think that this is either a secret dating line or a scam to get lonely people's money."

"And do you somehow convince them that you're not those things?" I asked. Just the act of conversation was having a profound restorative effect on me.

"All I can do is tell them how our little company came to be."

"How's that?"

"A very wealthy man decided a few years ago that America was slipping into a kind of melancholy," she said. It sounded as if this was a speech she had given many times. "People were getting fatter, becoming less active, concerned with the lives of characters on TV shows but completely unconcerned with the millions who die yearly from war and disease. This man felt that most people were unaware, or mostly unaware, of the sadness that was daily descending upon them.

"He knew that he couldn't address this emotional dysfunction directly. He knew that even his great wealth couldn't stem the tide of melancholy, so he decided to do what he could. He hired a psychological testing firm to locate and hire hundreds of persons who have empathy and care for people with problems. Not psychologists or professional counselors, but people who feel compassion for others.

"He started this hotline so that people could call, not necessarily when they were in an emergency but when they just needed a friend to talk to."

"You're kidding," I said. I was holding the big toe of my left foot with my right hand like I had when I was a child.

"No," Cynthia said, "I'm not kidding. And so if I think your family would be better for you to talk to, I'll tell you that."

"Wow," I said. I rolled onto my side. "How much time do I have?

"As much as you want, Cordell. But you were going to tell me about your family."

"My brother's in the army," I said. "Special Forces. He's always off in some foreign country either killing people or showing others how to kill. We haven't spoken in seven years. He believes America is doing great things and I don't. Not . . . not that I do anything about politics. I don't even vote. It's just that I don't believe that the government cares for everyday people.

"My sister and I just don't hit it off. She was angry at me for not making my marriages work. She's married. They live in Utah and have very little time for anything but their children and their church.

"And, and my mother is in a senior apartment complex in Connecticut. It's not a medical facility, and my mom is okay on her own, but she won't talk to me about anything important. If I bring up something that makes her uncomfortable, she gets confused and starts talking about the old days when Eric, Phoebe, and I were kids."

"What about your father?" Cynthia asked.

"He's dead."

"But our parents are close to us our entire lives," she said. "Your father will be with you until the day you die. What would he tell you about your girlfriend and her lover?"

In the wake of Cynthia's question, a wave of deep exhaustion washed through me. I yawned and pulled the pillow under my head.

"All of a sudden I'm really tired, Cynthia," I said. "I can hardly keep my eyes open. I guess talking to you relaxed me. Thanks a lot, but I think I have to get off."

"If you want to talk to me again," she said, "when they ask you to enter my code—just spell out my name, Cynthia, C-Y-N-T-H-I-A with a three at the end of it."

I nodded and then hung up.

I don't remember anything after that until the dawn light shone in my open window. I suspected that Enoch and Cynthia were the product of my sleeping imagination.

I got up, stumped into the living room, and realized that my experiences from the night before were real. Enoch was in the same position I'd left him. I was still dressed in the clothes I'd worn the day before.

I showered and shaved, put on clean clothes, and brewed a strong pot of French roast coffee. As I was pouring my first cup, Enoch wandered into the kitchen. Across his shoulders he wore the camel-colored cashmere blanket I'd covered him with.

"Good morning," he said, his greeting couched on the bed of a wan, sensual smile.

"Hey. You back with the living, huh?"

"How did I get here?" he asked.

"Last night you stumbled down to my apartment and knocked."

"I must have been really drunk."

"Oh yeah," I said with a smile. "I didn't understand a word you said. And then you just fell asleep."

"Did I say anything coherent?" he asked, staring into my eyes.

"No. You want some coffee?"

"Where do you live?" I was asking Enoch Bennett.

He sat at the small table next to the dishwasher in my kitchen. It was 6:36 AM.

"I live in L.A. with my mom," he said. "I'm planning to move out soon. But you know, rent is so high out there, and you really have to be careful about where you live."

I remembered that Sasha said he was thirty.

"Has it been fun visiting here in New York?" I asked.

"Yeah. Sasha's a blast, and I really love it here. But New York's even more expensive than L.A."

He seemed to be on the verge of tears.

"You better believe it," I said. "I'm from San Francisco originally. I'd leave, but I came here so long ago that I couldn't even imagine where else to live."

He smiled, his eyes welling with tears.

At that moment, someone knocked at the door.

"Excuse me," I said, rising to go see who it was.

Enoch sighed, glad, I was sure, to be left to his internal devastation.

Sasha was standing at the front door. All she wore was a lacy nightgown that went down to her knees and showed a good deal of cleavage.

"Is he down here?" she asked me. Her voice was flat and uninspired.

"Yeah," I said. "He came to the door, cried for a few minutes, and then fell unconscious on my couch."

"What did he say?"

"Nothing I understood."

103

"Not a thing?"

"No. Mostly he just cried, and the words made no sense in English, French, or Spanish."

Sasha smiled at my translator's note.

"Sasha?" Enoch was standing behind me at the entranceway.

"What happened, Inch?"

Instead of answering, he ran to her and threw his arms around her neck. He cried as hard as he had the night before. She put her arms around his back and held him loosely while he blubbered and wailed. Her face was without emotion as she held him. For her, you could see that this was just another phase in a very complex play.

After a minute or so, she patted his shoulder blade and said, "It's okay, baby. It's all right."

Her eyebrows rose in mild perturbation at his childish behavior.

"Thanks for taking him in, Cordell," she said. "Inch gets emotional sometimes when he drinks."

"No problem," I said.

"Come on, honey," she said to her brother. "Let's go upstairs."

For a moment Enoch resisted. He turned his face toward me, and there was real fear in his eyes.

"Come on," Sasha said. "Cordell has his own life to take care of."

"Yeah," Enoch said, still looking at me. Then he turned away, and the door closed behind them.

I took in a deep breath that trembled on its way back out. The passion between the brother and sister was dark and bottomless. I realized that the trouble I had with my siblings was nothing compared to what it might have been.

I made my bed and opened the windows wide again. I wrote down Cynthia's name and number. I thought about her seeming concern with whom I had in my life. Just remembering our conversation cooled the sexual tension that had colored every moment since I'd seen Jo and John Fry. Even then, when I remembered their sexual abandon, I had no emotional response.

Maybe, I thought, this time I could break it off with Jo. I had Cynthia now.

I wondered what the professional phone-friend looked like. Was she tall? Pretty? Asian? But I was happy to realize that it didn't matter what she looked like; Cynthia was a pure friend, an ideal friend, someone who cared about me for me. The money I paid meant nothing. I looked at it like a contribution to a charity committed to the eradication of loneliness and melancholia.

Cynthia was my social worker— that's how I saw it. Whenever I needed her, she would be there in my corner, asking questions about my well-being, my family, and my heart.

With those thoughts in mind, I lay down across my bed and slept for hours with no concern about Sasha and Enoch, Jo and Johnny, or Lucy and Billy.

I was a lone craft floating on a sea of unconsciousness. I had no destination, no point of origin. I didn't have a job or a girlfriend. I had no appointments or bosses to tell me what I should or shouldn't do.

When I woke up, the sun was shining on my bed—not directly on me but at my side, like a disembodied sacred lover, a goddess who graced me with her intangible presence for a few moments while I slept.

It was early afternoon by then. I took out the fax from Brad's office and called half a dozen galleries. I presented myself as Cordell Carmel, associate of Brad Mettleman. I told them that I'd been working for Brad for some years and now I was going out into the field to help him with a new stable of exceptionally talented young artists.

By 2:00 I had four appointments to show Lucy's works.

I took the subway up the Westside to Jo's neighborhood. As I walked through the door of her building, I glanced at my watch. It was 2:58. It struck me that I was always on time, never late a moment, until the day I didn't go down to Philadelphia.

I couldn't understand when other black people talked about CP time: colored people's time. I was never late. And so many of my childhood friends had joined the armed services. You couldn't be late in the army.

Maybe punctuality was part of my problem, I thought. Maybe I felt oppressed by everyone else's needs. If I started to live by my own schedule, maybe people I worked with and people like Jo wouldn't feel that they could walk on me.

Robert the doorman was at his post.

"Yes?" he asked me.

"You don't know me, Robert?" I asked back.

This retort made him a little wary.

"You're here to see—Miss Joelle?"

"Yes," I said, and I made to walk down the aisle toward the third bank of elevators.

"Wait," he said.

"Wait for what? I always go right up. You know that."

"I have to call."

"Fuck that," I said, and moved toward the elevators.

As I walked, I heard him ring the intercom bell. He muttered something; I'm sure it was a warning for Jo, who must have had John Fry up to her place on many weekday afternoons.

But even this did not shake me. I was a bit angry at Robert for being so obvious about Jo's indiscretions. He should have let me go and then called so she and John could come up with some kind of plan.

I rode the elevator wondering who I would be when she opened the door and also who she would have become. We seemed to change with every meeting. There was anticipation in my chest and a tap dance in my heart. Who knew what would happen next?

Jo came to the door wearing a semiopaque white dress with nothing underneath. Her pubic hair and large brown nipples were as evident as her smile.

"Hi," she said, bowing her head slightly.

"Take it off," I replied.

Without hesitation she pulled the dress up and over her head. I closed the door.

She reached for me, but I said, "Put your hands down."

When she faltered, I said, "Put your fucking hands down and let me look at you."

A smile appeared on her lips and then went away.

As I stared at her lovely form, she began to tremble.

I could feel my nostrils flare. My cock was pressing against the fabric of my pants.

"Will you take off your clothes?" she asked humbly.

"No."

"Can we go into the living room?"

"No."

"You just want me to stand here?" she asked.

"Turn around. I want to see your ass."

"Don't talk to me like that," she said, and I slapped her.

It wasn't hard. It couldn't have stung. It was just a brief touch

107

with a violent gesture leading up to it. But her eyes opened wide, and she turned around holding her backside high for my inspection.

After a minute or more she said, "L."

"Shut up and lift that ass higher."

When she did as I said, a big grin formed on my face. In my imagination I looked like a hungry hyena about to tear into some dying creature's flesh.

This notion frightened me. What was I becoming? For a moment I considered turning around and leaving—never talking to Joelle again.

There was something happening in me that I was barely aware of, some emotion that was forming into actions without my permission or control.

"Spread your ass," someone said. After a moment I understood that that someone was me.

Jo grasped her buttocks and pulled them slightly.

I slapped her right butt cheek hard and said, "I want it wide open. Wide."

She groaned and pulled her cheeks as far apart as Lucy had.

When I got down on my knees, I noticed that wetness was coming from her vagina, making her inner thighs a slick and shiny brown. I stuck my tongue as deeply as I could into the aperture of her ass.

"Oh my God," she moaned.

When she tried to move away, I slapped her damp thigh. It made a wet sound, and she yelped.

"Move back on my tongue," I said.

She did this timidly and moved off an inch—waiting for further instructions. Her breath was coming fast and her toes were gripping and releasing the carpet.

"Fuck my tongue with your ass," I told her. "Make it go in and out."

At first she went slowly, groaning each time her anus enveloped the tip of my tongue. But then she started going fast and hard. Her groans became barks, and I could tell she was about to come.

I stood up quickly and opened the front door.

"What are you doing?" she asked, straining over the nascent orgasm roiling in her womb.

Without answering, I pushed her out the door and got down on my knees behind her. Instantly she began fucking my face again. The barking returned. She was just about to come when the bell on the elevator rang. She froze, and I rose up behind her, wrapping my arm around her middle.

"Come for me," I whispered into her ear.

"Oh God," she whispered hoarsely, and then she forced four fingers into her mouth. She was trembling and screaming into her fingers.

Down the hall, the door of the elevator opened.

I waited until I could see the woman coming out before pulling Jo back into the apartment and slamming the door.

Jo fell on the floor writhing, wrestling with her orgasm.

"Fuck me!" she pleaded. "Fuck me right now!"

She arched up on her feet and shoulders, making a perfect presentation of the bushy mound.

I looked down on her and sneered. Sneered.

"No," I said, and I walked away into the living room. There I sat on the lush brown leather chair that faced the window. This was Jo's favorite chair, the chair that she'd sit in when she wanted to read or when she needed distance from me. I never sat in that chair. I never touched her when she sat there.

Jo came in and jumped on my lap, straddling me and pressing

109

her breasts against my chest. It felt very sensual for her to be naked while I was fully dressed—down to my shoes.

I threw her off, and she tumbled onto the carpeted floor, only to get up and jump on me again.

I threw her off.

When she was just about to rise, I pointed at her and said, "Stay."

Her eyes widened filled with both rage and desire.

When I grinned, surprised fear came into her visage.

"Please," she said softly.

I unzipped my pants, allowing the rock-hard erection to emerge.

When she sat up on her knees to regard the cock, I noticed that both of her copper calves were wet from her vaginal discharges.

"You can come look at it," I said. "But don't touch it until I say it's all right."

Obediently she sidled up next to me, touching my knee with one hand while letting her other hand and forearm settle gently on my thigh.

"It's beautiful," she said. "It's throbbing."

"Dominating you makes him want to sing," I said in a voice much lower than normal.

"It's wet at the slit," she said.

"He wants to come down your throat."

"Oh, yes," she whispered. "Does he want me to lick off that drop?"

I paused a moment before saying, "No."

"I want to kiss him," she said. "He's so dark and thick and hard."

"He could split your pussy wide open," I said.

She groaned again.

"Doesn't he want me?" she begged.

"Not now."

"When?"

"He won't say."

"But he's going to fuck me soon isn't he?"

"Not this afternoon," I said, and she whimpered pitifully. "He has other things on his mind."

"What?" she asked. "What is he thinking?"

"He's thinking about a man standing behind you. A man with a huge hard cock. A man who wants your pussy as much as you want this cock right now."

Putting her hands against both my knees, she got to her feet, her head not more than an inch from my straining member. Her butt was up in the air in preparation for the man I spoke of.

My heart was pounding then. It was difficult for me to maintain my dispassionate tone.

"His cock is thicker than mine and more than twice as long."

"Oh yes," Jo whispered. "I want it."

"And suddenly," I said, "without warning, he plunges the whole thing in you, all the way in."

Jo began to come again. She moved her hips from side to side and leaned forward to take my cock into her mouth. But I put my hand against her forehead to hold her off.

"He's pounding against the backs of your legs with his muscle-hard thighs," I said. "You can feel it all through you."

I perceived a light in the dome of my skull. It was bright yet not at all an optical experience.

"L!" Jo shouted.

When I looked down, I saw the thick white come erupting from my dick. It was shooting up and running down the shaft. The light was getting brighter, and I experienced very little physical

111

sensation. All I felt was my ass clenching, squeezing out the great quantity of come.

Jo's head was pressing against my hand, trying to get at the ejaculation, but I held her off. It seemed so perfect to have an orgasm without any tactile sensation.

Jo rolled onto the floor, grabbing at her pussy with both hands.

I stood up and looked down her rocking from side to side, grimacing as if there was something inside her that she was trying to pull out. A thick dollop of milky white semen leaked from my cock onto her cheek.

I went to the bathroom. There I dampened a washcloth and wiped the sputum from my pants. Then I held the still-hard penis in my left hand and washed it gently with my right. I stood there rubbing the rough cloth lightly upon the oversensitized skin of my manhood. It looked beautiful to me. It felt connected to every part of my being.

I had a college education. I learned that human beings were sexual creatures. But I had never experienced that knowledge. At that moment I knew that every step of my life was leading to this tableau. It wasn't about Jo. It wasn't about her affair with Johnny Fry. That's what started it, but the door that trauma opened led to another place completely.

I laughed.

There I was, dick in hand, philosophizing about sexuality.

"What's funny?" Joelle asked.

When I looked at her, I could feel the cock stiffen. And also I became aware of a sharp pain in my head that had been there since that light shone in my mind.

"Get dressed," I told her.

"Aren't we going to bed?" she asked, the disappointment all over her face.

"My head hurts and I'm hungry," I said. "I haven't eaten yet today."

"I need to fuck somebody, Cordell Carmel."

"Get dressed."

She gasped and then smiled.

"Didn't you hear me?" she asked.

"If you don't cover that ass, I will turn you over my knee and give you something to complain about." The familiar words fell easily from my lips. I could almost hear my father's voice a room or two away, down the hall.

I suppressed the urge to go look for him.

Instead I took a step toward Jo, intent on making my promise real. She yelped and jumped away. Within three minutes she returned wearing a plaid skirt and pink blouse. She had on black high heels and no hose. I couldn't tell if she was wearing underwear.

"Let's go," I said.

She put her arms around me and kissed me. Then she looked into my eyes.

"What's happening to you?" she asked.

"You."

"What do you mean, me?"

"Let's go," I said again, and she began to cry.

The tears weren't from sorrow or pain. It was just too much feeling. She felt like I did: like a cork on a rushing river, like a plastic bag caught in an updraft, finding itself thousands feet above the ground.

I took her by the arm and pulled her toward the door.

"I can't go out like this," she said.

"Sure you can. It's just your heart beating." I had no idea what I was saying. But my words seemed to mean something to her. She grabbed my arm with both hands and pressed her head against my shoulder.

As we went out the door, I felt that there was more love between us than there had ever been—more love than there ever would be again.

We walked out of the building with her head on me, her tears running down my breast.

"My toes feel numb," Joelle was saying. "It's what you do to me. It's just like . . . crazy good."

We were walking up Broadway a little past four in the afternoon.

"I have the worst headache that I've ever had in my life," I said.

"Where does it hurt?" she asked.

"The dome," I said. "Right up in the top. It feels like it's gonna explode."

Jo pulled on my arm, and we stopped. She got in front of me and began massaging my temples with the fingers of both hands. We stood there in the middle of the street facing each other sensually while dozens of people walked around us, furtively glancing at the shameless lovers.

"Is this helping?" she asked.

"It feels great," I said. "And I don't really mind the headache."

I took both her wrists in my hand and we walked half a block. She didn't resist the handcuff grip.

When I let go, she put both arms around me, hugging me as we went.

Cicero's is a small Italian restaurant above 93rd on Broadway that doesn't close between lunch and dinner. The waiter seated us at a corner table in the back of the empty dining room. I ordered a plate of antipasto for two and a carafe of red wine.

Jo sat close to me and held my hand. Now and then, she'd kiss my puffy knuckles. Whenever she did this, my erection throbbed under the table. It felt like a moan, like movement under the ground.

"Are we going back to my place after we eat?" she asked, after the waiter served our sliced meats, cheeses, and olives.

"I need you to wait until tomorrow," I said.

"I can't wait, baby," she said. And when I didn't answer, "My pussy is throbbing."

"Is it wet?"

"Yes. Very, very wet."

"It was dripping down your leg while I was licking your ass," I said.

"When I was fucking your face with my ass," she said correcting me.

"I never saw you that wet," I continued.

"Please stay with me tonight," Jo pleaded.

"Will you go fuck someone else if I don't?"

"No, baby," she said. "There's no one but you."

"How can I be sure of that?" I asked, trying to sound playful.

"Why would you even think such a thing?"

"You're a sexy woman, Jo. I only just realized how hungry you are for love and sex. In the park, in the hall, in your ass. How can a woman like that have just one man?"

"I did all that with you."

"But what about the last eight years? Eight years, and all we had was straightforward intercourse. Missionary position and, every once in a while, doggy-style. That's not much."

"Your wine," the waiter said. He was standing there next to us. He'd probably heard me. "Shall I pour?"

"Just leave it," I told him.

115

He smiled. He was a young Asian man with brownish skin, maybe Vietnamese or Cambodian.

"I've loved you all that time," she said.

"But couldn't you love me and someone else too?"

"No," she said with absolute certainty.

"What about kissing someone?" I asked. "Could you kiss a man?"

"Why are you asking me all this, L?"

"Robert."

Fear etched its lines into her face. I realized that I had never seen Jo really frightened before. But I could tell by those well-worn furrows that dread was no stranger to her.

I felt a pang of guilt. I'd thought that Jo was strong and unaffected by anxiety.

"My, my doorman?"

"Yeah. Him."

"What did, what did he say?"

The guilt in my heart was replaced almost immediately by a feeling of dominance and malice. The Rolling Stones' song "Under My Thumb" came into my mind. My mouth salivated over her trepidation.

I swallowed and smiled. I waited.

"What did he say?" Jo asked.

"Nothing."

"Then what does he have to do with anything about me?"

"He didn't want to let me up to your apartment."

"What?"

"Most of the times I come to your place on the weekend, Robert is there at least once. He sees me and waves for me to go up. When I knock at the door, you're always busy and take a while to answer. That way I know he hasn't called you."

"So?"

"But today, on a Monday, I come to him, and he says, wait. And when I ignore him, he calls you immediately."

Passion was completely gone from Jo's face. She stared at me with real concern.

"Is that all?" she asked.

"I figured that you had a weekday boyfriend, and Robert was worried that he was up there with you."

"But no one was there," she said.

"Robert didn't know that."

"Is that why you made me take my clothes off in the doorway?" she asked. "So my secret boyfriend couldn't get away. So you could fuck me while he hid in the closet?"

"I took you there because whenever I see you, I lose control. You are the most beautiful woman I've ever known and you have been the only woman in my life. No. No. You have been the only person in my life. My only friend. Really the only one I can talk to. But, obviously, I never knew anything about you."

"What do you mean?" she said. "You know everything about me. You've met my mother and my sister, my friends. You know about every job I do."

"But I didn't know how sexual you were. I didn't know that there's something you're frightened of."

"I'm not afraid of anything," she said defiantly.

"Why didn't Robert want to let me up?"

"I have strict rules that nobody comes up on weekdays without being announced," she said. "Not my uncle. Not my house-keeper."

"And not me."

"I never said anything to Robert about you, L. You never come during the week. Robert was just trying to do his job."

117

I didn't want her to confess about Johnny Fry. I wasn't ready for that kind of confrontation. All I wanted was for her to squirm a little.

I tried to smile, but instead, a spasm of pain rippled under the top of my skull.

"What's wrong?" Jo asked.

"My head. It really hurts."

"Are you seeing things?"

"What do you mean?" I asked.

"Things floating in front of your eyes, lights?"

"No," I lied.

If her life was a secret, so should mine be.

"If you need to go home," she said. "I'll wait until tomorrow."

"At three?"

"If that's when you want me."

I felt that last sentence in the center of my heart. It was a small expansion, a swelling of passion. She made herself into an object for me. It wasn't unlike me standing in her bathroom holding my half-swollen cock as if it were some kind of philosopher's stone.

"It's just that I didn't get much sleep last night," I said.

"Why not? Your headache?"

"I had a visitor."

That afternoon Jo's usually calm visage was like the New England weather. It went from cloud-filled to light to stormy in quick succession. My mention of a late-night visitor piqued her jealous sky.

"Who was that?" she asked.

"Enoch," I said dryly. "Enoch Bennett."

"Who's that?"

"You remember I told you about the woman who lives a couple of floors above me?" I said. "Sasha."

118

"Not really."

I told Jo about my adventures with Sasha and Enoch. Meeting them on the street, dragging him to the bed, the late-night visit and the confession about incest.

"Sasha once told me that her mother and she were feuding over something—I'm not sure, but I think it was a man," I said. "Maybe she's getting back at her mother through her brother."

"When he woke up, do you think he'd forgotten what he did?" Jo asked. The worry lines had returned to her face.

"No. I'm pretty sure that he remembered the act, just not the confession."

"That's too bad," Jo said. "Forgetting something like that would be best."

The woman who had been thrashing about on the floor in masturbatory orgasm just an hour before now seemed years older and fragile to the point of breaking under her own weight.

"What's wrong, Jo?" I asked. It was the first time I had been truly concerned about her in days.

She poured a glass of wine and downed it; poured another. When that glass was through, the rigidity in her limbs released a bit.

"You were right when you said that I haven't told you everything about me, L," she said. "I have one secret, a secret that I've never told anyone before."

"What's that?" I asked in a whisper.

"You asked me about why I'm so sexual lately," she said.

"Yeah?"

"It has to do with Enoch."

"Enoch? How do you know him?"

"I don't know him," she said. "But I know what he's going through."

"What do you mean?"

119

"Do you remember . . ." she said, and gulped. "Do you remember I told you six months ago about my uncle dying?"

"Your uncle, um, uh, Rex?"

"Yes."

"Yeah. I remember."

She hadn't said more than a few words about her father's half brother, Rex. There was a letter from her aunt Jemma telling her that he had died in their home in Hawaii.

"When my father died, Rex put us up in an apartment in Baltimore. I was fourteen, and he told my mother that it was time for me to learn an instrument. He taught piano before getting into the roofing business. So I'd go over there three days a week and take lessons . . ."

It was obvious where she was going.

". . . At first it was just lessons. He was a good teacher, and I still like playing the piano. But one day he told me that he loved me and that he needed me to be his girlfriend. It was very strange. He didn't touch me or anything. He just explained that we were going to have a relationship where I would be like a wife to him, or else he would stop paying for our food and our rent.

"My mother had a nervous breakdown after Dad died. She couldn't work, and I was too young to get a job. My sister was younger than I was . . .

"My uncle told me to think about it, and if I wanted to keep my mother out of the street, all I had to do was show up in two days for the next lesson."

All of this she said looking down into her glass. Then she looked up. The face she presented was another woman completely: a beautiful woman who had been defeated by her own good looks.

"I went back on Wednesday," she said. "He told me what to do. He, he did it to me again and again. I never saw a man who could

120

have sex so long. Some days he would come a dozen times. If I was ever late or tried to hold him off, he would beat me with a thin leather strap and then, and then sodomize me."

I reached out and took her hand. Her tears fell on the table.

"What finally happened?"

"Uncle Bernard, my mother's brother, sent for us. He let Mom live in his house and paid for me and August to go to college."

"And you never told anybody about this?"

Jo shook her head and let go of my hand.

"Not even your sister?"

"No. He wrote letters for years afterward," she said. "He wanted me to come back to him. He honestly believed that he loved me and that our relationship was somehow consensual. He told me that he needed me."

"Did you ever see him again?"

"No."

"Did he . . . damage you? Physically, I mean."

"He did love me, you know," she said.

"No. He raped you."

"Sometimes I'd looked forward to seeing him," she said reaching out for my hand again. "Sometimes I'd fight him on purpose so that he would punish me."

"He was fucking with your mind," I said, but she wasn't listening to me.

"It felt good when he punished me," she admitted. "Sometimes he'd drink water all day and when I'd get there he'd make me get into the bathtub and, and urinate on me because I was so disgusting."

"It's lucky the motherfucker's dead," I said. "If he wasn't, I'd kill him."

Jo looked me in the eye right then. Her gaze was clear and innocent.

"He couldn't help it," she said, shaking her head slightly. "His stepmother, my grandmother, kicked him out when he was only twelve. He went to live with his grandmother, who beat him and sold him to men and women for sex. He didn't know how to have normal love.

"Over the years, I learned how to deal with him. And I knew how to get him to give my mother what she needed."

"I'm so sorry, baby," I said. "I never knew."

"For many years, I never so much as went out on a date with any man," she continued. "And when I did start dating, I never liked anyone. I never let them get close. Then, when I met you, I knew you were the perfect man for me. I didn't want what I'd had with Rex. If I needed to be alone, you let me be. If I wanted to make love, you were gentle and kind.

"But when Rex died, something happened. After all those years, the hunger for crazy sex started to eat at me. That's why when you changed, I was so wild for you. I needed you to do what you did to me in the park. That's why when you pretended to slap me, I got so excited."

And that's why, I knew, she had started the affair with Johnny Fry. She needed to be abused and humiliated. She needed to be treated like an object—the object of lust.

"Do you want me to come home with you?" I asked.

"No. I want you to go home and think about what I've told you," she said. "I've told you a lot. You have to think about it. And I can tell from the way you're blinking how much your head hurts."

"I am in pain. But I wouldn't leave—"

"Don't talk about it now," Jo told me, bringing her finger to my lips. "Just go and come back tomorrow at three . . . if you still want to be with me."

★　　★　　★

122

Even though my head hurt terribly, I decided to walk. With each step on the hard concrete, I could feel and even hear the reverberations going through my body. It was like the pounding of great bass drums.

I wasn't walking in a straight line. I drifted from one side of the sidewalk to the other, looking at dogs on leashes and clouds in the sky. For four blocks, between 62nd and 59th, I counted the black splotches of dried chewing gum on the white concrete. I counted 292 before the headache got too bad for counting.

I went into Central Park for a while, hoping that sitting under the trees there would ease my pain. But the headache got worse and worse. The light in the dome of my head glimmered, and flashes of imagined lightning flickered in among the boughs overhead.

When I even thought about standing, I got nauseous. I had other symptoms too: my heart was pounding, I was dizzy, and now and then my hands trembled uncontrollably.

I hated those splotches of gum. For some reason I blamed them for my malady.

Hours later, the sun began to set. With the night, my symptoms eased up just a little. I was able to make it to my feet and stagger to a cab in Columbus Circle.

"What did you say?" the cabbie asked three times before he understood my slurred speech.

It was an $8 ride, but I gave him a twenty and told him to keep the change.

It took a quarter of an hour for me to find and work the keys on the doors to my building and my apartment. By that time, the pain in my head was worse than ever. It hurt so badly that it seemed to be making a sound, a deep humming note fluttering through the folds of my brain.

I found the slip of paper that had Cynthia's number on it and punched it into the keypad of my phone with great difficulty.

"Enter code or wait for first operator," the voice told me.

It took much longer than it should have. There were flashes in front of my eyes, and momentary dark spots. It's a wonder that I wasn't frightened. I could have had a brain tumor or some parasite or virus. But the only thing I cared about was getting Cynthia's name into that phone.

"You have entered the wrong code," the man's voice told me, and the line was disconnected.

I hit the redial button, and even though the memory held more numbers than I needed, the phone rang again. The man told me to enter the code again.

By this time pain was dripping from my eyes, nose, and mouth. When I pressed the pound key on the phone pad, it felt like the last thing I would ever do.

I knew that I was going to die but I wasn't exactly sure why. It had something to do with me not being responsible. There was a phone ringing somewhere. I was drifting slowly toward the floor. It was a known fact that once I'd rolled out of the chair, I'd never get to my feet again.

"Hello?"

"Cynthia?"

"Cordell? Is that you? How are you?"

How are you?

All it took was her asking after my well-being, and the pain lifted—completely. I wiped the mucous, tears, and drool from my face and took a very deep breath in through my mouth. The air felt really good in my lungs. The world was filling with possibilities.

"Cordell?"

"Yes, yes, Cynthia. I'm sorry if it's late, but I just had to call. My head."

"What happened?"

I told her about my talk with Jo, about her uncle and her brave sacrifice to keep her family alive.

"So I couldn't tell her about what I knew," I said at the end of the long tale. "I mean, she was in so much pain already, and obviously she couldn't control herself."

"It sounds as if she's in full control," Cynthia said. "She said that she couldn't get a job."

"She was only fourteen," I said defending my girlfriend as a child.

"When it began," Cynthia said. "But she was seventeen when her uncle . . . Bernard?"

"Yes."

"When her uncle Bernard took the family away. A seventeen-year-old could have found a job. And from what you said, she felt that she had some power over Rex. She never told anyone and she received his letters without turning him over to the police. It would be interesting to know what he wrote in those letters."

"It doesn't matter," I said. "She was a victim of sexual abuse. She couldn't turn him in because of what he did to her mind."

"That's no excuse for what she did to your trust," Cynthia said with conviction.

"You're a woman too," I exclaimed. "How can you say such a thing?"

"Because," Cynthia said, "if I forgave her, then I would have to forgive Rex for his actions. He was abused you say. He was sold into prostitution and mistreated by his grandmother. Can I tell you that he should therefore be forgiven for what he did to your girlfriend?"

125

"That doesn't mean that Jo is not a victim. I don't care about Rex."

"I don't either," Cynthia said. "Neither do I care about Joelle. All that concerns me is you, Cordell. You are the one in pain. You are the man in need of trust and love. I feel for the pain you brought to me when I first heard your voice tonight."

"Yeah," I said. "Why did it just go away like that? I thought I was gonna buy it before you answered."

"Because you know that I am here for you," she said. "I'm not going to lie or try to fool you out of your money. I'm not going to betray you. Your pain was the onset of the despair we experience when we are marooned in life."

"Are you sure you're not a therapist?" I asked the dial-a-friend.

"No," she replied. "The benefactor who funds this service doesn't want psychological professionals manning the lines. He wants people who will listen and also care."

I inhaled again, taking in a great quantity of air. Then I began crying and couldn't stop. I fell onto the floor and rolled into fetal position. My chest was wracked with sobs. My face hurt from the contortions it went through.

When the bawling began to ebb, Cynthia asked, "Can you talk now, Cordell?"

"Call me L," I said. "And yes, I can talk some."

"Are you angry at your girlfriend?"

"I don't know. Yesterday I would have said yes. But now . . . I don't know."

"What about her boyfriend?"

"I hate him," I said. "I hate him. But I can't pay attention to that."

"Why not?"

"Because the more I feel, the crazier I get. All the wild sex I'm

126

having with Jo, and then there's the night with Lucy. And my obsession with *The Myth of Sisypha*. I'm losing control."

"What's that last name you said?" Cynthia asked.

"It's this X-rated film I bought, *The Myth of Sisypha*. There's a woman in it, the star. I can't explain it, but she seems to understand."

"Understand what?"

"I only watched a few scenes," I said, "but I can't stop thinking about the woman and what she's doing to her husband. It's brutal, but I keep thinking that he needs someone, that I need someone to, to . . . I don't know—to wake me up."

"Hm. You say that you're losing control," Cynthia said. "But maybe what you're doing is finding your way."

"This isn't my way, Cynthia. I don't have semisecluded sex in the park and follow after another man with my own girlfriend. I don't quit my job on a whim and start a new profession that I know absolutely nothing about."

"But you have done all of that," Cynthia said. "I think what you have to do is trust your own heart. You're alone, L. You're looking for contact somewhere in the world. Sex is the first step to that contact. Don't abandon it. Jo hasn't. She found a lover to fill the void of her loss and longing. She took you where she needed you to be."

I couldn't argue. If I was to forgive Jo, then I'd have to forgive myself too. And I was lonely, desperately lonely.

"But isn't indiscriminate sex using people?" I asked.

"People work together all the time," Cynthia replied. "They use each other to make their lives whole. A mother walks down the street with a year-old toddler in her arms. The baby sees a big beautiful woman and reaches out his arms for her. The baby hugs this woman's neck and kisses her cheek. But the child has not abandoned the mother. The beautiful woman is elated by the love shown her through this child. There's nothing wrong with people helping each other, loving each other."

"I guess I never felt anybody loves me like that," I said feeling simultaneously shy and self-absorbed.

"Then it's time you felt it," Cynthia said. "Take your journey, L. Don't be afraid to reach out."

On the answering machine I had three messages. One was an offer to consolidate my credit card debt into a new card that would charge only 2 percent interest for the first sixty days. The second was from Sasha Bennett.

"Hi, Cordell," she said. "I just sent Enoch off in a taxi. I'm in my apartment all night. Any time you'd like to drop by, I'd be happy to see you."

The third call was from Jerry Singleton again.

"I can't believe that you're being this unprofessional, Cordell. I've had to scramble all week just to get somebody to cover this meeting. You should at least call me to explain yourself."

After erasing those messages, I was worried that the headache would return. I was expecting pain but all I felt was depletion. Every part of my body, down to my fingers, felt weak and tired.

Still I managed to call a number.

"Hello," she said on the third ring.

"I love you, Jo," I said.

"Does that mean it's over?"

"No. Why would you think that?"

"I thought you were going to say that you have to let me go because of what I did, because you're so disgusted with me."

"No," I said. "I'll be there tomorrow at three."

"Oh," she said. "Oh. Are you sure?"

128

"Of course I am. It's not your fault what your uncle did."

"That's not what they used to say in my mother's church," Jo whispered.

"No? What did they say there?"

"That a man couldn't be evil alone," she said. "Men create evil between themselves."

She answered the door only moments after I knocked. All she wore was a white T-shirt that came down to just above her knees.

"I was expecting you," she said.

It was 2:22 in the morning.

Sasha took my hand and led me to a brown chaise longue that sat near an open window. The apartment was lit by several dozen candles and four glass-encased oil lanterns.

"I lit all the lights for us," she said. "Enoch left early, but I didn't care. All I've been thinking about for days is getting together with you."

She stood at the end of the backless sofa and reached down to the hem of her white T-shirt. Two of the lanterns stood on a table to the right, and so, when she pulled the shirt up to her belly button, I got a clear view of her wide hips and dense pubic hair.

Sasha wasn't fat but she had a generous woman's figure. She sat back on the chaise longue, bringing her left foot up so that her vaginal lips and clitoris were presented deliciously.

Without a word, I sank to my knees and gently sucked the engorged clitoris into my mouth, enough to get my tongue up under the hood.

Sasha let out a groan that reverberated around the gutted apartment.

I spent many long minutes in that groaning room licking and sucking her perfectly formed pussy. It was leaking big dollops of

129

tangy fluid. When I would get down and run my tongue from the bottom back up to the clit, she'd say, "Swallow the come, baby. Drink it all down. I want you to eat me up."

I swallowed as she commanded, smacking my lips so that she knew what I was doing.

While I was still flicking my tongue over the erect clit, Sasha moved back and sat up.

"Stand in front of me," she said.

I did as she asked, and she pulled down my pants and underwear with one expert yank. I realized then that I had lost weight in the last few days.

My cock was standing straight out. I stared down at it and at Sasha's face beyond. It seemed to me a miracle to be there. The fact that Sasha wanted to be with me was what made me so hard.

There was a small drawer in the table next to the chaise. This she opened, taking out a rubber dildo, a ceramic cup filled with some kind of fluid, and a small square packet containing a condom.

She ripped open the condom and took hold of my erection, gently looping the rubber over the head.

While she rolled the band down on me, she said, "The dildo has been boiled and washed. It's completely sterilized."

"What are you going to do with it?" I asked her.

"Put that big fat cock inside me," she commanded.

I got on top of her and did what she said. It surprised me how tight she was. Much more so than Jo or Lucy. I imagined that all her lovers had small members, and this for some reason excited me.

"Not so fast, Cordell," Sasha whispered in my ear.

Instantly I slowed my beat.

"Look at my right hand," she said.

I saw that she was holding the dildo, dipping it into the ceramic

130

bowl. When she took the thing out, I could see that the liquid was thick and viscous.

"It's the best lubricant," she breathed.

Then she moved the dildo behind me, where I couldn't see it. But I felt the thick oil falling into the crack of my ass and flowing down over my balls. There it seemed to heat up a little.

I groaned loudly so as not to increase my pace.

"That's right," Sasha said. "Fuck it slow like you love that pussy. Take it all the way out and then come in again like your big dick is kissing it again and again and again."

Every time she said the word, I reentered her. This obeisance caused both of us great joy.

"It's so tight," I hissed.

She got more oil and dribbled it over my ass.

The heat became greater.

Then I felt the head of her dildo press against my rectum.

"Get ready, baby," she said. "I'm gonna shove it all in, all at once. Then you're going be in control. If you don't want it too deep, don't pull out so much when you fuck that cunt. If you can keep it to short deep thrusts, you won't have to take too much."

"What if . . ." I said, and then she pressed the full length of the phallus into my rectum, filling it up.

It didn't hurt exactly, but felt like I had to defecate. It was as if an empty space that I had never considered was suddenly completely filled.

"Do you feel it, baby?" Sasha whispered in my ear.

"Yes."

"Then fuck it. Fuck it hard."

Her words were in complete control of my mind. I rose up above her and pounded down on her sex like that was my one purpose in life. When I was just about to come, she moved the

131

dildo around in a wide circle inside me. It was as if someone had grabbed me by the insides and pulled me back. My body faltered and my cock came out of her, hovering above the opening as I tried to compensate for the new feelings inside me.

"I'm going to move it around again," she whispered. "Okay?"

I nodded, holding my breath.

I thought that I'd be ready the next time, but the broad arc of the dildo made me grunt like a wild boar. Before the spasms left my body, Sasha whispered, "Fuck me, Daddy."

Daddy.

As I came in and out of her tight pussy, her dildo went in and out of me. The harder I fucked her, the more she plunged the gray-and-white phallus into me. Whenever I began to cry out, she moved the thing in a circle, effectively stopping any orgasm.

"How does your cock feel?" she asked.

"Bigger than it's ever been."

"Tell me you love me."

"I love you," I tried to say but the words got stuck on a sob in my throat.

At that moment, she pulled the dildo out, and my rectum went into a painful spasm.

"Keep fucking, Daddy," Sasha ordered.

I tried to do as she said, but the pain threw off my equilibrium. I jammed myself into her and then stopped, pulled out again, went in again, came out and stopped. By then she had sopped her dildo with thick oil again. When she pressed the thing back into me, my beat came back—hard.

"You need that to keep you fucking me fast," she said smiling up at me.

"Yes Mama, yes Mama, yes Mama, yes," I chanted.

And for a maybe three minutes I experienced pure sex. My body was slick with sweat. Hers was too. There were pains in my back and left foot, but I couldn't stop bucking on top of that woman unless someone was to knock me off.

When my beat went off again, and I began to cry out in a language I knew but did not understand, I thought that she'd moved her dildo around to stop me from coming. I was expecting the broad, painful sweep, but instead Sasha said, "Stand up quickly."

I obeyed, teetering a little on my feet.

With her teeth Sasha ripped off the head of the colorless condom. She held the base of my cock with her left hand and used the right to massage the shaft. Almost immediately I felt the orgasm begin. My rectum tightened and the dildo popped out of my ass. When I began to ejaculate, Sasha squeezed the head so that the thick white fluid came out in a powerful stream, as if I were urinating.

I screamed out in pain and ecstasy. Sasha loosened her grip and the come flowed out onto her face and breasts.

"You come so much," she said, and I howled trying to come up with words to excite her as much as she did me.

The tremors were still going through my abdomen when she lifted my cock and sucked my tight balls into her mouth. She was rough with my testicles, and I thought it would hurt so much that I'd lose my erection quickly. But then she put her finger up my rectum and pulled violently on my cock again. Within seconds I was having another orgasm, this one so powerful that I was afraid that the light in my mind would return and the headache would come back to finish killing me.

I fell down next to her on the sofa and hugged her close to my chest. My shoulders jittered and the tendons in my neck thrummed.

"You come a lot," she said in my ear before sticking her tongue in there.

I tried to speak but the sensation was too great.

After a moment or two, I said, "I never came like that before."

"Never?"

"No."

"Has anybody used a dildo on you before?"

Mel and Sisypha came to mind with her question. I had so identified with him that for a moment I almost answered yes.

"No," I said at last, "never."

"Just before you came the second time, your prostate got real big. I could tell that you were gonna let go another big load."

What could I say? A week ago, if I'd heard a woman talk like that, I would have run away. But now I could feel the stirrings of yet another erection.

For a while after that, we didn't say anything. My right hand and her left played with each other. She was gentle with the bruised hand. Now and then a big truck would rumble down the street. There was a light on in the building across the way.

I thought about my call to Joelle, telling her that I loved her. That act felt in perfect balance with me lying there with Sasha.

"Did Inch tell you what happened?" she asked.

"Yes."

"What did you think?"

"When he came downstairs, he was so upset that I was sure he'd killed you. So when he said that you'd had sex, it didn't seem so bad."

Sasha grinned and moved up to kiss my lips.

"We've been fucking since he was twelve and I was fifteen," she said. "He says that I make him but I don't. He always comes on to

134

me, and I tell him no. Then he says okay and gets us both drunk. Then . . . well . . ."

"So you like it too?"

"I love sex," she said with a sneer.

The phone rang. It was a cordless phone on the floor just next to the chaise longue. Sasha picked it up nonchalantly. That was a few minutes before three in the morning.

"Hello?" she said.

"Oh. Hi, Martine . . ."

Martine Mocking was the neighbor who lived between our floors, a black woman who was my age and worked for a theater producer on Broadway. We'd never said more than *hello, how are you* in all the years we'd been neighbors.

"Oh no, honey," Sasha said. "That was just Cordell from down below you, he was coming . . . Uh-huh, yeah. He comes really hard, and a lot too . . . Uh-huh. All down between my tits and to the floor . . . Thick and black . . . I know it's funny but all black men are like that, huh? . . ."

It was odd lying there next to Sasha listening to her gossip about sex with me to a woman I hardly knew but whom I saw at least twice a week.

"I don't know," Sasha said. "Let me tell you."

She got on her knees and reached out for my cock (which had been stiffening while she talked). She held it and squeezed.

"There we go," she said smiling at me. "I can just barely touch my fingers . . . uh-huh, it's very thick . . . Let me see . . ."

She leaned over and took the head of my hard-again penis into her mouth.

"Just a little salty and very smooth," she said and then she put her mouth on me again.

It felt so good that a moan escaped my lips.

135

"Did you hear that?" Sasha asked. "He loves sex . . . I know you'd never think it by looking at him. Hold on a second. He wants me to suck his cock a little."

Instead of that, she looked up at me and shoved the tip of her tongue into the slit of my urethra.

"Oh God," I called.

Then she took the whole thing into her mouth and down into her throat. It felt hot and slick in there, as if I were inside her vagina. I pressed my hips forward and she began to fuck me with her mouth.

I tried to keep quiet, but it felt so good. She kept going up and down for a minute or so and then she leaned back, pulling on my slick cock and grinning into the phone.

"It's all slick now," she said. ". . . what? . . . Okay, I'll ask him. Martine wants to know if I can fuck you now while we're still on the phone."

Her hand was moving very fast and light on my thing. It felt so good that I couldn't get the words to come out from my lips.

"He says okay, Martine," Sasha said.

I expected her to lean over to the table and pull out another condom, but she didn't. She just straddled my hips and came down, enveloping me in one motion.

"Oh God yes," I cried.

"It's just so thick," Sasha crooned into the phone. "My pussy has never been stretched so wide." She was going up and down slowly, alternating between biting her lips and smiling. "Oh yeah, yeah. It's hard as rock . . . Uh-uh, it doesn't bend at all . . . Uh, uh, uh. That's him pushing it up inside me. Oh yeah, yeah . . . Every time he does, I have a little orgasm . . . Oh yeah. I sure am." Then to me, "Martine wants to know if I'm gonna jump off and eat your jism when you come." Then into the phone, "It had a tangy flavor. Yeah, yeah, drink it down."

136

For a while she fucked me sitting straight, going up and down. Then she leaned over me, rocking back and forth. The whole time she talked to Martine, telling her how everything tasted, felt, and smelled.

She was looking lovingly into my eyes while saying, "Oh yeah, you took the dildo up in your ass. Didn't you, baby? Didn't you?

"At first he struggled, but I made him take it."

By then my groans were coming quickly, and I was thrusting up as hard as I could. Sasha put the phone next to my head and gripped my shoulders so that she could fuck hard and fast. She began yelping.

"Sasha," the phone squeaked in my ear. "What's happening now?"

"She's fucking me hard," I told Martine. "She's holding on to my shoulders and can't hold the phone."

"Is she coming?"

"I think so. I think so."

"Is she taking your whole cock?"

"Yes," I said. "I can feel her ass slapping down on my balls."

"Oh God," Martine said. "And what are you doing?"

"I'm trying to get as deep inside her as I can. I'm fucking her."

Hearing me talk must have excited Sasha more, because her cries got louder.

"What are you doing?" I asked Martine.

Silence.

"Tell me what you're doing, Martine."

"I have three fingers of my right hand inside my, my pussy," she said. "And I'm massaging the clit with my left."

"Are you coming?"

Silence.

"Are you coming, Martine?"

Sasha was sitting halfway up, actually crying, actual tears coming from her eyes as she slammed down on me again and again.

137

"Yes, I'm coming," Martine shouted.

"It's me down there fucking you," I said. "That's my fat cock up inside you."

"Oh. Oh. Oh," came over the phone.

Sasha screamed.

My body went stiff, and Sasha jumped off me and hurried to grab hold of my erection. I could see her licking the come as it cascaded off the head of my cock. The whole time, Martine was moaning and calling out in one-syllable words and sounds.

"Oh that's right, baby," I said, and both Sasha and Martine groaned in pleasure.

Sasha kept licking my dick well after the last drop of come was gone. Then she rubbed it against her cheek, closing her eyes with the feeling.

"I'm going to give the phone back to Sasha now, Martine."

Picking up the phone, Sasha smiled and said, "Thanks for calling, honey . . . Okay I'll tell him."

She disconnected the call and snuggled up beside me and said, "Martine said thanks for such a wonderful time." Then she turned her back to me, and we fit together like spoons.

I reached down and positioned my half-hard erection, then entered her.

"Oh," she said. "Oh."

"I want to go to sleep with my cock inside you," I said.

She shuddered in response.

For a while I got very hard, and Sasha pressed against me. But finally we both fell asleep. I awoke only once in the night when I fell out of her with the most excruciating wave of ecstasy moving between my shoulder blades.

★   ★   ★

138

That night I dreamed about a beach. I was much younger and naked, walking along the white sand shore. There were large fish jumping out of the water, and bright-colored birds, flamingos, soaring across a cloudless sky.

I wondered how I ever got to such a place. I knew that I had always wanted to be there, naked and young. But I also knew that I was never supposed to arrive; instead, I was meant to wander endlessly in the jungle that called to me at the edge of the sands.

I sighed in the dream and awoke on the chaise longue alone. The candles had all been extinguished and Sasha was nowhere to be seen. Tacked to the front door was a note she'd left.

My Dearest Cordell,

Thank you so much for your uninhibited passion and your spirit. The whole night my heart fluttered next to you. And even after you were asleep you stayed hard. I tried to go to sleep myself but first I had to have another orgasm while you slept and stayed hard. I've never been with a man I enjoyed so much and I hope that you will see me again.

I'm off to work.

I love you

(really),

Sash

My mind had taken a turn somewhere. I appreciated Sasha and her kind words, but as soon as I was down in my apartment, I forgot her.

It was just shy of noon.

I showered and shaved and put on my gray suit with a black silk T-shirt instead of a collar and tie.

I took a taxi to the Stowe Gallery on East 63rd Street.

139

A very prissy young man named Roderick glanced through Lucy's photographs and said, "Not for us."

He didn't offer any explanation or criticism. He didn't say he was sorry or suggest any other gallery that might be interested. He just said, "Not for us," and, when the phone rang, "I have to get that. Good day."

I stopped at a Galaxy Coffee Shop franchise on Madison. There I took out a plastic pencil and began to write in a small bound book of blank paper that I'd carried around in my briefcase for years. I'd bought the journal in a shop in Provincetown six years earlier, thinking that I'd write down my feelings. I carried the book everywhere, but the words always eluded me. Many a time I had sat in a coffee shop or restaurant with the book opened to its first blank page—but no words had ever come.

That day was different. I started writing immediately about the children of Sudan. It wasn't so much prose that I jotted down as notes to myself about what to do with those children. How could they be used to explain something that these gallery owners didn't know? How could those children, their plight, open a door for them to pass through?

By the time I got to the Nightwood Gallery, four blocks away, I had completely redesigned my approach. With Roderick I'd just laid out the portfolio and stood back, expecting him to be moved by the subject of the pictures if nothing else.

But now I was ready to fight for my client.

The person I met at Nightwood was Isabelle Thinnes, the owner. She was a white woman in her sixties, well-preserved, tall, thin, and aristocratic—definitely a WASP. Her long gray hair had strands of black shot through it and was tied into a feathery bun at the back of her head.

I sat across from her in the gallery at a desk that had a green, white, and black marble top. I put the portfolio down and placed my hand on it, letting her know that I had something to say before she saw the work.

Isabelle and Brad Mettleman were good friends, and so she was willing to hear me out. But this brash gesture caught her up short. Suddenly she was forced to wonder who this man sitting in front of her was.

All of this I could see, or believed I could see, in her eyes.

"Before you look at this work, I have to tell you something, Ms. Thinnes. The pictures you see here will affect you. They are of children, most of whom are probably dead by now. You will see the death in their living eyes. You will know that there was no saving them. They are victims of their own people and of the neglect of the rest of the world. You will see them carrying guns and dolls and standing in front of burned-out buildings and on fields of slaughter. There's a lot of smoke in these photographs, smoke rising from broken-down hovels where these orphans live, smoke from explosions, smoke clouding the eye of reason in anyone who lived in this world.

"But none of that matters."

"No?" Isabelle said, her intelligent, blue eyes trying to decipher my meaning.

"No," I said. "You can find pictures like these anywhere. Maybe not as well presented, maybe not with the same impeccable eye that Lucy has. But there are pictures of dying children on TV every night and all over the Internet. In one photograph you'll see here, there is in the foreground a doe-eyed girl-child who can hardly stand, she is so hungry and frail. Behind her an American flag is fluttering proudly in the wind. Now, who knows why the flag was there? Maybe it was a camp that we built to help the children. Regardless, your clientele will see it as an indictment of them. They haven't done anything to help those children, and anything America has done is too little and too late."

"You're not doing a very good sales job, Mr. Carmel," Isabelle Thinnes said very seriously.

"That's not the sale, Ms. Thinnes. That's just the setup. You and I both know that this is business we're talking here. Art business, yes, but business still and all.

"I believe that Lucy Carmichael is one of the most important young photographers to hit the New York scene in the last decade, but that doesn't mean a thing if the pictures don't sell."

"You're blunt, Mr. Carmel," the gallery owner said. "But I can't say that you're wrong."

"That's why," I said, "I've had Lucy form a nonprofit corporation that is to receive half the profits from the sale of these photographs. I know that the standard cost for the work of an unknown like Lucy would be twenty-five hundred dollars. But in this case I want to charge six thousand."

"Six thousand!"

"Yes. Because for every picture sold, three thousand dollars will be donated to the Lucy Carmichael Foundation for the Children of Darfur."

"So you're saying that these photographs will cause guilt in the people who see them—"

"And then offer them a way to assuage that guilt," I said, finishing her thought.

Ms. Thinnes peered at a point above my head, her face devoid of any discernable emotion. Then, suddenly, she broke out into a smile.

After that, showing her the photographs was a mere formality; the sale was already made.

Within the next hour, she'd agreed to represent Lucy for a fifty-

142

fifty split after the monies that had been deducted for Lucy's foundation. I would be paid by taking a percentage of Lucy's share. Ms. Thinnes promised to have the papers ready by Saturday. We shook hands on it.

As I was preparing to leave, she said, "Excuse me, Mr. Carmel."

"Yes, Ms. Thinnes?"

"Why haven't I heard of you before? I thought that I knew every photographers' agent in America."

"I've worked with and for Brad for some years, ma'am. It's only now that he's so busy that I'm getting out in the field."

"You're very good at it," she told me.

There was a look of real admiration in her eyes.

I'd worked as a translator for twenty years and no one had ever shown me as much regard or respect.

"Thank you, Ms. Thinnes. I really appreciate that . . . more than you can know."

When I got to Jo's house, she was wearing a formfitting buttoned-up white blouse and lime-green cotton pants. Her fiery brown skin looked lovely against those light colors.

She looked at me with trepidation and suspicion.

I smiled and took her in my arms. I was excited from the moment I saw her. Her fear of my rejection was like gasoline on the flame.

From the hug I lifted her into my arms and carried her into the den.

The den was a narrow room with a big brown couch and a small TV and stereo system on shelves. I sat down on the sofa, positioning her between my knees. I unbuttoned her trousers and pulled her pants down to her ankles. She was wearing green thong panties. These I also pulled down.

"Shouldn't we talk about yesterday?" she asked.

I turned around and sat her on the sofa. Then I stood and let my pants drop.

When faced with my erection, Jo took it in her hand and lifted it. I thought she was going to take my testicles in her mouth as Sasha had done, but instead she put her nose into the crease between my hard shaft and loose balls. She breathed in deeply through her nostrils.

"I love the way you smell," she said.

I took a condom from my pocket.

"Put this on me," I said.

"Why?"

"It cuts the feeling a little, and I want to fuck you a long time."

Joelle grinned and did my bidding. Then I got behind her on the sofa and plunged right in. She was very wet and I think, judging from her song, she came right then.

With my injured right hand, I reached over and took both breasts into my grasp. Then I wound my left hand in her hair and pulled hard. The whole time I was sliding in and out of her at a very slow pace.

I waited for her second orgasm before speaking.

"Have you had any other lovers since we've been together?" I asked, fucking her at the same slow pace.

"No," she moaned.

"Never?"

"Never."

"Have you ever wanted to? Is there any man you wanted?"

"No."

"Never?"

She began pushing back against my cock. She didn't answer.

"Never?" I asked again.

144

"Once."

"When?"

"Six months ago."

"After your uncle died?"

"The next day or, or maybe the day after that."

"Who was it?"

"A man," she said, and then she gasped as I pulled on her hair. "George Leland."

"The Italian tie importer?"

"Yes."

"He wanted you too?"

"Yes."

"Tell me," I said, pushing all the way inside.

She grunted twice and then said, "I was there one night, talking to him about presentation," she said all in one breath. "It was late. We had two drinks. And he, and he, he kissed me."

"On the cheek?" I said on a slender breath.

She shook her head and said, "Down my throat."

"Did you like that?"

She nodded and pressed back against me. Her thighs began to quiver.

"What happened then?" I asked.

"I kissed him for a while and then I pulled away. But he grabbed my hand . . ."

"Why did he do that?"

"To show me how hard he was."

"Did you hold on to it?" I asked. My breath was coming faster.

"It was very, very big, long and thick. He asked me, he asked me if I wanted to see it."

"Is that what you were thinking about while I was talking to you about the man standing behind you?" I asked.

145

She nodded, pulling her own hair as she did so.

I was fucking her faster now, with short punctuated strokes.

"Did you want to?"

She nodded.

"Did he take it out?"

She shook her head, no.

"No?" I asked, both relieved and disappointed.

"No, I . . . I got down on my knees and unzipped him."

"Did you suck it?"

"No. I told him I wouldn't."

"What happened then?"

"He made me lie down on top of him fully dressed. I even had my stockings on. I squeezed his thing between my thighs and he moved it back and forth."

"Like I'm doing to you right now."

"No," she said. "He wasn't inside me. He was too big."

"What happened?" I asked.

"He came doing that. It was all over the back of my dress and in my hair."

I pulled her hair again.

"And did you come?" I asked.

She went silent, and I began moving in and out very hard and fast.

"Did you come?"

"Yes," she shouted, and she came then too. "I came and came and came."

And I did too, so hard that we fell off the couch and onto the floor. I couldn't stop humping her. I was pulling mightily on her hair and yelling out, "Like this, like this, like this?"

"Yes," she said. "He kept coming and every time I felt his cock pulse against my clit, I came too."

146

My orgasm had run its cycle, but I couldn't stop humping her. My half-hard erection came out, but I kept rubbing it against her ass. She pushed back against me and reached behind to caress my head.

Then she stood up and pulled me to my feet. She got down on her knees and took my penis in her two hands. The condom came off, and she wrapped the dick between her palms.

"He was still excited after all that, and so I got down like this and started jerking him off." She held on to me and moved her whole body in a slow and rhythmic rocking manner. "It had a big purple head that was so shiny that I could almost see my reflection." She worked faster. "He kept begging me to let him inside me, but the more he begged, the harder I pulled. Finally he put his hands on my shoulders and I knew he was going to come. I held his shaft next to my ear, and when he came, I could feel the come splashing down on my ankles."

I came again even though I didn't expect to; I didn't even want it. But from force of will she made me.

I sank down on the floor beside her and we hugged, two tired comrades after a rough journey over treacherous and uncharted terrain.

When I woke up, it was three minutes after midnight. I didn't remember climbing up onto the couch with Jo, but there we were, wrapped in the same embrace. I sat up and looked at her face, thinking that I had never known her, but that she was the only friend I had.

As I stood, Jo turned over and began to snore. She was always a heavy sleeper, and once she began snoring, I knew she would stay out till sunrise.

I lumbered into her kitchen, turned on the light, and sat in a chair by the window, thinking of everything that had passed.

It was as if I were adrift—but not yet dying—on a lone raft in the middle of a tranquil and treacherous sea. There was no one coming to save me. There was no land in sight. But I wasn't yet thirsty or hungry. I was just fine there but also on the verge of death.

It was a silly image that I couldn't shake. There was no saving me. But, I told myself, there was Lucy and Sasha, Cynthia, and my new profession as an art agent. I had a life spread out before me. I had hope, and Jo obviously loved me. She was afraid to tell me about her indiscretions with Johnny Fry, but that was understandable.

Bleep-bleep.

It was an odd sound but familiar too. While I sat there trying to remember what it was, it sounded again.

Bleep-bleep.

I walked down the long hall, past my snoring lover, into the small room, closet really, that she used as an office. There her computer sat alight. Her Internet connection was on. There was an instant message from JF1223.

Are you there? The first message read. It was posted at 7:25.

I ache for you, JJ, the next message read at 8:14. *These days apart have shown me how much you mean to me. Bettye means nothing now. I'll never see her again.*

At 10:47 JF1223 wrote, *Have you thought over meeting me in Baltimore? You don't have to worry. I won't let Cordell know what we're doing. I know you need to be with him too. I respect that.*

The second-to-last message said, *My cock is aching for you too. I haven't even masturbated since the last time. I still remember how you strained and choked to hold it down.*

Finally, contrite, he wrote, *I'm sorry about that last message. It's just that I sit here every night waiting for your decision. I think about your skin and your touch. I think about you bringing me to your home that night we*

met at Brad's party. I have never been so overwhelmed by a woman. I think
I would die without you.

I sat there in front of Jo's computer, wondering what it all meant.

I remembered the night she'd first met Johnny Fry at Brad Mettleman's Brooklyn apartment. He had said something flirtatious to Jo when he didn't know that she was with me. She laughed him off, and he asked her what she was drinking.

I told him that I'd get her drink and I supposed that that had ended his attempt. But a while later, Brad asked me to come to his den. He'd received a letter from a Spanish photographer that he needed to get the gist of. I read it over twice, no more, and told Brad that the artist, Miguel Rios, was willing to have Brad be his only representative in the U.S. The whole exchange between Brad and me could not have lasted more than twelve minutes.

Twelve minutes. When I came out, Jo came to me and said that she had a migraine coming on.

"I'm feeling it in the center of my head," she'd said, pointing at the place where her third eye would have been.

Twelve minutes. Seven hundred twenty seconds, and a man she'd never known before had convinced her to get me to put her in a cab so that she could rush home to give him better sex than I had ever known.

The next thing I knew, I was standing in the kitchen with a butcher knife clenched in my fist. I don't to this day remember walking there or pulling open the drawer.

Then I was standing over Jo with the knife gripped tightly in my hand. Her pants were off but she still wore the white blouse.

I worried for a moment over the bloodstains that wouldn't come out of her shirt. Then I raised the blade. But the thought of those stains stayed with me—blood on her shirt and carpeting.

149

Blood never washes clean; that's what my mother, when she was still clearheaded, used to say.

Then I was standing in the bathroom in front of the open medicine cabinet. There was a small prescription bottle in my hand.

Jo took the popular sleeping pill now and again when she had to work late. Something about staying up after midnight made her wired, and she needed sleep aids.

I took two of the oval tablets and then went to lie beside her.

I lay there next to her, staring at her face. At first I felt nothing, not hatred or jealousy or betrayal. But then I remembered JF1223 talking about her choking to keep him down. I rose up on one arm, intent on strangling her in her sleep. But the sleeping pills hit me, and I fell back, trying to rise up out of the black pit that was engulfing me.

I awoke to the sound of Jo making noise somewhere in the house. The events of the night before came back to me in snatches and glimpses. I remembered the knife and the sleeping pills. I remembered—

"L?" Jo said. She was standing in the doorway with the butcher knife in her hand.

"Hey."

"I found this in the bathroom," she said holding the knife out to me with open palm held upward.

"I, I couldn't get to sleep," I said. "So I was going to take your cough medicine. But the bottle wasn't open and I couldn't twist it off, so I got the knife to pry it. But then I saw the sleeping pills."

She looked at me with curiosity but no suspicion in her eyes.

"I sure didn't have that problem. I went to sleep without even turning off my computer."

"So that was all that bleeping," I said.

"You heard it?"

"Yeah. I heard something but I didn't know what it was. I tried to wake you up but you were dead to the world."

"Huh. What would you like for breakfast?"

"I better rush, honey," I said. "That vinegar book won't translate itself."

When I stood up, she walked into me, putting her hands on my chest.

"You aren't going to leave me?"

"No. Why do you ask?"

"George Leland," she said, looking down, pressing her forehead against my chest.

I lifted her chin and kissed her nose.

"You had just heard about your uncle, right?"

"Yes, but—"

"There hasn't been anybody else since then, has there?"

"No," she said. "No one."

"What can I say, when you told me about George, I got so excited I couldn't stop. It was like you found my switch and jammed it to the *on* position."

"So we're still together?"

"Yeah. Sure we are," I said. "Till death do us part."

Back at my apartment, I was trying to figure out how to extricate myself from the unerring call of death.

Death followed me, a silent but sure companion. Cynthia had told me that Jo was responsible for what she did. And it was obvious that she was still considering being with Johnny Fry.

It wasn't that I had it in mind to kill Jo or Johnny or anyone else; it's just that there I was with the knife in my hand. Murder

151

rose up in my heart when I thought of the intimacies between them.

I knew that I had to break it off. I had to stop seeing her.

I picked up the phone, intent on calling her. But all that I had in my mind was her name—her name and his. I put the phone down and concentrated, finally recalling the phone number. I picked up the phone again.

"Hello," Joelle answered.

"Hi, honey," I said, my tongue as fat as a cow's cud.

"Hi, baby," she said.

"I wanted to tell you something."

"What's that?"

I cleared my throat and shook my head vigorously.

"It's about what we were talking about the day before yesterday."

"What about it?" Jo asked.

"Maybe you need a break from me," I said. "Maybe this thing about your uncle means that you need time to figure things out. You might need therapy or someone other than me."

"That's so sweet, L," she said. "No, baby, you're what I need. You're proving that right now by showing me real love. You care about my needs over yours."

How little she knew. I was trying to save myself from murdering her, and she was thanking me. I wanted to speak up, but the words were buried under a lifetime of numbness. My emotions were like lava flowing under a fallow landscape. I was filled with rage and impotence too.

"L?"

"Yes, Jo."

"I thought you'd drifted off."

"No, honey. I'm right on course."

★　　★　　★

152

A week before, I was barely alive and didn't know it. I didn't know what sex was or what love was. I didn't understand hatred or desire. I had no notion of the bloodlust that thrived in my heart. If only I could have turned around, walked back through the days to the time I was supposed to be on that noon train to Philadelphia.

Standing in the kitchen with a knife in my hand. How did I get there? Shouldn't a sane man remember the steps that brought him to the brink of murder?

I was sitting on the sofa in front of the great plasma screen. I thought maybe Sisypha had an answer for me. I reached for the remote control, and the phone rang.

Stop, the jangling bell screamed.

"Hello?"

"L?"

"Oh. Hi, Lucy," I said.

"You sound funny."

"I'm anything but funny," I said.

"Are you okay?"

"Sure. Sure. Fine. My heart's beating hard. The blue in the sky is no longer just a memory." I was speaking freestyle, the way I had been writing in the coffee shop.

"What does that mean?" she asked.

"You know when you look at something you've seen a thousand times," I said.

"Like this cup sitting on my desk?" she asked.

"Yeah. Like your cup. If you're just looking for something to drink out of, you glance over at it, you think you know what you're looking at, but you don't really."

"Why not?" she asked, obviously taking my words quite seriously.

"Because the cup is in your mind," I said. "A kind of imperfect memory—or maybe an ideal memory. You've probably never looked at that particular cup very closely. You've owned it and used it for years but you never noticed the little bump near the base of the handle or the place where the glaze bubbled up and left the clay underneath uncovered."

"You're right," she said. "I'm looking at it right now. I got it at a pottery sale in Northampton when I was spending a semester at Smith. I think of it as a blue cup, but now that I look at it, only a part of it is blue. The other half is a sea green. And the green has tiny gold flecks in it."

"You could probably spend the whole day looking at that piece of pottery and you'd come up with something new every few minutes. There's probably a whole novel in there."

I thought to myself that this was just college stuff, the kind of thinking that kids discover—or rediscover—the first time they're away from home. But it meant more to me. I felt what I was saying to Lucy. I'd skimmed across the top of things my whole life, never looking deeply, never knowing what it was that I experienced—what it was I had missed.

"I called to talk to you about something," Lucy said.

"Sure," I replied. "The art galleries . . ."

"No," she said. "No. I don't expect you to get anywhere with them for a while yet."

I was about to contradict her, but she went on. "It's about the other night."

"Oh?"

"I wanted to talk to you about what happened."

"Sure," I said, thinking that maybe this would distract me from my morbid thoughts. "I hope you aren't too upset with me."

"Oh no," Lucy said. "No, not at all. I'm surprised that it happened with someone so much older than me, but I'm not

154

upset with you. I was hoping that you didn't think I was some kind of slut."

"I think you're some kind of wonderful," I said, feeling foolish at expressing my feelings through the lyrics of an old-time song.

"Me too."

"You what?"

"Billy came to see me the other night," she said. "He spent the night, and I realized that he has no idea about women and the way we feel. He's a nice guy, and I have a lot of love for him, but he's never really touched me. Do you know what I mean?"

"Like looking at the cup?"

"Yeah," Lucy said. "You have to listen to me, L. I'm very, very embarrassed by how I'm feeling. I have always believed that men and women are equals and that we have to treat each other in some kind of egalitarian manner. But that night I wanted Billy to ravish me, and all he did was go through the motions. I, I slapped him . . ."

"Why?" I asked.

"I don't know. I was on top, and he was looking up at me with this puppy-dog grin, and I lost my temper and slapped him. And when he whined and asked me why, I slapped him again."

I covered my mouth to keep her from hearing my laughter.

"What happened then?" I asked.

"He didn't know what I was talking about. I told him that I wanted passion. I said I wanted him to hurt over wanting me. I wanted him to hit me back. I kind of lost my mind. And then I realized that I wanted him to be you, Cordell."

"Me?"

"I . . . I want you to start up from where we left off. I need you to listen to me," she said. "I don't think I could say these things to anybody face-to-face. That night when we were together, I could see you in the mirror on your door."

155

I tried to think of where we were and what she would have seen, but failed.

"I don't remember," I said, "where the mirror was in relation to us."

"You wouldn't have seen it," she told me gently. "Hold on a second."

A muffled sound came over the phone a moment, and then she was back again.

"My supervisor wants me to do something, but I told her I need to finish this call," Lucy said.

It surprised me that she was sitting at a desk at work talking so seriously about sex.

"I have always had a big butt," she said. "I never liked it, and I have done exercise my whole life to make it smaller."

It really wasn't so big, but I liked hearing about it. Lucy's voice was a lifeline leading away from my sinister thoughts. I would have begged her not to have gotten off the phone right then.

I was a year shy of twice her age, and I felt every minute of it. But somehow we were equals on the telephone. Not even equals. Lucy was the leader, the more articulate of us peers. She was leading me to where I wanted to be, but I doubt that she had the slightest notion of the power she wielded.

"When I looked into that mirror, I didn't feel like that any-more," she was saying. "You know why?"

I smiled because the breath was stuck in my lungs for a moment. I had to cough before saying, "No."

"Because your face was up between the cheeks of my ass," she said; there was a slight leer in her otherwise innocent voice. "And I could feel your tongue burrowing inside me. When I saw my butt covering up your face and I felt you pressing to get even closer, I fell in love with my butt . . .

156

"L?"

Again my breath was gone.

"Wow, Lucy," I said. "Wow. I, I, I don't know . . . I don't even have words to tell you . . . Can we see each other?"

"That's why I'm calling," she said.

As she prepared to finish her thought, I became petrified. Lucy coming over to my place was all I could think about. If she didn't come, I'd go out and kill Johnny Fry that very day.

Kill Johnny Fry?

"I can't get being with you out of my head," she said. "Even just sitting down makes me excited. The pressure down there is you, you on your knees kissing my ass. That's what I want. I want it right now."

"What about Billy?"

"I don't give a fuck about him," she said. "I have to have you. I don't have anything against Billy. For all I know, we'll stay together and get married and have kids. But I need your big dick in my ass tonight. There . . . I said it. I have never said anything like that to anyone . . . ever. I need you. Do you understand me, L?"

"Yes. Yes I do."

"So what's it going to be?" she asked.

"I'm gonna get way up in there," I said. "I'm gonna open you up like a ripe fig."

"All night?"

"And the next morning too."

"I have to go to work tomorrow," she said.

"No you don't."

"I don't have any more sick days or personal ones. I would stay but I can't."

"I got you a gallery," I said. "I'll advance you five thousand

157

dollars and you can quit and start to get the photos ready for hanging."

"You . . . you're kidding."

"Are you still coming over?"

"I'll be there in fifteen minutes," she said.

She hung up the phone in my ear, but I wasn't angry.

An hour later, the newly unemployed office worker Lucy Carmichael was lying naked, slathered with a shiny coat of massage oil, on my futon couch. I was naked too, and my cock for the first time in years was tilting up.

I had forgotten the butcher knife and the bloodlust. I had forgotten Johnny Fry and my translator's dictionaries. I was rubbing my thumbs down the muscular inside cheeks of Lucy's ass while she whimpered with pleasure.

I had on a bright-yellow condom.

I poked my point finger down into her rectum.

"Is this what you want?" I asked her.

"I want your big fat cock," she said. "I've been thinking about it every minute."

"You were thinking about it when you were fucking Billy?"

"Yes. Yes. Yes. The only way I could come with him was to think about you."

"On my knees kissing your ass?" I asked, positioning myself above her.

"Yes. Now do it."

I sank into her like a bullet into the well-oiled chamber of a gun. The sound she made was a low roar. There was more satisfaction in her call than I could have imagined. She arched up, pressing back against me, taking the two inches I spared her. She groaned,

158

bellowed actually, like some large woodlands creature in ecstasy over the wild.

I moved hardly at all, just hovered there above her, with my entire erection buried and hot. She moved her butt up and down in small circular motions, grunting at each small shift.

"That's good," she said in a vibrating tone. "That's good."

Still I stayed motionless, allowing her to find the sweet spots inside her; she gasped with short breaths every time she found another place of pleasure. She began writhing beneath me. Her shoulders twisted and her feet kicked up. At one point she moved almost on her side, straining at my erection. "Uhh," she groaned in a deep voice— almost bass, almost impossible. Then she turned back on her stomach, pushing her butt up against me with short, fast thrusts.

"Is that what you've been thinking about?" I asked.

"Yes, baby. Yes. Oh yes. Just like that. Just hold it in me and let me dance with it."

"Squeeze your butt cheeks together," I told her.

"Ohhhh," she replied, doing as I asked.

I pulled my cock out of her while her sphincter gripped me. She cried out in pain, the feeling thrumming through her. She flopped on the couch like a mackerel on the deck of a fishing boat.

"Put it back," she sobbed. "Put it back."

I did as she said, and she hissed at me, "Don't take it out again or I'll slap your face."

We kept that up for over an hour. I withdrew my erection twice more, and both times she sat up and slapped me. I hardly felt her blows, but that doesn't mean she didn't hit me hard.

Whenever she hit me, I threw her down and gave her what she wanted.

Finally, Lucy put her hand back against my navel and said, "I can't do it anymore. I'm sorry."

159

I raised up and took her into my lap. She put her head on my shoulder and brought her knees to her chest.

"I have needed that as long as I have been alive," she said. "I needed a sweet man to get down and nasty with me. I needed you."

I couldn't force even one word from my throat. Lucy had taken all my passion. It was odd, because there was no notion of orgasm for me in our struggle.

It was, in a way, a conflict—a battle that seemed to fulfill some forgotten rule.

"You're a child," I whispered.

"And you fucked me raw," she replied.

"I'm twice your age."

"And your dick is still hard."

She got down on her knees in front of me, pulled off the condom, and clenched the hard thing in her hand. She poured half the bottle of massage oil on it, ruining the futon and letting it spill off onto the floor, but I didn't complain. She jerked on me almost halfheartedly, looking at me with a careless expression that a stranger might have handing you a package that you dropped.

But all that deep ass-fucking had had its effect on me. I became aware of a rumbling. At first I thought it was a subway underground or maybe an earthquake. But then I realized the shuddering was inside me. My diaphragm was moving in and out. Before I could identify the feeling, I jumped to escape it. I tried to get to my feet, but my equilibrium was gone. I fell to the side, landing on the floor.

Lucy was laughing. She hadn't let go of my slippery erection. She gripped it as hard as she could, and the semen started gushing while I called out in fear.

Ignoring my fright, Lucy was saying, "That's right, baby. Give it to me. Let me have that." And then, "Look at it come."

I looked down at my cock clinched so tightly in her grip. The ejaculation seemed to be going on forever. This also scared me. I felt that I had somehow lost control.

"You can come again, baby," Lucy said. "Come on. I didn't come all this way for you to give out on me."

Sweat was dripping from her face. Her visage was one of ferocious exultation. Seeing her in this half-feral light, I came again and called out again. Spasms went all through me, and I jittered on the floor in a fit worthy of epilepsy.

"Wow," Lucy said when my convulsions subsided. "I've never seen a man lose himself like that before."

I shook my head and tried to grin. Who knows what I looked like?

"Get up and carry me to your bed," Lucy commanded.

And even though I didn't know if I could stand anymore, I made it to my feet and hefted her in my arms.

When we got into bed, she turned me on my stomach and licked my rectum with loud relish. It wasn't sex but just to show me that she was willing to go as far as she wanted me to go.

We lay next to each other for hours, spent but unable to sleep.

"Don't you feel like you might die?" she asked late into the night.

"Yes," I said. "Sure do."

"Doesn't it feel wonderful?"

"And scary."

"You don't have to worry about me, L. I don't want anything from you but that you do it to me for hours and then come so hard that it shakes the floor."

"But don't you wonder what makes us need this?" I asked.

Lucy didn't answer the question because she had fallen asleep.

161

In my living room at three in the morning, I called a number that I knew had no phone attached. When it rang, I was certain that Joelle's computer was not online.

I signed onto her Freearth account using my plasma TV as the screen.

There were three e-mails that she'd received and read from JF1223, and two responses from her.

JJ,

I know that in the past I wanted you to leave Cordell. I see now that you can't. I am willing to share you. I have given up Bettye. I will never see her again. Even if you don't ever come back to me I won't see her. That is my gift to you—my sacrifice.

If you forgive me, I won't complain about Cordell again. I won't get in the way of your loving him. But please don't abandon me. Don't leave me like this. It's just as if we were making love and just about to come and you stood up and walked out of my life without a word.

You are everything to me. You are my heart. I cannot smile or sing or do anything else without you.

I love you,

JF

This e-mail, titled "Lost," was not answered.
His next communication, "Found," read:

JJ,

For the last two hours I've been sitting here in front of the computer waiting for your answer. I know you're online. I know you read my message. It's been strange sitting here waiting for you. I've been thinking about you, about how

162

you always told me that you couldn't stop yourself from being with me. You said that you didn't want to be with me but you couldn't pull away. That's some powerful stuff.

Many of the things you had me do to you I didn't really want. The spankings, the bathtub . . . But I did it all and I would do more because I love you. I love the curve of your neck and the way your eyes get tight when you're reading something important. I love the way you fold the towels in my bathroom whenever you go in there. And I love how you never allow anyone in a store to cheat you.

I love your butter-brown skin and eyes that see past what I say.

While waiting for you to answer, I've been thinking about all those ways I love you. The crazy time with your uncle's strap and the roses you bought me the next day. I know now that I love you most because you trusted me in the most intimate and scary part of your life. And I know that if I really love you, I have to stop thinking about what I need and let you move on.

Good-bye, Joelle. I release you from my desire.

JF

Jo had shared her secrets with Johnny Fry long before she'd ever told me; that much was clear from his e-mail. And even though I knew that she was using him to work out her dark obsessions, the jealousy awakened in me felt like a fully revved engine impotent because it's left out of gear.

I wanted them both dead but I didn't necessarily want to be the killer.

Jo's first reply to JF1223 was titled "Re: Found." For a long time I resisted opening that epistle. But finally I couldn't hold back anymore.

163

john-john,

I appreciate what you wrote. I know how deep the wound is. I have been bleeding from it my entire life. When I met you I needed something and you gave it to me. It was something that I had never told anyone about. It was like a tumor in my core, and you clawed it out of me. You made me whole—if only for a moment. And because of that I will always . . .

I was going to say that I will always love you, but that would be too easy. Everybody talks about love: mothers and fathers, grandmothers and grandfathers; there's love of country and love of race. There's the needy love children have for their parents, and you can see lovers walking up and down the street of any city in the world. Love is commonplace, but what I feel for you is anything but common. What I feel for you aches deep in long-healed wounds; it bruises my thighs and eyes and flows from me like blood. If you were a deer, or I was, the other's blood would run freely from the wolf's fanged embrace; that wolf is the passion between you and me.

You are a pain deep inside of me, an agony that I cannot ease. And your words, setting me free, hurt more than I can say. But if I've learned anything from you, it is that I can feel the pain and survive.

jj

That was when I decided to kill Johnny Fry, when I knew for certain that he had gotten closer to her than I ever could. He had given up everything just to tell her that he loved her. And she had professed a feeling for him that belittled my most powerful emotions. Jo and Johnny Fry humiliated me with the breakage of their union, and I hated him for that and hated him all the more for the demotion in my own eyes.

164

I almost logged off then. What more could I gain from her second e-mail? Reading this much had already made me a second-class citizen in the province of my own imagination. But I couldn't turn away without reading her last communiqué. Maybe, somehow, this note would resuscitate my self-esteem.

This e-mail was titled "wait."

I wrote the last note and sent it quickly. After that, I took your shirt out of the bottom drawer and breathed in your scent, then I balled it up and squeezed it between my thighs. I came twice and then called up the words I sent you . . .

I can't end it, john-john. I can't say goodbye. The pain you've brought into my life is the sweetest thing I've ever known. It doesn't matter about I, or Bettye. It doesn't matter that you're white and unrepentant. It doesn't matter that we love, actually love, other people. Even when I sit here and think of your pain at our separation, I get a feeling inside me that no cock or tongue or even having a baby could make me feel.

I think about that time you hired that guy in Atlantic City to do me while you sat at the foot of the bed and watched. My eyes were on you the whole time. My passion was you making me submit to a stranger.

I will go with you to Baltimore next week. I will submit to you and master you and our hearts will vomit out of our mouths. The police will find us and wonder what sick vows we took.

Johnny Fry answered this last communication in less than a minute. It had no message line.

i'll be there

JF

I had pocketed Jo's sleeping pills. There were eighteen left in the bottle. I would have killed myself right then if I hadn't had it in mind to kill Johnny Fry.

Instead I took two pills and lay down next to Lucy, who slept, peacefully nude, on top of the covers. The window shade was up, and the nearly full moon shone down on her skin, making it seem preternatural—luminescent like a goddess's breath.

I reached out to touch her naked shoulder but pulled back.

I was wondering why I had to kill John Fry. It wasn't his fault, obviously, that Jo's needs were so deep and dark. He said that he did what she wanted in order to be with her. She said that she didn't love him . . .

The moonlight was moving on Lucy's pale skin.

I thought of the young photographer then, undulating under me in pain and ecstasy. She still loved Billy, but the need inside her negated this feeling; his needs came second to hers. She wanted something that I had, but it wasn't necessarily me. I gave to her the same way John Fry gave to Jo. And Jo took from him the way Lucy did from me.

She knew I had a girlfriend but never asked if this was okay. It wasn't her job to worry about Jo's feelings. She had an itch, and I had knees to bend.

It wouldn't be my fault when I killed Johnny Fry . . . The moonlight was resplendent, but that radiance would have come to nothing if Lucy's skin were not there to receive it . . . In her dreams Lucy had been in a desert dying of thirst, when a stranger, an enemy of her people, let's say, stopped on his camel and gave her a gourd filled with ice-cold water . . . Somewhere Johnny Fry refrained from masturbating so that he could come in great gushing spurts down Jo's clenching throat . . . Somewhere Jo was shivering in anticipation of returning to the arms of the man who made her feel that even love was commonplace . . . And at some moment in the past I was reaching for a knife, walking down through time in order that I might arrive at the proper instant where he is sleeping next to my woman . . . Her first waking sensation would be his warm blood on her skin. And when she rose in shock, the only thing left of me would be a door slamming on the sham of both our lives . . .

I jerked from the sleeping-pill-induced stupor; the door slamming seemed almost real.

Almost real . . . I was coming to reality. So far my life had been a dream, a wan thought about someone named Cordell Carmel. A brief imitation of manhood in a world that took everything from me before I knew what loss was. I was coming to be real, a knife in my hand and blood ready to spill . . .

The next morning, Lucy woke up to the feeling of my engorged cock sliding into her still-oiled rectum. She took in a great gulp of air and exhaled, "Oh, oh, oh, oh."

I was hard and cold, taking deep satisfaction in her writhing rapture.

This time it was me moving back and forth; it was me finding those sweet spots and pressing them home.

Lucy grabbed on to my biceps and dug her fingernails in. I fucked her harder then and she screamed but did not try to stop me.

Fifty minutes later, we were showered and powdered, sitting at the breakfast table with French roast coffee brewing by the sink. We were fully dressed, ready for the civilized world. She apologized for making me bleed. I told her that it was worth every drop.

Now we sat at the table going through her responsibilities to the gallery. She would choose fifteen photographs to put on display and decide on what kind of frames to use. I would stay on Ms. Thinnes and make sure that the contract would come by Friday.

I wrote her a check for $5,000.

"This is the advance," I said, handing the note to her.

"You don't have to give me all this," she said.

"Take it. It's the beginning of your life as a photographer, and anyway you'll need it for the accountant."

"What do I need an accountant for?"

"In order to convince Ms. Thinnes to take the photographs, I told her that you had your own foundation to help the orphaned children of Darfur. Instead of selling the pieces for twenty-five hundred dollars, she'll be charging six thousand, three thousand of which will be going to your foundation."

"Per picture sold?" she asked.

"Per picture sold."

A blank expression folded over Lucy's eyes. She stared at me with her mouth agape. The water percolating on the kitchen counter was the only sound.

"That was my dream," she said haltingly.

"If the dream is strong enough, it comes real," I said, thinking that the same was true for nightmares.

Lucy stood up over me, her hands unconsciously balled into fists.

"That was my dream," she said again. "I can save children, support a small orphanage. I could, I could . . ."

She put her arms around my head and plopped down into my lap. She began crying. I couldn't understand the things she was saying through her tears.

168

Nor did it matter what she said. I hadn't set up the notion of the charity for any good reason. I simply knew that making the white patrons of that gallery feel that they could assuage their guilt meant that I would make out. I was a sham and a liar, no matter what good came from what I'd done. That young white child cared more for Black Africa than I did. She cared more for my people because I had no people. All I had were the echoes of lost heart and fading images that I now knew were never love.

But even that didn't matter anymore, because now I was dedicated to the slaughter of Johnny Fry, the man who took my fantasy of manhood and mashed it into pulp.

Lucy went off to the bank. She asked if she could spend the night again, but I told her that an old man like me needed to take time off between sessions like we had.

"I have to rest up," I said. "You know I got twenty years on you."

"That's not all you have on me," she replied.

I hustled her out the door so that I didn't drag her back to my bed.

After that I called Linda Chou, Brad Mettleman's receptionist.

"I was wondering if I could come over and talk to you after five," I said, knowing that Brad left the office every day at four.

"Of course," she said brightly. "I work every night until seven or later."

Outwardly my daily life seemed to be the same. I had the same apartment, and me being home at noon was nothing new, seeing as I hadn't had a day job in many years. I wore the same clothes, used the same phone, Jo was still my girlfriend—in name. My life, to

169

anyone looking in, was just as boring and mundane as it had been in all the twenty years that led up to that day.

But inside there was a new man—not a better man by any means. I was no better but I was different because I was going to commit a murder; that set me apart from all those other common lovers that Jo talked about walking down the street.

I sat there on my oil-soaked sofa feeling gravity working on my bones. I was a force of nature now. I was ready to take the ultimate step. The plan was already in play, and I hadn't even left my apartment.

Time was passing, but I felt unhurried and calm. I wasn't eager for love or sex or success. I had it all or I would never have it—either way, there was nothing for me to desire.

As the minutes clicked by in bright-red numerals on the digital clock of the cable box beneath the plasma TV, my thoughts began to evaporate. They winnowed down to words: murder, life, sweet, sex. The words were solitary and meant little in my mind. They were the moments before sounds. And later on they weren't even that.

Waiting, waiting, waiting.

When the telephone rang, I jumped to my feet. My mind had become so disconnected that the jangling sound seemed impossible.

"Hello?" I said, stunned by the intrusion.

"Hello," a sultry woman's voice said. "May I speak to Cordell please?"

"That's me."

"Hi. My name's Brenda. I was asked by a friend of mine to give you a call."

"Who's your friend?" I asked. I was calming down back into the meditative state of my previous reverie. The woman's voice was low and sensual like the interior of my newly attained serenity.

"Cynthia," she said.

"Cynthia who?"

"Her last name is Cook, but she doesn't give that out on the dial-a-friend line."

"She . . . she asked you to call me? Why?"

"She thought it would be good if we talked."

"Why?" I asked.

"I don't know. All I know is that she called me up and said that you needed to speak to me in order to work something out."

"I don't know you, do I?" I asked.

"I don't know you," she said rather mysteriously.

I was perturbed, because the serenity I'd reached after deciding to kill John Fry was being tested by Cynthia's betrayal.

"She didn't do anything wrong," Brenda said as if reading my thoughts.

"Why'd she give you my number?"

"Because she said that you were going through a rough time and she thought you'd like to talk to me."

"Why?"

"Listen, Cordell, if you don't want to get together, we don't have to."

"Get together? I thought you wanted to talk," I said.

"I don't want anything," Brenda said flatly. "Cynthia called, said that you might get something out of a little meal together, and asked me to give you a ring. I know almost nothing about you other than your name."

Something about the way she put words together gave me pause. I felt as if we had talked before but I knew we had not.

Maybe Cynthia knew something that would help me. Maybe I wouldn't have to kill Johnny Fry if I spoke . . .

"When would you like to meet?" I asked.

"I'm only in town for a few days," she said. "Tonight at ten would be great for me."

"Where?"

"Michael Jordan's Steak House."

"At Grand Central Station?" I asked.

"See you there at ten," she said, and hung up.

I put the phone down and slipped back into the trancelike mood of disconnectedness. Brenda's call left me like a dream. It was less than a memory. I didn't need Cynthia's help. All I needed was to kill Johnny Fry—not because that would get Jo back; Jo was lost to me now. To her I was a house pet, while Johnny Fry was what she craved.

No. I was killing Johnny Fry because he was a parasite that had burrowed under my skin. He was an infection that had to be dug out and crushed, a fat white larva filled with sickly yellow puslike blood who believed that my flesh would sustain him.

My hands were numb, and so were my lips and toes. My breath came slowly as I sat there . . . waiting.

When the digital clock read 4:09, I stood up and went out of the door.

On the street everything was just fine. I was walking one step after another on numbed feet toward the subway.

In the underground train I sat next to a young black woman who was writing in a French workbook, solving the conjugation of verbs.

When she did one wrong, I interrupted her and told her the correct past tense. She thanked me and went on working, but after a while, she turned away from her book.

172

"Are you from another country?" she asked.

I wondered if she had ever read the novel.

"No," I said. "I'm American, from San Francisco originally, but I've lived here in Manhattan for over twenty years."

"Oh," she said, smiling, nodding almost dismissively. She was darker than Jo, both shorter and thicker. Her lips were large and well formed. If you looked very closely, you could make out the most lovely freckles on either side of her nose, these just slightly darker than her deep-brown skin.

"I was thinking that you were from a francophone country because you helped me."

"Language major," I told her, "at UC Berkeley."

"Wow. I'm studying French at City up in Harlem. I want to live somewhere else than here in America." She sighed and glanced out the subway window into the swift darkness.

"Why?" I asked.

"To find a good black man."

"There aren't any good ones here?"

"Uh-uh," she said, her upper lip curling in disgust. "All the men I meet are either dogs, on the down low, dealin' or doin' drugs, or expect me to pay for dinner *and* the rent."

"All men are dogs," I said. "Frenchmen included. And Africans and Jamaicans and even Pygmies, whatever language they speak."

The young woman grinned, and the train began to slow. I became worried that the next stop was where she'd get off. Her smile made me want her to stay.

"Is this your stop?" I asked.

She was about to say something then refrained. Then she said, "No. Is it yours?"

"No."

She smiled while people moved all around us. The car was very crowded, and we were pushed closer to each other on the light-blue plastic bench.

"So learning French won't help me?" she asked, as the warning bells rang and the doors stuttered because of people holding them open to get in and get out.

"It'll make you smarter," I said. "But knowing things is often worse than not knowing them."

"I want to know things," she said, looking up into my eyes.

Her red-and-yellow blouse opened a bit, allowing me to appreciate her cleavage. I tried not to be obvious about looking, and she didn't turn away.

"We always say that," I said. "We want to know things, but then one day your mother says that your brother is her favorite. One day your wife says that she'd rather sleep on a bed of glass than with you. The doctor, the official letter, the bank . . . We want to know things, but only those things that make us happy or don't touch us at all."

"That sounds so sad," the young woman—I pegged her at twenty-seven—said. "Are you sad?"

"Yeah," I said. The feeling tingled back into my hands and feet. "I'm very sad, I guess."

"Why?"

"What's your name?"

"Monica. Monica Wells."

"I'm Cordell Carmel."

Monica held out her hand and I shook it.

"Pleased to meet you, Mr. Carmel," she said and I could hear the invitation in her voice.

I looked at the pretty, chubby little woman and wondered. I thought, very clearly, almost crazily, that a man on foot could only travel one path but that in his soul a man could be going in two opposite directions at the same time.

Here I was, bound for the execution of Johnny Fry, but at that simultaneous moment, I was on a train destined to try to get Monica Wells to smile at me.

"Only part sad," I said.

"What part is that?" she asked.

"The one not talking to you."

"What does that mean?"

"I'm at a transitional crossroad in my life, Monica," I said, consciously using her name. "I've been a freelance translator for nearly the whole time I've lived in the city, but last week I stopped that. I also broke up with a girlfriend a while ago and I've been seeing different women. It all sounds like fun but really it isn't. I quit my job on a whim. My girlfriend, although she won't say it, is in love with another man—"

"That's too bad," Monica said. "Has she been seein' him?"

"I don't know. Maybe."

"Can you pay your rent wit' no job?" she asked.

"I got another job. It might make more money than the last one. But it's just, uh . . . confusing."

"Yeah," she said. Her hand moved as if she wanted to touch my arm, but she held back.

"What about you?" I asked. "What's your life like?"

"I live in the East Village with my mom," she said. "An' my li'l girl."

"How old is your daughter?"

"Five."

"That's nice. She's walking and talking and going to the bathroom by herself but she does what you tell her to—most of the time."

"Yeah," Monica said, tucking in her chin and grinning. "She's a good girl. She misses her daddy, but we can't do nuthin' about that."

175

"He left?"

"He's in prison."

"Oh. I'm sorry to hear that."

"It's alright," she said, raising a hand either in prayer or dismissal. "He always wanted to be runnin' in the street with his friends, an' it finally caught up with him."

"He's in for a long time?"

"Uh-huh. You know, that's why I started goin' back to school. I want my baby to know all kindsa people with all kindsa lives. I want her to go to a French school, what they call a lycée, here in New York. That way she'll have a whole 'nother world to be thinkin' 'bout."

"I know a woman who's connected with the Lycée Français," I said. "I've done English-to-French translations for her."

"Is she a black woman?" Monica asked.

"No. Her name is Marie Tourneau, and she's there most days. You could call her and tell her I said to come see her. She'll call me and I'll give her all kinds of glowing praise."

"You don't even know me," Monica said.

"I probably know you better than anyone giving an interview," I replied. "I know you're trying to make a better life for yourself and your daughter. I know how much the school means to you. What's your daughter's name?"

"Mozelle."

"Okay then, tell me about Mozelle."

For the next ten or twelve stops, Monica talked to me about her only child. She was short like her mother and athletic like her dad—Ben Carr. She loved crayons and yellow paper and music. She helped her mother and grandmother with dinner every night and knew how to boil an egg if somebody was in the kitchen with her.

176

Every weekend, mother and daughter went somewhere special: the Bronx Zoo, the Museum of Natural History, the Metropolitan Museum of Art. They rode the Staten Island Ferry one weekend after visiting the Jewish Museum downtown.

"I want my girl to know everybody's history," Monica said. "Because she needs to know where we come from—all of us."

The train came to a stop at 135th Street. When Monica stood up to get out, I did too.

"You goin' to City too?" she asked, with maybe a hint of trepidation. After all, she didn't really know me—only the words I had said.

"I was going to Fifty-ninth," I admitted, "only I enjoyed talking to you so much that I stayed on. I'll just cross over to the other side here and go back down."

"You got to pay again here," she told me. "If you stay on up to One-forty-five, you don't have to."

"That's okay," I said. We were already out of the car. "I'll walk you across the street and go down over there. It's worth the extra fare."

At the crosswalk I said, "So, Monica. We agree that all men are dogs. I freely admit that I'm going out with many women. You know I have a job. I'm not on the down low, or dealing drugs, or taking drugs, and if you agree to go out with me, I'll be happy to pay for dinner."

The light turned green, but she didn't step into the street.

She was quite a bit shorter than I and not nearly as stout as I had thought.

"Why you wanna go out with me?"

"Because when I told you about why I was sad, you almost put your hand on my arm to tell me things were okay but you didn't because you didn't know me well enough."

177

"I sure didn't." The smile came up in her brown face like light on the darkness of morning.

"So I figure if we meet for dinner, then you could get to know me better, and the next time I'm sad, you could pat my arm."

"Is that all you want?"

"Right now I'm just happy standing here with you."

"Tonight?" she asked.

"Tomorrow."

"Where we gonna eat?"

I gave her the address of the Italian bistro on Sixth.

"What time?"

"Seven?"

"Okay. I'll be there." She put one foot in the street, but the light had turned red again. A speeding car honked, and I grabbed her by the arm, pulling her back on the curb.

Instead of thanking me, she asked, "Do really know that woman, that Marie Tourneau?"

"Yes, ma'am."

The light turned, and I let go of her arm.

We walked together to my subway entrance and there we parted. She was halfway up the hill toward the college before she looked back. I waved at her, and she laughed out loud, doubling over.

"I thought you were coming at five," short, sweet, and light-olive-hued Linda Chou said to me at the third-floor office door of my old-time friend Brad Mettleman.

She unlocked the door when I knocked. I could see that she had recently reapplied her ruby-red lipstick and the razor-thin eyeliner at the outer edges of her eyes.

She was twenty-five, no more, and thin. Not malnourished like the children in Lucy's pictures but wiry like those old men and women who outlive their children while existing below the poverty line on farms perched at the outskirts of rural America—where people still thrill when they think about God and sin and George Washington.

"Sorry," I said. "Really. I was on the subway . . . just thinking . . . and then it was One hundred thirty-fifth Street."

"You went all the way up there?" Her eyes could get wide.

"I'm sorry," I said again. "First I'm rude and then I make you wait."

"That's okay. The flowers were nice. You wanna see 'em?" She smiled and let her head slide to the side a bit.

She took the sleeve of my tan jacket in a playful grip and pulled me from the entrance area into the larger room that contained her reception desk.

The yellow roses really were lovely. Their long, trimmed stems stood straight in a slender glass vase, unadorned with the usual green flummery that so many talentless florists use.

"They fit you," I said looking at her.

She bit her lower lip, and I regretted having to meet Brenda, whoever she was, later on.

"What did you want, Mr. Carmel?"

"Why don't we sit down?" I suggested.

There were two guest chairs in front of her Arts and Crafts oak desk. She sat on one while I took the other. Our knees were only inches apart.

My life would end soon, I knew that for sure. I could kill Johnny Fry, but I doubted that I would manage to get away with it. The police would arrest me or shoot me down; the court would sentence me to death or life.

It's funny how none of that bothered me. I guess I was kind of

179

crazy. And I loved it that every moment I spent seemed to be filled with so many of the glorious details of life.

I could almost hear Linda's heart pounding with interest.

My nostrils flared, and she smiled for me.

"I made a deal with Ms. Thinnes to represent Lucy Carmichael's work," I told her.

"You did?" Linda's eyes and mouth made three perfect circles. "She's really hard. Brad's only had two shows with her in the last twelve years."

"I appealed to her political side," I said. "I told her that Lucy had a foundation for the orphaned children of the Sudan. It seems that Ms. Thinnes likes to think that she can make a difference."

"That's kinda cynical, isn't it?" Linda asked, crossing her legs. She was wearing a mid-thigh bright-orange silk dress that had the outlines of yellow fish drawn here and there. The hem fell in just such a way as to make you feel that you were seeing more thigh than she was actually showing.

The look excited me, but it was the word, *cynical*, that caught my attention. Not the word, exactly, but the challenge it held. She was confronting my contempt of the elder Ms. Thinnes's intentions.

This reminded me of my father.

I had a momentary glimpse of him in the living room of our apartment on Isabella Street in Oakland, California. I had told people I was from San Francisco for so long that I sometimes forgot our little back-of-the-building apartment on Isabella.

My father was sitting in the ratty old maroon sofa chair that he'd found in the street in the rich white hills that lay between Oakland and Berkeley.

Brain is the only defense a niggah has, he was saying in the reverie. Only he was saying it very fast, as he always did, and the words

180

blended together. *White man love ya. White man hate ya. It's all the same. 'Cause you know he ain't evah gonna feel like you. Uh-uh. No, no. Not even for a minute. White man ain't nevah gonna know you and so he won't evah do nuthin' you want on purpose. He cain't. So you got to think like him and find out what it is in his mind that he's thinkin' so you can get him to do sumpin' and make that sumpin' what you want too.*

"Yeah," I said to Linda. "You're right. I gave her a chance to think that she could help the people of Sudan by throwing money at a white girl who had been there. I got her to agree to charging six thousand dollars for Lucy's photographs."

"Six thousand?" Linda said. "Dog."

"Lucy thinks she can help people too," I said, with a smile on my face that might have seemed sad.

"You don't think so?" Linda asked, uncrossing her legs and leaning forward with her elbows on her knees in a masculine pose.

"You're very pretty, Linda Chou."

"Is that the answer?"

"No," I said. "I guess . . . I guess I don't believe that we, I mean none of us, understand how far down the pain goes for others. We think things and believe other people think like us. We feel things and think other people feel like us. But we're just making it up most of the time. Our beliefs are like the dust falling on mountains, like sunlight at the bottom of the sea."

My words surprised both of us.

"That's kinda heavy," Linda Chou said, and I smiled.

"Have you ever been in love with somebody and then broke up with them and realized that you never knew who they were?" I asked.

"Yes," she said with renewed interest.

"You look at them and wonder what could you have possibly been thinking when you got together? How could you kiss

181

them or talk to them? They were never what you thought they were."

Linda was biting her lip again.

"What does that have to do with the people in Darfur?" she asked honestly expecting an answer.

"It's like humanity was a body," I said, thinking that I wanted to get on my knees and bury my face in her orange and olive thighs. "Not some people over there and some others over here. I hurt my hand the other day. I was in pain, and even though the doctor looked at that, he had to consider everything about the injury. For instance—why had I fallen? Did I have fever? Was there an obstruction in my brain? If I'd had an infection, he wouldn't have injected my hand. That would have hurt too much. We are a system, all of us, but we don't think like that. We blame and feel sorry for and ignore. That's why I have no faith in the intentions of people. People are blind and even worse, they don't know it."

"Not you," Linda Chou said, and I didn't know if she was making fun of me.

"Will you go out with me sometime?" I asked her.

"Out where?" she asked back.

"I don't know. Dancing?"

"You like to dance?" she asked.

"I've never been dancing in my life. I sure don't know how. But you look like a dancer to me, and I'm willing fall down a few times."

"But then, what if you have a fever or a tumor?"

"I'll die dancing," I said. "What could be better than that?"

Linda laughed very loudly. I think she was nervous because the conversation took her off guard with its intensity. I remembered how Lucy had arched her body when I entered her as she slept. She wanted what was happening, but at the same time it was too much.

"Okay," she said. "When?"

"Not tonight. I'm meeting someone about business later on. But the day after tomorrow would be fine."

"Okay," she said, giving in with a shrug and smile. "I'll find a place and you can pick me up here at nine."

"I have to go to the bathroom," I said then. "Do you mind if I use Brad's."

"No. Go on."

Brad's office door was frosted glass. Linda could have seen me moving around through it if she stood up to look. But I didn't close it anyway. I walked into the large, modernist office and went to the bathroom door. I leaned in, turned on the hot and cold water so that they made a lot of noise, then I got down in half-lotus and opened Brad's bottom drawer.

I knew he kept an unregistered pistol in there. A .32 caliber gun that he bought from a junkie client of his. He told me that he bought it to give the guy something to eat with and to save him from killing someone else or himself.

The junkie died of an overdose three weeks later. Brad made over $100,000 on the canvases he'd gotten. The junkie didn't even have a girlfriend to pay off.

I put the small, unloaded pistol in the left inside breast pocket of my jacket and the box of bullets in the right. Then I went into the bathroom, flushed the toilet, turned off the spigots that looked like silver lizards, and came out.

Linda was sitting behind the desk now. She had out three legal-looking forms.

"These are the boilerplate contracts we use with all of our clients and dealers," she said. "You should take them with you and read through them. When are you meeting with Ms. Thinnes again?"

"Saturday."

"Go over them and we'll talk about what you should ask for when we go dancing."

"Maybe," I said.

"What do you mean?"

"Well . . . I wouldn't be a very good date if I made you work for your dinner and dancing."

"Don't worry," she said, with a delicious smile. "I intend to work your butt off on that dance floor."

I walked the young receptionist to her subway stop and kissed her cheek good-bye. I looked forward to seeing her again, but I knew from the weight in my pockets that I might be dead before the time our date rolled around. For some reason, this made me laugh.

I walked through Central Park again, over to Fifth Avenue and then down. It was a sultry night, and people were out in droves. Secretaries and fat businessmen, displaced cigarette smokers, taxis and limos ferrying people from one door to another, lovers— commonplace lovers.

I stopped at a phone booth and called Joelle.

"Hi," she said in a way that seemed she was expecting the call.

"Hi."

"Oh . . . L."

"You were expecting another call?"

"No, no."

"I could get off and call you later."

"No. Where are you?" she asked. "You sound like you're outside."

"I'm on Fifth Avenue. My guy down in Philly is leaving tonight at ten from Penn Station. I'm going down there to deliver my pages. What have you been doing?"

"Nothing. Working."

"Anybody interesting call?"

"No. I . . ."

"Yeah?"

"I have to go down to Baltimore next week. They're having the service for my uncle."

"So long after he died?"

"It . . . My family from Hawaii is in town and we, my sister and I, thought that it would be a good time to, to say good-bye."

"Why would you want to do that?" I asked.

"I feel that I must do this," she said, with an odd articulation.

"I'll come with you," I offered.

"No."

"I think I should. I mean, after we talked about it the other day, I feel that it has to do with me too."

"No, L. Please don't ask me. This is something I have to do alone."

"Oh. Okay. Well, I better be going."

"Come by after your meeting?" she asked so sweetly that for a moment I forgot how humdrum and ordinary our love was.

"Okay," I said. "I'll come."

I got to Grand Central Station a little after 8:30. Rush hour was winding down, but there were still a lot of people there.

I wandered into the bookstore and looked for some novel that I could read while waiting for my meeting with Brenda. I thumbed through John Updike, Colson Whitehead, Philip Roth, and a sex book penned by a popular TV sex star. All of them had their merits, but I realized that I wasn't in a reading mood.

185

I was angry and feeling betrayed by Cynthia. And the more I thought about it, the angrier I became.

Why couldn't I trust anybody?

Why did everyone betray me?

I went to a phone booth and entered all the right numbers. Her phone rang three times, and a message machine came on.

"This is Cynthia. I'm busy on a call right now, but I'll be happy to ring you back if you just leave a name and number."

"It's Cordell," I said without inflection. I left the number of the pay phone and hung up.

Thirty seconds later, I was thinking that I was a fool to expect her to call back, then the phone rang.

"Hello?"

"Cordell?"

"You called?"

"I've been expecting you. I checked the call-waiting to see if it was you, but the number was blocked, so I waited for the message. How are you?"

"Feeling a little let down by you, I guess."

"Oh don't," she said. "Don't feel like that. I thought long and hard before calling Brenda. I knew that you needed to see her, to talk to her. I could tell."

"Who is she?"

"Someone who will help you on your journey."

"What is she? A therapist? A prostitute?"

"She's a very powerful woman. A woman who will understand your grief."

Grief.

"Cynthia," I said. "You couldn't possibly know me well enough to set me up on a date."

"This is no date," she said. "It's nothing like that. This meeting

186

you have with Brenda could very well be a turning point in your life. It could open you up to understand just how important your receptivity to the world can be."

I wanted to be angry but I couldn't hold on to the feeling. The concern in Cynthia's voice was real, and that was all that mattered to me.

"I hope you're right," I said. "Because I've been beginning to think that I won't survive this trauma of Jo's."

"Have you told her?"

"No."

"Has she gone back to her lover?"

"I think she intends to. They're going down to Baltimore to attend the service for the uncle that molested her."

"How does that make you feel?"

"Like shit."

"What are you going to do?" she asked.

"Some things I cannot share with you, Cynthia. I hope you understand that."

"Absolutely. But you need to know that you can tell me anything. Anything. I will always be in your corner."

That was an emotional time for me. The tears came up and out. I didn't know which way to turn, and so I said, "I gotta go," hung up the phone, and hurried out into the night. I walked down 42nd Street toward Broadway looking into storefronts and wondering about love. I thought about my mother in the Connecticut retirement community. I called her once every two weeks to talk for three minutes or less. I asked her how things were going and if she needed anything. Things were always fine and she had enough.

"I love you," I would say after saying good-bye.

She'd hesitate and then murmur, "Uh, oh yes. Bye."

But Cynthia, whom I had never met, was willing to try to make

187

some commitment to me. She was looking for my number on her line.

It was no wonder that Jo thought me at best common. I couldn't even respond when I saw her with her lover. He was fucking her ass like it was his and his alone. She was nodding and calling him Daddy. And what did I do?

I felt for the pistol in my pocket. At that instant, a raindrop splashed against my cheek. I had a Brookstone umbrella in my briefcase. By the time I had it out, it was raining hard—a downpour.

My feet were getting wet, but that was okay. The rain fell straight down, and the design of the umbrella made it quite wide when open, despite its compact size.

At Sixth Avenue I found myself standing next to a young black man, no more than twenty. He wore black slacks and a loose T-shirt and was getting soaked by the rain.

"Which way you goin'?" he asked me rather sheepishly.

"West."

"Can I . . . ?"

I gestured with my briefcase, and he huddled under the comparative shelter of my umbrella.

We walked side by side, close but not touching, together by circumstance, not speaking a word. Around us people ran and stood in doorways. One extremely fat man carried an umbrella so tiny that was of little more use to him than a hat would have been.

After a few blocks, the young man said, "I'm goin' to Billy's Burgers, past Tenth. You goin' that far?"

"Sure."

It felt odd walking with someone I didn't know, sheltering him. It made me think of those glass-eyed wolves at the Museum of Natural History. Some things are done from instinct—precious in the so-called civilized world . . .

When we got to the door of the fast-food restaurant, the young
man asked, "Where you goin'?"

He had a lazy eye and one silver tooth.

"Just out walking," I said. "Killing time."

"You wan' somethin'?" he asked me.

"Like what?"

"A blow job?"

"Uh . . . No . . . No thank you."

"It wouldn't cost nuthin'. You live around here?"

"Sorry . . . no."

"M'kay. Thanks for walkin' me."

He turned and went into the restaurant, where other young
men greeted him and kissed his cheek and lips.

The rain started coming down even harder.

On the walk back toward Grand Central, I thought about the last
time I'd driven up to visit my mother. She was having a nice time.
The only thing my siblings and I agreed on was making sure that
our mother had a comfortable place to retire. We all chipped in for
the monthly payments and her government income covered the
rest. There were bingo games and nightly movies in the small
auditorium. She had a white boyfriend who still played tennis and
ate dinner with her every weeknight.

"Would you think of marrying him?" I asked my mom during
one of our three-minute talks.

"Oh no, Eric," she said. She often called me by my brother's
name. I wondered if she even remembered that she had two sons.

"Oh no," she repeated. "I never even married your daddy."

"What?"

"I never married him. I'm a free woman. He can't own me.
Nobody can own me." She was very animated, angry even.

189

"So you never wanted to be married?"

"No sir. Not me."

"Yes, sir?" the young Hispanic hostess asked.

"My name is Cordell," I said. "Hers is Brenda. We were to have dinner at ten."

The handsome young brown woman looked down at her computer screen and smiled.

"Your guest is already at the table, Mr. Cordell. Just walk past the bar and turn to your right."

At the entrance to the dining room, a chubby white girl in a flouncy blue dress smiled at me.

"Right this way," she said holding the menus to cover her ample cleavage.

The restaurant was divided into sections. The first one was smaller but with large tables and a banquette for eight or nine couples. The next room, where our table was, was open, looking out onto the main floor of the station and up at the roof, which was dark turquoise and had the creatures of constellations painted on it, with small yellow lights to indicate the position of the stars.

The waitress was bringing me to a table that was perched at the outer wall, giving the best view of the floor. I was so happy about the placement that I didn't pay close attention to the profile of my blind date.

She was black, that is to say, Negro; her coloring was caramel, and her dark hair was straightened. She wore a red dress and seemed to have a nice figure.

The waitress brought me to the table and set down the menu. It was only then that I got a clear view of Brenda's face.

"Have a nice dinner," the waitress was saying.

190

"Uh . . . huh . . ." I said, gawping at the woman who called herself Brenda.

"Maybe you should sit down, Cordell," my date suggested.

I realized that the hostess was holding the chair for me. I tried to show some decorum sitting, but I went down too fast and stopped the chair before she could push it fully under me.

"That's okay," I said. "I'll get it."

The buxom hostess moved away, and I gazed into Brenda's radiant face.

"I can't believe this," I said.

"You know me?"

"I, I, I . . ." I said. Then I took a breath. "You're a dream, not a person—not a living, breathing, smiling, eating person."

Her smile was certain and sharp.

"Am I your fantasy?"

"Was Mel an actor or someone who didn't know what he was in for?" I asked.

"You could tell that?"

The surprise on her face sent a wave of glee down into my intestines. I had to use all of my strength not to giggle and jitter in my chair.

"How did Cynthia know?" I asked. "How did she know to send you to me? And why would you, *you*, agree to meet with me?"

Sisypha's smile was intelligent. Her eyes defied my humility.

"I'm a woman and you're a man," she said. "Nothing's gonna change that. Cynthia used to be a sex worker a long time ago. We were friends in West Hollywood. She's always had my number."

"And she just called you and you came to New York?"

"That was serendipity . . ."

Just her use of the word elated me. My right foot was tapping out her name in Morse code: my first foreign language. I used to sit at the dinner table tapping out *fuck you daddy asshole* while my father lorded over dinner.

". . . I had to be in New York for the games," Sisypha was explaining. "Cynthia knew I'd be here, and she called and said that there was someone who was on the edge of something wonderful or something bad. She said that you had seen my film, *The Myth*, and that it intrigued you."

"You made him submit to you," I said.

"Is that what you want?"

I brought my hand to my face and then put it down again. I looked for a waiter, but there wasn't one around.

"What, what are the games?" I asked, hoping that my heart didn't leap out of my throat.

Sisypha (I would always know her by that name or some derivative thereof) sat back and smiled, showing her teeth.

"The Sex Games," she said. "They're held in New York every three years. There are twelve major events and twice that many entertaining performances. They also have mixers very late at night, after the competitions are over."

"I've never heard of them," I said, and her smile broadened.

"No. You wouldn't have. They bend a few rules and so they're kept quiet. Tickets are a thousand dollars each and the events are held in special warehouses in Brooklyn and the Bronx."

"And you, you like to go to, um, the events?"

"I'm a judge," she said. "I score a few competitions every season."

"I was walking down the street just now," I said. "And it was raining, and this young man asked me if he could walk with me because, because I had an umbrella."

Her face was hard in places but the underlying beauty was undeniable. I wanted to keep her attention on me, on my words.

192

"And?" she asked.

"When we got to where he was going, he offered me a free blow job." I whispered the last words.

"Did you take it?"

"No. No I, I wasn't interested."

"Oh. I see. So why are you telling me this?"

"My whole life up to last week was as plain as a brown paper bag," I said. "I had missionary sex with my girlfriend, with some slight variations here and there. I had never been approached by a woman sexually, much less a man. And I never met women like you at all."

"And what am I like?" she said with a hint of danger in her tone.

"You're a person who lives in the world. You make your own decisions and live by them. You take your feelings and make them real. You are everything I want to be, but I never knew it before."

"You want to be a woman?"

"No. I want to be free."

A spark of something beyond humor and indignation showed in Sisypha's eyes. She regarded me closely and clasped her hands before her.

I noticed that she wore no jewelry.

"Aren't we all free in America?" she asked.

"Freedom is a state of mind," I said, wondering where I had heard it before, "not a state of being. We are all slaves to gravity and mortality and the vicissitudes of nature. Our genes govern us much more than we'd like to think. Our bodies cannot know absolute freedom, but our minds can, can at least try."

"That's very wordy, Cordell," Sisypha said, and then she looked up behind me.

"Anything to drink?" the waiter, dressed in black and white, asked.

There were nicks on his newly shaven face. He stood close enough to me that I could smell the cedar fumes in the fabric of his jacket.

"Just water," Sisypha replied. "And I'll have the Caesar salad with chicken."

"Pork chops for me," I said, "with green beans and that stacked-up bread you have."

"Very good," he said without writing anything down.

I waited for him to leave before starting up our talk again.

"Too wordy, huh?" I said.

"Freedom is also an exercise," she said. "You have to practice it to master it."

I breathed in and for a moment forgot how to exhale.

I wanted to tell her about how I intended to kill Johnny Fry, but I held back.

"Would you like to come with me to the games tonight?" she asked.

"Yes," I said knowing nothing about what I was agreeing to. "I'd love it."

This seemed to make Sisypha happy. Maybe she thought it was a submission. Maybe it was.

After the salad she ordered the cheesecake.

"You should have some coffee," she said. "The games are pretty late. They don't start till after midnight."

I ordered a triple espresso and flan. They were both delicious.

Over the meal Sisypha talked about ordinary, even dull topics. She was from Milwaukee originally and had three years of college, where she studied accounting. She owned almost every image of herself in existence and therefore made a good living over the Internet.

"My audience is small but dedicated," she told me at one moment. "They like the serious bent in my work. I always try to make some kind of point somewhere, either about love or loss or how impossible our desires are really."

"You mean because we want one thing and also the opposite of that same thing?"

She smiled and said, "Cynthia didn't tell me that you would be good for me too."

"When do we leave for the game?"

"Games," she said. "I don't know. In a while. I guess we could take a walk after dinner."

"If it isn't raining."

The sex star smiled, and I knew it wouldn't be raining.

"What was Cynthia talking about?" Sisypha asked me.

We were walking down Sixth Avenue nearing 40th Street. Cars were rushing up the avenue, but there were no pedestrians other than us two. The bleak street had a hard-edged beauty to it—a quality of waiting that resonated with my emotions.

"I found my girlfriend with this guy," I said. "This white guy named Johnny Fry."

"And you were jealous?" she asked. Her tone was nonchalant.

I looked at her sleek figure, thinking that any boyfriend she had could see her with dozens of men. He would know that when she left for work in the morning she was going to have sex with any number of powerful, well-endowed lovers.

No. Not lovers. Something other than mere love.

"He was fucking her, and she was looking at him like he was some kind of god . . . Then he turned her around and fucked her back there. It destroyed me," I said.

The woman named Brenda put a hand in the crook of my

195

elbow, stopping me. She brought her fingertips together under my chin and turned my face. I thought that she was going to ask me a question, but instead she just stared into my eyes, looking for something.

After a moment she said, "Go on," and we continued our slow walk.

"Nothing else to say," I said. "She was my girlfriend and my only friend. There's nobody in my life I could talk to about this. I mean really talk to. Someone who knows me."

"That's why you called Cindy?"

Just the mention of Cynthia made me nervous and light-headed.

We were passing a little bistro called Trente-Sept. It was closed, but they had a small wooden bench out in front, chained to the metal bars that protected their glass door. I took two uneven steps and then fell onto the bench. I was breathing hard. My chest was quivering.

Sisypha sat down next to me, her warm thigh pressed up next to mine. She put her hand to the side of my face, molding her palm to the dimensions of my jaw.

"Did you, did you do something?" she asked.

"No. No, I didn't do a thing. They didn't even see me. I just walked away." I hesitated. "He was so big. It made me feel like nothing."

"And you're afraid she'll leave you if you tell her you know?" Sisypha asked.

The tone in her voice was gentle. I turned toward her. She was gazing at me with deep concern.

"I feel like I don't have any skin or bones and all that's holding me together is her. If she leaves, I'll fall apart. A big pile of blood and guts on the ground."

Sisypha took her hand from my face and laid it across my bruised

196

knuckles. There was no sexual tension between us. I felt as if there was nothing separating us at all.

"Will you tell her?" she asked.

"I don't think I can."

The thought of killing Johnny Fry seemed ludicrous to me then. He didn't matter, not at all. Nothing mattered except for that bench and the feel of Sisypha's hand on my pain.

"Why not?" she asked in a whisper.

"Her uncle," I said.

"What about him?"

"He raped her . . . a long time ago, when she was a kid. He died, and she needed something . . . something I don't have."

"Lots of people have it hard when they're little," Sisypha said. "That's not your responsibility."

"That's what Cynthia thinks. She said that everybody is responsible for themselves."

"Damn right," Sisypha said with surprising emphasis. "A black woman taking a white man up in her ass, and her man comes in on it? Her black man? She should expect a bullet."

"Yeah," I said, still whispering. "But don't you see? When I saw them together, I knew somewhere deep inside that she needed more than I had. I never even suspected what was going on in Jo's mind. Johnny saw her one time and knew how to get there."

Sisypha's indignation melded into wonder.

"You knew that?" she asked.

"Yeah. I knew. And I hated them both, Johnny especially, but at the same time I knew, I knew they weren't afraid to go after what they needed. And so when Jo took me and made me do what Johnny had done to her—"

"She what?"

197

"But don't you see," I said to the sex worker, "I couldn't have gotten there by myself."

"So why are you so upset? Shouldn't you be happy that you know all this now?"

"Yeah, but I'm not. I quit my job and started a whole new life. I've had two lovers. But . . ."

Brenda caressed my hurt hand with both of hers.

"Are you giving up?" she asked.

"I don't know what you mean."

At that moment a white stretch limo pulled up to the curb in front of us. I expected someone to get out, but the big Lincoln just sat there as if waiting for us.

"Are you running away from life?"

"I have no life to leave," I said. "There's nobody there."

"But it's her fault that you feel like that."

"If there was a hunger deep inside you and, and, and then one day you saw what you needed, would someone you love hold you back from that?"

"They'd want to," she said. "They'd want me to be with them."

"But you'd already be gone."

Sisypha/Brenda gasped and put her hands over her lips. Again I thought she was going to ask me something but she didn't.

"What?" I asked.

"I want to ask you for something, Cordell. But it's too soon."

"What is it?"

She smiled and stood up.

"Shall we go?" she said gesturing at the car.

On cue, the driver's door opened, and a tall, extremely handsome Asian man got out. There were a few strands of gray in his shoulder-length black mane. His face was completely without emotion. He wore a driver's uniform and cap and had very muscular hands.

"This is your car?" I asked Sisypha.

"Of course."

"How did he know how to find you?"

"I carry a small device that he can track. All I do is tell him when to pick me up. He appears wherever I am.

"Miss Landfall," the driver said in greeting.

"Yes, Wan," she said. "This is my guest—Cordell."

He nodded and opened the door.

We climbed into the backseat facing forward. The seats opposite were taken by a couple, a man and woman. The woman was white as anything, from her platinum hair to the satin slip she was using as a dress. The man next to her was as black as a blindfolded vision of midnight.

"Caesar, Inga," Sisypha said in greeting. "This is my friend Cordell."

Caesar's white teeth were a shock next to such black skin. I thought that his eyes were probably white too, but the sunglasses he wore hid them.

Instead of saying anything, Inga pulled down her bodice, exposing two very firm and upstanding breasts.

"I like a dick between my tits while I'm getting fucked, Cordell," she said with a sneer.

The car moved from the curb.

"Uh-uh, no," Sisypha interjected. "I have no intention of smelling your pussy all the way to Brooklyn. If you want to ride with us, Caesar and you both have to keep it in your pants."

"Snap!" Caesar shouted.

"I don't have any pants on," Inga said, looking me in the eye.

She couldn't have been more than twenty-one. But her eyes

199

were much more experienced than I would ever be. There was power in her.

I was glad that Sisypha had interrupted. Sex had brought me to that car, but I wasn't interested in Inga. She was only flesh, and I had come to believe that I was looking for something else.

I turned to my hostess. "What were you going to ask me?"

"Later," she said, patting my hand. "Maybe."

On the ride over, Caesar talked about his African ancestry. His people had been nomads two thousand years ago, and their history had been, he claimed, passed down unbroken since that time.

"Seventy-six generations back," he said. "My ancestor lay with Julius Caesar. All of the firstborn male children in my lineage bear his name."

"And what brings you to the Sex Games?" I asked.

The big African cocked his head as if trying to discern an insult. He took off his glasses, showing that he wore bloodred lenses over his eyes.

"Sex," he hissed. "Long, hard campaigns in the bedrooms of the most beautiful people in the world." He reached around Inga and took her breasts into his large hands. She closed her eyes, transported by his touch.

"The games," he continued, "are the only reason I don't drive a knife into my belly."

"Oh God," Inga moaned. "I can feel him even when he's not inside me."

The red-eyed black god grinned at me, and my mind wandered back to Mel. Was I in for the same treatment?

I was slightly worried that I might have taken the same wrong turn as Mel, but I was more concerned that I had made that turn on purpose. Maybe Sisypha was right. Maybe I was looking for punishment the same way Jo had done with Johnny Fry.

Once again, silently, I committed myself to killing Johnny Fry.

The block-square warehouse that Wan brought us to was in the middle of a whole district of warehouses. Now and then you saw a homeless man walking his shopping cart down a vacant street, but otherwise the area was dead.

The green metal front door opened as we approached it. Two women—one white, the other brown, neither one wearing a stitch—smiled at Sisypha and hugged her.

We all walked down a long, dusty hall to a rickety old platform elevator that had an uneven floor made from planks of wood. Wan worked the lift while the naked young women chattered at Sisypha.

I didn't listen because I was trying to control my breathing.

I was petrified. All the tranquility and calm I'd gained from the decision to kill Johnny Fry was gone. People were touching each other and looking frankly at me. The man next to me had red, red eyes and counted his relations all the way back to Imperial Rome.

The lift came to a stop, and Wan rolled the door open.

The huge room we came into was filled with light of every color. There were at least three hundred people in there, either sitting in the twelve-row-high collapsible bleachers or milling around the circular platform at the center of the room.

Almost everyone was scantily clad, even the older and fatter among them. In one corner, I saw a man and a woman having slow, serious sex on the floor. Just beyond them, a man was on his knees giving another man oral sex.

The smell of the room was strong with the odor of sweat and a cloying sweetness too.

I began sweating. All the sex and stories I had experienced before that moment were mere fairy tales at kindergarten recess. This was more serious than I believed I could take.

"Here," Sisypha said to me. She was handing me a little pink pill.

"What is it?"

"Something that will keep that paleness out of your face." She smiled and made a kissing gesture.

When she moved away, I saw the young man yanking on his partner's cock. The standing man began to ejaculate, and three women standing around them applauded and cheered.

I swallowed the pill and asked, "Where are we sitting?"

"This way," Sisypha said.

She led me to a table near the platform. After I was seated, I put my head down into folded arms, waiting for the drug to do something, anything.

Amid the milling throng, I heard sporadic moans and grunts. There was the scent of sex in the air.

I didn't raise my head for a very long time.

I could tell that more and more people were coming in by the sound of footsteps and the rustle of clothes. But the louder sounds were subsiding. By this I assumed that people were getting seated in the bleachers.

Not only was my head buried in my hands, but my eyes were also shut tightly. Everything I had experienced since seeing Jo and Johnny Fry together came down on me. I couldn't see the light for the darkness in my mind.

"Come on," Sisypha said, her cool voice like a tender hand at the back of my neck. "You'll be okay now."

I raised my head, realizing that though the fear was still in me, it had somehow been muted.

The seats were all filled with men and women ready for a show.

"What's it gonna be?" I asked.

"It's like the Olympics," Sisypha told me. "They come here to find out who's the best."

"The best at sex?"

"Kind of," she said turning to me, her café-au-lait face as beautiful as the memory of childhood.

"What does that mean?" I asked.

"Sex is all kinds of things. For some men, it's their mothers, and for a lot of women, the father is the ideal. I know men who won't even look at a woman unless she's got tremendous boobs. She might not have brushed her teeth in a year, but if he can put his head between her tits, she's got him for the night.

"There's all kinds of obsessions and perversions, and this series of contests is how we say what is the best among them.

"For instance, this morning we had to choose who had the biggest cock among all the contestants. That's a hard call."

"Why?" I asked. The drug had hold of me by then. "All you need is a ruler."

"Some guys have long ones but they aren't very thick," she explained. "Others have big ones that never get really hard. A guy could have a two-pound salami, but if it can't stand up, it loses points."

"I see," I said.

I put out my fingers to touch her cheek lightly.

Her face hardened, and she said, "Don't touch me unless I invite it."

I pulled my hand away and put it under the table.

"What is the next contest?" I asked to cover my embarrassment.

"Cock fight," she said.

"What does that mean?"

"You'll see."

The lights went down, and a spotlight hit the back end of the slightly elevated platform. The six blocks of seating stood in arcs of three—one arc before and the other behind the raised dais.

The man who stood in the beam of light was the same man who bound Mel in *The Myth of Sisypha*. He was wearing purple hot pants and a red velvet shirt that had generous sleeves longer than his arms. His red hair was cut into a Mohawk that looked like wind-tossed wheat at the tips.

He raised his arms, and the red sleeves fell down to his elbows. You could see that he wore a ring on every finger.

"Sluts and pimps," he cried. The crowd cheered. "Harlots and masochists, molesters and molested, fuckers and fucked, welcome, welcome, welcome . . . welcome to the main event."

He bowed so low that his forehead nearly touched the ground. His crop of hair actually did brush the floor. People jumped to their feet and hollered. They threw flowers and kisses. They bared their breasts and cocks and asses to him. They danced in place. There were flaming cigarette lighters held high in praise.

One woman was actually weeping. Many were laughing.

The sex clown waited for the cheers to subside. The derision in his scornful gaze somehow transformed into praise. I thought about Sasha looking at her brother's blubbering sorrow. That, I realized then, was her love for him.

"This is it," the sex clown cried. "This is the main event . . . the cock fight."

Another round of exuberant cheering followed this claim.

Again the clown waited.

"For the past three days, heterosexual men have been competing in Greco-Roman wrestling to see which two were the best. Sixty brawny, brawling, bulldozing, bullying men have struggled to make it to the top of this competition."

Two more spots came on; one on the left and the other on the right of the dais. These lights illuminated two men, one black and the other white, both of them swaddled in luxurious robes. The black man (he was really black, not brown) wore a creamy white robe, while the white man wore a forest-green cloth that sparkled in the hot light.

The audience was yelling now.

"I'm sorry," Sisypha whispered into my ear.

When I turned to her, she kissed me, pressing her tongue into my mouth and holding the back of my neck with the tips of her fingers.

It was that kiss you yearned for as an early adolescent. The kiss that women gave on movie screens and in magazine stories about love. It was a soulful and resounding call to my manhood. The crowd's yells receded. The vestiges of fear evaporated.

Sisypha leaned back and regarded me.

"I'm sorry I told you not to touch me without an invitation," she said. "I'm an icon in certain circles, and men reach out for me without regard for my dignity or my independence. They want to pull me out of my life and into their fantasies."

"I didn't mean that."

"I know," she said, and then turned her attention back to the dais.

". . . these men have been tested for STDs," the sex clown was saying. "They were all kept in isolation for a week before the event. As I said—they are all straight men. But even a straight man can get his blood boiling over battle . . ." The crowd's cheer was

205

deafening. "Even a straight man can get it up when Dr. Themo-polis gives him his magic injection."

The nude young women who greeted us came up then, and pulled the fine robes from the contestants' shoulders.

Both men were naked, powerful, and muscular. Their chests were heaving with anticipation for their competition. They were oiled and shining. And both of them had large and upstanding erections with cock rings to help keep them hard.

Men and women hooted and hollered their approval.

I turned to Sisypha to ask her a question, but she put her finger to her lips. At that same moment, the sex clown raised his hands to the sky, and the audience went silent. It was to me as if Sisypha's small gesture had hushed them.

"Let the contest begin," the sex clown said, bowing low as he backed off the dais.

Without further ceremony, the men ran at each other, their bodies slamming together with an audible impact. They struggled and grabbed, but the oil they were covered in made it hard to hold on. The white warrior struck the black man with his fist, knocking him down. The crowd cheered. The white man jumped on the black one's back, but was shrugged off when the darker man stood. They were breathing hard and harder, thrashing against each other, trying to get and keep a hold.

At one point, the white man again got the black one down on his belly. People behind me rose to get a better look. The audience was mostly silent, but there was great anxiety among them.

The white man was thrown off, and people regained their seats.

Four times the white man struck the black one with his fists. But the black man never struck back. In my confused excitement I thought that maybe this was a political rule—giving the advantage to the white man as he had in the world.

But this was not the case.

The fight went on without a break for twelve minutes by my watch. The sound of the wrestlers' ragged breath filled the large room. Now and then they would back away from physical contact, circling one another and breathing hard. But whenever they came together, great force was exerted. The black man was bleeding from his left nostril. The white fighter limped slightly.

And then, shockingly, the black man backed away from a hold and struck out with his fists, hitting the white one three times in the abdomen.

Most of the audience leaped to their feet. The white man crumpled to his knees, where the black man slapped him, knocking him down on his belly. Then the black man got on top of the white one, holding him in an armlock. He positioned his still-hard cock over the prone man's clenched buttocks, then he looked up at the audience.

"One!" they cried in unison, and the black man drove his engorged member all the way into his defeated opponent.

The white man cried out in agony.

As soon as the black man pulled fully out, the audience screamed, "Two!"

Down again the black man went. Now his opponent was struggling hard to get away and yowling.

My fists were tight, and all I could do was hope that it would soon be over.

The black man pulled out and swiveled his grinning face to see the standing crowd.

"Three!!" was hollered out, and he went down for the final time and then jumped to his feet, his hands in the air. The white man had rolled into a ball and seemed to be crying.

With a roar, the crowd rushed the stage.

"We better get out of here," Sisypha shouted in my ear. "Everybody's fair game now."

It was true. People were rushing the stage, ripping off the few clothes they wore as they ran. They were cheering, kissing, even fucking already. Two men were fighting. The sex clown (later I found out that his name was Oscar) was jumping back and forth, shouting and slapping people as if he were anointing them.

The winner of the cock fight was fending off male and female admirers. They wanted him to have sex with them, it seemed. But he was still feeling the ecstasy of having won the contest, shouting unintelligible words and raising his fists high.

I couldn't see the white wrestler.

"Come on, quickly," Sisypha said, pulling me by the arm.

Ahead of us were the naked girls who had ushered us through the doors. They led us to a corridor behind the far stand of bleachers and slammed a door behind us before any other revelers could follow. We went down the long hall and into a large room that was connected to a broad wooden stairway.

"It was so fast," the Hispanic girl said as we went. "I thought Mike Dour would have had more in 'im than that."

"Yeah," the white girl agreed. "He just doubled over like a pussy."

"Peanut hit him hard," Sisypha told the girls, neither of whom could have been older than nineteen.

"He really fucked him good," the brown girl said with a grin. "Fucked him up."

We went down flight after flight on the wide wooden stairwell. We were at least twenty floors up.

When we finally got to the bottom, the girls threw the doors open and led us into the dark street. Wan's white limousine was waiting there for us.

"Good-bye, Miss Landfall," the white girl said.

"You girls should come with us," she said.

The expressions on the nude beauties were of honor.

"That would be wonderful," they both said.

"Wan," Sisypha said. "Get them something to wear out of the trunk."

The expressionless chauffeur opened the doors for us and then rummaged around the back until he returned with simple white smocks for the girls.

"What are your names?" Sisypha asked them as the car took off.

"I'm Krista Blue," the white girl said.

"And I'm Freefall," the Hispanic child responded. "Freefall La Vida."

"And your ages?"

Krista was eighteen; Freefall nineteen.

They had both worked for a guy named Andy in the sex worker business up and down the East Coast, sometimes as models, sometimes as nude waitresses. And of course they were prostitutes now and again.

"People never want to understand when you try to explain it," Freefall said to me as we were crossing the Brooklyn Bridge. "They think if you fuck for a living that that's all you are. But people can be all kinds of things. A woman can be a mother and a doctor and a dancer and a prostitute. A prostitute could paint a good picture, she could have a smart little girl that she loves and cares for."

"Yes," I said, and she smiled brightly for me. "I'm sure that most people are much less than that, and because they are less, they think that they're better."

"I like this one, Miss Landfall," Freefall said. Her sparkling eyes, slightly intoxicated, shone on me. "Is he yours?"

209

"I don't know," Sisypha said, speculation in her tone. She and Krista were leaning against each other, back to back, in the seat across from us. "Are you mine, Cordell?"

"Heart and soul," I said. "Gut and butt."

"Oooo," Sisypha crooned. "I like the way that sounds."

Freefall leaned way over and kissed me.

"Where do you girls want to go?" Sisypha asked them.

"We have a place in Newark," Krista said. "But if you wanted to party, we'd be happy to."

We drove to a private club on East 33rd Street. The only thing to mark the nightclub's existence was a small, removable brass plaque, no more than six inches square. The plaque was attached to the wall next to a very ordinary-looking door. The Wilding Club had been three apartment buildings that were now connected.

It was inconspicuous and thriving.

The entrance was a small foyer of dark wood and blue velvet manned by a sixty-something white gentleman in coat and tails. He wore white gloves and had white sideburns. His eyes were at once grandfatherly and foreboding.

"Miss Landfall," he said, staring at me.

"It's okay, Winter," she said. "Krista, Freefall, and Mr. Cordell are with me."

"I know the ladies," the tall sentry said.

"He's from the other world," Sisypha said. "But he's okay."

"Raise your hands, sir," Winter requested quite respectfully.

Still under the effect of the drug I'd taken, I put my hands in the air, like a criminal in an old-time TV melodrama.

When the sentry took out the pistol and ammunition from inside my coat, I was mildly surprised. I wasn't wholly unaware of the weapons, but they seemed out of place somehow, like I was

210

out of place in that posh club in the early hours of a weekday morning.

"Did you know about these, ma'am?" Winter asked Sisypha.

"He often carries a small weapon," she said. "Yes, I knew, but I didn't remember to ask him to leave it in the car. He's never been here before."

"I see," said the guardian, who seemed to grow taller by the moment.

I got the feeling that he was more than just some hired hand. Sisypha, who usually maintained a superior air without a trace of haughtiness, showed him great deference.

"I will have to ask you to check your weapons until you leave, Mr. Cordell," he said holding the devices as an appraiser might.

"That's fine by me, Mr. Winter."

"Just Winter," he said.

He put my stolen goods in a drawer in a cloak closet and handed me a card, the eight of clubs, for my chit.

While this transaction was going on, Krista and Freefall were taking off their borrowed smocks. These they handed to Winter. He stamped their hands with number and suit so that they could claim their belongings without having to carry a playing card.

After that we went through the swinging blue-velvet door behind Winter's post and were transported to another world.

The first room we encountered was mostly dark except for five spotlit alcoves in which various combinations of people were having sex.

The first recess had a very fat, middle-aged man fucking a small young woman who was hanging, spread-legged, from a harness that he stood before. His erection was of a moderate size, but he had to hold his stomach up to enter her when she swayed onto him. Every time he entered her, she would swing a yellow fiberglass rod, hitting him on the thigh or butt or back. The white man had many, many red welts on his ample flesh, and every time she struck him, he cried out in real pain.

"Hurt for me, Jerry," she said each time she swung her yellow stick. The woman, who was Asian, seemed completely focused on this man. She watched his face like a cat looking for a mouse to stick its head out from a hole. She had no reaction to him entering her, but when he shivered from her blows, her toes curled and a satisfied grimace spread across her young face.

"Come on, Cordell," Sisypha whispered. "It's only the first step."

"But she, but she seems so happy," I said. I could tell that I was intoxicated by the drug as well as the sex.

"Does that make you happy?" she asked, taking my chin with one finger and moving my head to face her.

"It makes me wanna cry, but, but I don't know why exactly."

The next niche had one woman with two men. The room was a shower with a glass door for us to peer through. The water was on, and the woman stood between the men. She was somewhere in her forties with a normal body—white skin with slightly sagging breasts and a homely face made interesting by the deep pleasure she was experiencing. The man behind her was skinny and tanned. He was maybe fifty with faded, indecipherable tattoos on his forearms. He wasn't a good-looking man by any means.

The ugly man was fucking the homely women in the ass—very, very slowly. He'd press himself all the way in and out about six times, taking a minute doing so, and then he'd come out completely, rub some kind of cream on his small member and then enter her again. At the same time a beautiful blond boy with big

212

muscles and a great hard cock kneeled before the woman, soaping her breasts and legs, washing her with a huge sponge. The woman was staring at the boy astonished, almost in tears over his gentle strokes. He would smile and nod, encouraging her every time she came.

The next nook contained two men in business suits. They were sitting on a faux park bench, kissing. Their kisses were passionate and profound. Now and then they'd lean back to look at each other and then they'd lunge into another hungry osculation.

"Can we get out of here and get to the next part," I asked Sisypha, knowing instinctually that there was a certain structure to the Wilding Club.

"Does it make you uncomfortable?" she asked me.

"Very."

"The men?"

"All of it."

"Why?" she asked, standing in front of me, intent on blocking my way until I answered.

"There's too much feeling in here," I said. "I can't stand it."

"Why did you come here with me?" she asked.

"Because I'm obsessed with a story in my head."

From the next booth up a woman's frenzied cry issued: "Oh God, oh God, oh God!"

The cries made me think of Sasha and her story about her mother.

I glanced up.

"Don't look at them," Sisypha said. "Look at me."

I pulled my attention back to the golden-hued woman.

"What?" I said on a sob.

"What story?" she asked. "The one about your girlfriend?"

"No. I mean, I mean yes . . . in a way. But really it's about when I saw your movie. It was my story, only stronger."

"Better?" she asked, a child's grin on her face.

The whole time we talked, the woman kept calling for God.

"No. Stronger, scarier, something that I can't look away from. You."

She took my wrist and led me toward the exit. As we went past the booth from which the screams issued, I saw a black couple having vigorous missionary sex. You could hear their skin slapping in rhythm to his beat. Her face, the only one I could see, stared into his with fear and fascination as he kept hammering at her faster and faster.

We walked through the door at the end of the dark room and into a rather genteel-looking bar. It was then that I noticed we'd lost Krista and Freefall. I wasn't bothered that they'd gone off and so I didn't ask Sisypha about them.

This room was bright and might have been anywhere in Manhattan if it weren't for the occasional nude woman and the one man at the bar who was on his knees with his head up under a woman's chiffon gown.

While he performed cunnilingus on her, she was talking to another man.

"I'll meet you in twenty minutes in the green room," I heard her say as we passed them.

"Maybe we should have a drink," I suggested to Sisypha.

"It wouldn't mix well with the cocktail you've already had."

"What does that mean?" I asked.

She opened a white door and nodded for me to go ahead of her.

"The pill you took is actually four doses of different drugs that

214

will affect you in different ways . . . at different times," she said as we walked through another door. "The first dose, which will wear off soon, makes you relaxed. The second will intensify your mind, and the third will get you hard and horny."

"What about the fourth?"

"That one's a knockout drop," she said.

We were in a long, empty hall that was laid with small white and black tiles. The walls and ceiling were painted cherry red.

I stopped and took Sisypha by the arm.

"I better go home," I said.

"Why?"

"I don't know anybody here and I'm scared, at least I should be scared."

"I want you to stay with me for the night."

She was looking up into my eyes. Sisypha was no more than thirty, much younger than I. But to me she was like a goddess, a minor spirit in a great pantheon that mortals like myself were never allowed to see.

"Did Mel know what he was getting into?" I asked.

"Not consciously."

"Will you do that to me?"

"You aren't him," she said. "You don't need to be stretched out on a rack and have your ass reamed by a woman who gently strokes your face—do you?"

I moved my face very close to hers and grabbed her by both wrists.

"Don't destroy me, Sisypha," I said in a voice that might have been issuing a prayer.

The next room we came to was a restaurant. It too was bright, with twelve tables set for four and four corner booths that might have

215

accommodated six. Five or six of the center tables were inhabited, mostly by couples, but one table sat four.

Only one of the booths was in use. A man and woman sat there, but I couldn't see their faces.

"Miss Landfall," the maître d' hailed.

He was a portly Latino man. I would have said he was of Mexican descent, but I knew better than to second-guess the genes from south of the United States border. He could have been from Panama or Bolivia, Puerto Rico or Peru.

"Pero," she said in a perfect accent.

"Your booth?" he asked.

"A table will do."

Once we were seated with menus, Sisypha looked at me.

"What?" I asked.

"How much do you know about me?" she asked.

"I've only seen the first few scenes of your movie," I said. "I didn't look at any of the extras."

"But have you been to the blogs about me, or my Web site?"

"No."

"Do you belong to my fan club?"

I shook my head, then asked, "How many members are there?"

"At last count, eleven thousand four hundred and sixty-two."

"Wow."

"More than half of them women," she added proudly.

"Is it because you're so confident and dominant?" I asked.

"Do you want me to fuck you, Cordell?"

"No."

"To make love to you?" she asked, a little sarcastically.

"Not even," I said.

"Then what? What do you want from me?"

"You called me," I said.

216

"But you called out to me."

I was feeling, for lack of a better term, rather bold.

"I'm hoping," I said, "to learn from you. To get a, a grasp on your handle on things. My girlfriend thinks of me like I'm a favorite pet. Up until a week or so ago, she had me so well trained that I'd never even ask her could I come by during the week, when she was working. If we were on the phone and she said she had to go, I'd never argue, no matter how much I wanted to talk.

"She has another man who throws her on the floor and fucks her in the park and who hires male prostitutes to take her while he watches and smokes cigarettes."

I wondered where I came up with the smoking detail. Johnny Fry had never smoked in my presence.

"May I get you something to drink?" another waiter asked us.

I remember thinking about how many waiters and waitresses there were in my life. People who attended to my needs but who never knew me. This one was short and dark with tiny eyes and no accent.

"Water, Roger," Sisypha said. "And two green salads."

I didn't protest her ordering for me. I felt that I could break the table in two, but holding myself in check wasn't a problem.

"What's the gun about?" she asked then. I could tell by her eyes that she knew I planned to kill Johnny Fry.

Fuck you, I thought. *If you know all about it, I don't need to say.*

"I got it from a friend of mine," I said. "Sometimes I carry it around with me."

"For protection?"

"For fun."

"You feel the second drug now?"

"Oh yeah," I said. "I could pick you up and run around the block. But I don't have to."

217

She reached across the table and pinched the skin on the back of my injured hand—hard.

A typhoon of rage went through me. I bellowed and stood straight up, knocking my chair to the floor. Everyone in the room turned toward me, even the couple hidden in the booth. The woman, I noticed, even through the red fury, was quite elderly, while the man she was with couldn't have been thirty.

"Is something wrong, sir?" the maître d', Pero, asked, rushing to pick up the fallen chair.

"I, I, I," I said.

"His first time," Sisypha explained.

Pero held the chair for me. After a moment I obliged him by sitting down.

Sisypha was grinning.

"What is that you gave me?" I asked.

"Designer," she said. "The guy who makes it lives in Berlin. He's originally from the Bay Area but I think his passport is Brazilian. He has a thousand clients. We pay him a yearly fee, and he supplies us with drugs so secret and so new that they're never illegal."

"I still feel your pinch," I said. "It makes me want to get up and run through that wall."

"Maybe we should go to the Gym after we eat," she suggested.

"Let's go now," I said.

She smiled and nodded.

We left the room without paying. I guessed that Sisypha was a member of the Wilding Club. Her life came in a monthly bill, not pay-as-you-go.

We were walking down yet another empty hallway. Hallways and waiters, I remember thinking, they are the bulwarks of my empty life.

This passageway was carpeted in red, with walls painted brown. "What did you want to ask me?" I said to Sisypha's back. She turned to face me.

"I like you, Cordell." Her eyes fastened to me. "But . . ."

"But what?"

"I don't know you."

Before I could say any more, she turned away.

The Gym was more than I expected. There was a health bar and many exercise machines; they even had a sports ring for boxing or wrestling. As with every other room, there were lots of naked men and women posing here and there. But there was no sex. People posed and worked out, but that was all.

Sisypha and I sat at a small, white table at the health bar. She had celery juice, and I had Sleepy Helper tea. The drug inside me was like a wide-awake two-year-old looking for mischief in my hands, in my feet. I couldn't concentrate on anything but Sisypha for more than a few seconds at a time.

"What do you like about me?" I asked the woman known as Brenda Landfall.

She smiled and shook her head.

"Please answer me," I said. "I know it's stupid and childish, but I didn't know what this goddamn drug was gonna do to me."

"You're blaming the pill?" she asked with a smile.

"Please."

"Love, I think, is a material thing," she said, taking my hand and stroking the fingers lightly. "It's something made naturally every day, like tartar or blood or skin. Most people I know don't store it up; they give it away as soon as it's there. They give it to ungrateful children, unworthy lovers, to faithless friends, and strangers they meet each day . . ."

This was why I wanted to be with Sisypha. The knowledge she passed to me was like fresh, home-baked bread to a hungry man, or like penicillin to a mad fever born of infection.

"... But now and then I meet a man who has never tapped the love he creates. He's like one of those ants in the colony that become giant sacks of honey. All you have to do is stroke his neck, and sweetness just flows out of him."

She was still stroking my fingers. I, for my part, was staring hungrily into her eyes.

"A man like you is a treasure for women like me," she said. "Most people, men and women, only want to take from us. But every once in a while, we meet someone who only has love to give."

"Me?"

"Why not you?" she asked.

"I'm cold and boring," I said. "I'm, I'm commonplace."

"No, Cordell," she said gripping my hand. "You're special. You've had your ability to give love turned off, but never has your ability to make love been messed with. You're like a treasure trove. There's enough passion in you to keep someone rich for their entire life."

"I don't understand," I said.

"I know you don't," she said. "And I wish I could tell you, but . . . But I don't know you."

"What does that mean?" I asked. "Do we have to be friends for a while and then you'll know and then you could tell me?"

"I probably won't ever see you again, Cordell."

"Why not? I mean, can't we be friends?"

"Bren," a man said—a tall, black man dressed in metallic gold pants and a finely spun white cotton shirt. You could see the outline of his huge cock against the tight, shiny fabric.

"Hi, Maxie," Sisypha said, in mock submission. "This is my friend Cordell."

"Nice to meet you," the deadly handsome man said. He was bald, and his head was waxed. "Come on, Sis, let's go to the playroom."

For the first time that night, my date seemed uncertain.

"Um . . . I'm here with Cordell," she said.

"I'll bring you back in forty-five minutes . . . if you still want to come back, that is."

"Would you mind?" Sisypha asked me.

"Yes, I would," I said, with no hesitation. I wasn't going to be Mel.

"But you said you didn't want to make love to me."

"I want to be with you," I said. "Be with you all night."

Sisypha breathed in deeply and smiled for me.

"Sorry, Maxie," she said. "He needs me to be with him."

"He can come," Maxie said with a single shoulder shrug. "Maybe he learn sumpin'."

Sisypha shook her head and smiled. You could see that there was a history with this guy; she would have gone with him if I hadn't held on so tightly.

For a moment I worried that I was doing the wrong thing. Maybe I should have let her go off to the playroom and take his big dick up in her ass. But as I had this thought, I imagined Jo asking me if I minded if Johnny Fry climbed into our bed and she fucked him while I sat there and read the *New York Times* or watched *Seinfeld* on the TV.

The drug and the thought blended together in my sinews.

I jumped to my feet, shouting something stupid like, "Fuck no! Fuck you, fucker!"

There was actual fear in Sisypha's eyes.

221

"What?" Maxie said.

"I said, take your pimp pants and your fairy blouse and get the fuck outta here." They were words I would have spoken privately—thinking I should have said them but keeping the thoughts to myself. "I don't have to take your shit."

Maxie looked at me and then shook his head, dismissing my threats.

He turned to Sisypha and said, "What you gonna do, Bren? You know you supposed to be goin' wit' me."

"Didn't you hear me, man?" I said. "I said get the fuck out of here."

This was the person I always wanted to be. When my father slapped me or humiliated me or told me where I could go and how long I could be there even when I was sixteen—I wanted to be that man. When teachers refused to believe that I was smart and when the police stopped me for walking in neighborhoods where I had white friends. I wanted to stand up to my father and every racist and bully I'd ever known, but I'd never had the courage until that night. And if I had stopped there, it would have been enough to last me until my dying day. I would have been able to look back and say that, at least once, I was a man in the world—that I didn't let some motherfucker walk up and take my woman without a fight.

Take my woman. The words felt like rats scuttling down my arms. I jumped at Maxie with outstretched fists. I had no idea what I was doing, but the next thing I knew, we were on the floor, wrestling and trying to hit each other.

Looking back on it now, I can see how that was a very bad move. Maxie was four inches taller and at least thirty pounds heavier than I. His fancy white shirt was open, showing the highly defined muscles of his chest.

But I fought wildly until hands grabbed my arms and legs to pull

222

me back. I struggled against the men that held me. I almost broke free more than once.

Someone was talking to me. For what seemed like a long time, I couldn't hear him, because there was the taste of violence in my joints. I could feel my hands choking Maxie.

"Do you hear me?" the man's voice asked.

"*What?*" I said.

"Do you want to fight this man?" the voice asked.

"*Yes!*"

"Look at me," the voice said.

The command touched me. I turned and saw Oscar the sex clown standing there next to me. His hair was as wild as ever, but now he was wearing a dark suit that fit closely on his slender limbs and body.

"What?" I asked the harbinger of Sisypha's fantasies.

I wondered if this was all on camera. Would I be the victim of her new film? But that question gave way to the sound of blood rushing in my ears.

"You can fight Maxie Allaine in the ring, with gloves," Oscar said.

"Okay," I said, and then I leaped toward Maxie, who was also being held back, but the people holding us kept us from our goals.

I was taken to a back room, where men disrobed me and strapped boxing gloves onto my fists. Except for these I was naked, and breathing hard. Now and then a rush of blood went through my mind, and intermittently I wondered if this was all a show.

They took me to the ring and put me in a corner diagonally across from Maxie Allaine. He was huge. When I think back on that early-morning rage, I'm amazed that I wasn't injured for life or even killed. Maxie was six two and over two hundred pounds. He was, as I was, naked except for large, white boxing gloves. He had one other piece of clothing—his penis was so large that someone had taped it to his left thigh to keep it, I suppose, from being hurt. His biceps were like big stones and his abdomen was just as powerful. His handsome face was contorted into hate-filled desire.

But I wasn't afraid. All I saw was flesh that I wanted to rend. All I knew was that I wanted to kill this man. There was no reason for my wrath. I wasn't thinking about Sisypha. I wasn't thinking about how he ignored me like I was some kind of inferior being. All I wanted was to kill him for the pleasure of seeing him die.

"When I ring this cowbell," Oscar the sex clown was saying, "that's the end of the round. When you hear that," he hit the flat-toned bell with a spoon, "I want you to go back to your corners. The first man knocked off his feet is the loser. May the best man remain standing."

An errant thought went through my mind. I thought that Oscar was trying to give my opponent the edge by looking at him as if he expected me to lose and I wasn't even worth the consideration. But then a rush of blood flooded my ears like loud white noise on a radio.

Oscar was naked too. He was a white man in a white boy's body, but he wasn't really white at all. His skin had an orangish hue. His cock was crooked and pink. It was more than half erect too. He was going to enjoy our fight.

He hit his cowbell, and I ran out toward Maxie's fist, battered it with my face, and almost went down. He grinned triumphantly, but I don't think he counted on Sisypha's drug in my veins. I leaned backward as if I were going to fall, but the pain set off that rush through my brain, and this transferred the momentum of his blow to my right hand.

When I connected with the side of his head, I knew that I would never have a more satisfying sensation. The punch was flush and

224

solid. I heard him grunt, and I knew in my heart that he was going to go down. But when I looked at him, his face only registered surprise.

For a moment I was worried, but then came that rush again.

Maxie Allaine knew how to box somewhat. He threw jabs at my face and caught me about every third one. His arms were longer than mine, and even when I caught his punches on my gloves or arms I could feel them shudder through my frame. But the pain made me angrier, and every now and then I'd unleash a flurry of punches that would go wild, missing the target nearly every time.

He hit me again and again, but I stopped feeling it after a while.

I had a vision of my father trying to teach me how to fight in the backyard of our tenement building. There he was, a full-grown man, punching me with his fists and knocking me down. And now here I was with a bigger man trying to do the same thing.

I had boxed with my father and then a little at the YMCA in downtown Oakland, but all I really knew how to do was to hold up my hands and put down my elbows when he went for the body. It was working pretty well until he hit me with an uppercut that sent me into the ropes.

I loved those ropes. Their thick, rough fibers abraded my skin like the rough kisses of new love. Without them, I would have been on my back. Without them biting into my elbows, I would have slid down to my knees and then kissed the floor.

The cowbell rang, and when I looked up, three men were holding Maxie back, pulling him toward his corner.

Hands reached out for me, and then I was on a stool, wondering if I could even get to my feet again.

"Cordell," she called.

I turned to my left and saw Sisypha standing there, her red dress clinging to that perfect honey-gold form. She was looking at me, fear in her face, her hands clasped under those perfect breasts.

The love I felt for her turned into that white noise in my brain. I could feel my heart thunder, and then the cowbell sounded. I leaped to my feet and stalked forward with my hands down and my ugly face on.

It was all in slow motion, the whole rest of the fight.

Maxie had tasted my counterpunching, and even though it hadn't hurt him, he was moving counterclockwise around me, throwing jabs. I savored this punishment. Every time he hit me, I felt more powerful. Every time he moved his head back, just in case I threw something, I felt victorious.

But then Maxie landed three jabs on my nose and came in with a left cross that connected with the tip of my chin. I was lifted, still in slow motion, off my feet. I went backward a foot or so and came down like a building collapsing in on itself. I thought to myself as I was going down that if I fell all the way, Maxie would get Sisypha. He'd take that great big cock and fuck her till she shouted for him the way she did for the big Greek workman Aristotle.

By the time I was down in the crouch, ready to fall over, the second phase of the designer drug made its last hurrah.

With all the might in my thighs, I pressed against gravity to rise up from defeat. On the way I had the feeling of weightlessness. I realized that Maxie was just standing there—confident of his victory. But there I was, damn-near flying. All I had to do was put out my glove.

This time his grunt was from pain, not surprise. This time it was he who went backward into the ropes and slumped to the canvas. I was wobbling on my feet but I was still erect. Still erect.

Maxie bounded to his feet and rushed toward me, but half a dozen men moved in to seize him. Oscar ran to my side and raised my gloved hand in victory.

226

For the first time since the fight began, I looked out and saw that sixty people or more had come to see us. They applauded and cheered.

"The winner," Oscar shouted, "Mr. Cordell."

I noticed that the little clown had a full erection then. It stood up, in its crooked fashion, with the head nestled in his navel.

Men and women raised me to their shoulders and paraded around the room. From that height I saw Maxie arguing with Sisypha. He grabbed her, but Oscar got between them. The white man held his hands out, successfully warding off the much larger Maxie.

When the crowd put me down, Sisypha was standing at my side, grinning. In one arm she carried my clothes and shoes.

"Come on," she said, still smiling broadly. "We have to hurry."

Oscar helped me shuck off the gloves, and without putting my clothes back on, I followed the woman who had come to symbolize my life (and Johnny Fry's death). She led me into a narrow corridor that was painted black. Every ten feet or so a naked red bulb shone wanly.

"That was so wonderful," Sisypha told me as we went. "I didn't think you had a chance. And I was so sorry that you took that pill."

"What was Maxie talking to you about?" I asked.

"He wanted me to come home with him."

"Even after he lost?"

"He thought he had the right to take me," she said, flipping an upturned palm at her shoulder.

"Why?"

"He's my husband."

That piece of information was just sinking in when our path became blocked by a very large white woman. She was obese, but not disgustingly so. Her naked figure had shape to it and her skin was firm. She had a fair complexion and red, red lips. Her face was like one of those good girls in junior high school that boys masturbated about in the afternoon before their parents got home from work.

The hall was so narrow that Sisypha could barely squeeze by her. When I did so, we were pressed together. When our faces met, she smiled and gave me a brief kiss. I was thinking of getting past her when my tongue lanced out into her mouth.

For a few seconds we made out; the walls at our backs seemed to be pushing us together.

When the woman reached down and grabbed me, she said, "I like that."

Sisypha took hold of my arm and pulled me toward her.

"I'll do him right here, sister-girl," the fat white woman said. "The way he feels, it won't take long."

"Sorry," Sisypha said. "We have an appointment."

After a few more moments, we came to a door. Sisypha ushered me in. It was a small room that stood before a doorless doorway that opened onto an even smaller room. The smaller room had red carpets and red fabric paper on the walls and ceiling.

"I'm sorry," I said to Sisypha. "I mean, I didn't want you to go with your own husband, and there I am making out with that girl."

Sisypha kissed me lightly on the lips.

"That's okay. It's just the drug coming on. You need to fuck now."

Sisypha shucked off her red dress, and in the soft light of our alcove, she looked like my most closely guarded secret.

"Sisypha," I said. "I, I . . ."

She put a finger to my lips and said, "Don't worry, baby. I know you can't love me tonight. That's why I have Celia coming."

"Who?" I asked.

At that moment the door to our double room opened.

The woman who came in was from a place in my mind even deeper than the one Sisypha occupied. She was naked and short (not a hair over five feet tall), slight of build but buxom, with a generous, well-formed butt. Her skin was as black as skin could be but her big round nipples were darker still.

This woman was the epitome of blackness. Her dense hair was tied up into the shape of some kind of wildflower on top of her head. The only thing about her that wasn't black was her pubic hair; this she had bleached white and cut so that it was in the form of a flickering flame.

"This is my friend Cordell, Celia," Sisypha was saying.

"Hi," I said.

"Oooo, look how he holdin' his dick, Sissy," she said. "You want me, Cordell?"

I nodded, almost certain that the drugs flowing in me now would bring on a heart attack.

When she smiled, I could see that Celia had spaces between each of her teeth. She didn't have a beautiful face, but it was hungry and friendly in the way that that made you understand that no matter how long you knew her, you could always get to know her better.

"Let's go in the little room," she suggested, and the three of us did.

When we were standing there, Celia told me, "Get down on your knees, Cordell," which I did with a thump.

She leaned over me then, her ample breast pointing at me.

"Lick it light," she whispered, and I did.

"Oooo. That's nice. You see how it get a little harder an' rise up?"

"Yes."

"Lick it again."

Sisypha put a hand on my shoulder, and I let my tongue circle Celia's hardening nipple.

"Oooo shit," she said. "Just two licks an' it's full hard."

I tried to make my breathing regular but couldn't.

"Do it to the other one now," she said.

I followed her orders without having to be led. She made all the right noises, and Sisypha put a hand on my other shoulder.

"Uh, damn," Celia said. "Okay, Cordell. Now I got sumpin' for you. Sumpin' every man want even though he might never even think it. Do you want it?"

"Yes."

"Even though you don't even know what it is?"

"Anything," I said, looking up into the hungry young eyes that reflected my own desire.

"My titties are full wit' milk," she said. "Mother's milk."

I moved to take a nipple in my mouth, and she slapped me.

"I didn't say you could have it," she said in lecturing tone.

"Please let me drink," I said. I could see the pale liquid at the center of her ripe nipple. A drop formed.

Without saying another word, Celia pushed her wet nipple into my open mouth. I sucked on it twice, and a thin stream of warm, almost sweet liquid shot into the back of my throat. I drank from her while stroking my cock. Sisypha was rubbing the sides of my neck gently.

Then Celia pulled the nipple from my mouth. She did this while I was sucking on it, so it made a loud smacking sound.

She was pressing against the base of her breast, and so the nipple sprayed milk on my face and down my chest. I opened my mouth to catch it.

"Oh, baby," Celia crooned. "That's what I wanna see. Stick out your tongue. Get it all. Uh."

I was sure that she would offer me the other breast, but she didn't. Instead she said, "Lie back, baby. Lie down."

I was willing, but getting all the parts of my body to obey was beyond me. The taste of her milk in my mouth and down my throat caused a thrumming in me that interfered with my motor functions.

"Lie down," Celia commanded, and then she pushed against my chest.

I fell backward into Sisypha's embrace. She was seated behind me and put her arm around my head, holding me so that I was looking up into Celia's goddesslike face.

The black woman straddled me and leaned close to my ear. Her left breast was still leaking onto me and I wanted sex more than I ever had in my life.

"Sissy's gonna hold you down and I'ma fuck you," Celia said. "You hear that?"

I nodded.

"I want you to look up in my face, you hear me?"

I nodded again.

And then she lowered onto my erection. It was as if the notion of pure silk entered my mind, and also like a giant cruise ship coming into a port that was way too small. She was going up and down at a leisurely pace without letting me fall out of her perfectly smooth vagina.

"Open your eyes," she commanded, and then she slapped me.

I felt the thrumming again. This time it felt as if the whole room was on wheels. But Celia was fucking me faster now, and I couldn't be concerned with anything else.

When I'd tried to move my head, I found that Sisypha was holding me so that I could only look into Celia's eyes.

"You cain't move, baby," Celia said. "Sissy holdin' you down

231

an' I'm fuckin' you. You cain't get away from it. You cain't move."

I started bucking up into her then.

"That's right," she said. "That's it. Fuck it hard, Daddy. That's the only way you could go."

I lost control then and bucked even though there were pains all through my body from the fight with Maxie.

"Where you wanna come, baby?" Celia asked me. "My ass, my face? You want me to swallow your come like you did my milk?"

She was looking directly into my eyes, her words interrupted now and again by my strokes against her. Her face was tender, caring even. I wanted to answer her, but there were no words in my head.

Sisypha let my head go then and reached down, tweaking both my nipples very hard.

"Come," Sisypha said. "Come for her now."

I grabbed on to Celia's impossibly small waist and jammed myself as deeply into her as I could.

Through clenched teeth she said, "That's right, baby. Gimme it all. All of it. All of it now."

I didn't feel the ejaculation, but I know it was hard and a lot.

The applause didn't surprise me, really, but I didn't know what it was. I looked out into the larger room, realizing that the small red platform had somehow been shifted into one of the sex nooks at the entrance of the club. Ten or twelve people had been watching us. One, toward the back, was the elderly woman from the restaurant. There was a hungry look on her face. Something about her desire sparked even more passion in me.

"Fuck his ass, CC," Sisypha said. "He can do it again."

Celia got down on her knees at my feet and shouldered my legs apart. When I felt her tongue lance into my rectum, I was hard again immediately.

"Hand me that Vaseline, Sissy," she said, and a moment later her fingers were up inside me.

I tried to rise up, but Sisypha put me in a headlock. And then Celia was sucking my cock and moving her fingers around.

"Oh, baby," Celia said. "You right, honey. His come bubble's big and hard. Shit, he gonna explode."

And I came again while Sisypha held me down and Celia leaked milk on my balls.

"Yeah. Come on," Celia said.

The audience was applauding and murmuring.

I felt as if I would go unconscious right then. I was in a daze. The room rumbled again, and we were shifted back into the place we'd first entered.

Celia leaned down and kissed my lips.

"You are sweet," she said.

"Your kiss," I replied.

"What about it?"

"I don't know. I don't know anything."

"Oh, baby," she said, and stretched her ninety-pound body over me.

I closed my eyes and sighed.

"Is this your man, Sissy?" she asked my guide.

"I don't know yet," Sisypha replied.

"If he ain't, then gimme his numbah. Damn."

I dressed in a fog. Celia kissed me good-bye, leaving Sisypha to help me.

"I feel like my head is packed with cotton," I said.

"That's the beginning of the fourth cycle," Sisypha told me. "In an hour you'll be unconscious."

"Should I apologize?" I asked.

"For what?"

"For the way I lost myself in her love." I was a bad version of a seventies song.

"Do you want CC?" she asked.

"I drank her milk," I said.

"How did that feel?"

"Like the mother I never had," I said without thinking.

Sisypha was dressed in red again. She took my forearms and pulled until we were kneeling before each other on the floor.

"We don't have long," she said. "So listen and tell me if you will."

"Will what?"

"It has to do with your girlfriend."

"What about her?"

"My brother raped me when I was eleven," she said. "He was supposed to protect me but didn't. And then, when you told me about Joelle, I could see that you were protecting her, no matter how much she hurt you."

I was feeling the lethargy of the drug coming on, but her words still touched me.

"I'm so sorry," I said. "About your brother, I mean."

"That doesn't matter," she said. "He's dead to me. Him and all my family. I don't have any relatives as far as I'm concerned. But when we talked out there on the street, I had the idea that you could do something for me and maybe I could for you too."

"What could I do for someone like you?" I said. "I'm nothing."

"No," she said, shaking her head. "When Maxie wanted to take me, you wouldn't let him. You stood up to him even though you knew he could kick your ass."

"The drug," I said.

234

"That's not all of it," Sisypha said. "What I want to know, Cordell, is if you will be my brother."

She was looking right at me. Nothing that I was could escape that gaze.

"What does that mean?"

"That you will love me and protect me and call me on my birthday. It means that you will pull me out of the gutter if you see me there, and that we will never, never have sex."

"Yes," I said, giving a brief nod.

"You understand what I'm saying?"

"Sure thing . . . Sis."

She put her arms around me, and I wondered how any of that could be happening. But at the same time I knew that what she asked me for was another thing I had always wanted. Somehow I had been denied love. I'd had sex. I'd had friends and lovers and people who pretended to be those things. But I never had a sister who wanted me to be her brother. I had never had a woman who sought to make me happy.

"Does this mean you love me?" I asked.

"Love doesn't mean anything, Cordell. I'll be like a tree in your backyard," she said. "Like that old sweater you wear every fall. I will always be there, and so will you."

Exhaustion was pouring in from all sides. Brenda sat me down in a plush chair that sat alone in an empty room. She told me that she had to find her driver. I didn't want her to go, but once seated I couldn't even raise my arm. After a very long time she returned accompanied by Wan. Together they pulled me from the chair and led me out of the Wilding Club.

Wan drove me home. When he let me out of the long white limo, he handed me a brown paper bag, saying, "This is yours."

I staggered to my building and also up the stairs. I don't remember using the keys, but I must have. I don't remember getting into my bed, but I woke up there, still fully dressed.

In my sleep I imagined a loud TV somewhere. People were arguing. Doors were being slammed. The police were having a shoot-out with the bad guys . . . But when I opened my eyes, the only thing on my mind was Sisypha and her declaration of sisterly love.

Did she mean what she said? And if she did, what was the meaning of our new relationship? And why was I awake? It seemed early, and I didn't get home till nearly five in the morning.

I felt very relaxed—not hung over at all.

Everything in my life had changed.

I no longer needed to kill Johnny Fry. I wasn't mad at Jo for having to turn to him for release. She couldn't ask me to do the things he did without being asked. She couldn't help herself, despite what Cynthia said.

Anyway, I had been given the love that I needed.

The love I got from Celia was enough to last and sustain me— that's what I felt. I didn't know if my mother had breast-fed me or not, but I did know my life wasn't that of a child who had the benefit of a mother's love. Celia had given that to me.

She had asked Sisypha if I was free because she wanted me. Maybe that was all part of the game, but no one had played the game with me before.

There came a knocking at the door.

It seemed to me that this wasn't the first knock. Maybe that's what had awakened me.

I didn't have to dress, so I walked through the rooms to my entrance nook. I noticed the bag that Wan had given me sitting in the corner.

"Who is it?"

"The police."

Could they have heard about the fight with Maxie Allaine? Was that some crime?

I opened the door on five men. Two of them wore suits, and the others were in uniform.

"Cordell Carmel?" a man in a gray suit asked.

"Yes."

He held out a wallet that contained a badge and an identity card. I nodded, pretending it meant something to me.

"What's the problem, Officer?"

"Did you hear a disturbance last night?" he asked. He was tall and broad of shoulder but his gut stuck out too.

"No, sir. But I didn't get in until about four-thirty or so."

"And you didn't hear anything?"

"No."

There was silence there for a moment. I knew that the cops wanted something from me, that their silence was meant to rattle me. But I didn't know what I had to worry about.

"Your upstairs neighbor was killed this morning somewhere between five and six."

"Martine's dead?"

"Sasha Bennett," the officer said. I noticed that he had nicked himself shaving and that he had the sweet smell of cologne about him.

"Sasha? What happened to Sasha?"

"Did you speak to her last night?"

"No."

"When was the last time you spoke to her?"

"Two, three nights ago," I said.

"And what did you talk about?"

"It was late. I went up to her apartment and spent the night."

237

"She was your girlfriend?"

"No. No. That was our only time together. I was thinking of breaking up with my girlfriend, and Sasha said I could come up whenever I wanted."

"Did you go up there last night?"

"No."

"Did you talk to her last night?"

I remembered then that I was a black man in America. All of the policemen were white. Sasha Bennett was white. I had been upstairs fucking a white woman a couple of days before, and now she was dead, and the police were investigating me.

"No," I said. "I haven't talked to her since the night I spent at her place."

"Can we come in?"

"For what?"

"To look around." The cop—he had salt-and-pepper hair and was at least ten years older than I—was trying to sound nonchalant.

"Tell me what you're looking for, and I'll think about it."

"We can get a warrant easy enough," he told me.

"Okay," I said, and I moved to close the door.

"We just want to see the window to your fire escape," he said hastily.

"Two of you," I said.

He put his hands up in a gesture of supplication. "Come on," he said. "You don't want these guys to have to stand out here."

"Two of you," I said. "That's all I want in my house."

Finally the man in the suit and a young uniform came in. They went to the window that led to my fire escape. I could have told them myself that the window was painted shut.

He checked it out closely and looked out on the fire escape for something, I'm not sure what.

"Sasha is dead, and there's a young white man dead too," he said.

"White guy?" I asked. "Big lips, though?"

"Yeah. You know him?"

"Sounds like her brother. He came to visit last week, but she told me that he'd gone back to California."

"Can you think of any reason that he'd kill her?"

"Not offhand," I said.

Suddenly the reality of Sasha's death hit me. I ran into the toilet and vomited up what was left of the bread and pork chops from the night before.

While I was washing my face, the policemen stood behind me.

"When's the last time you saw her?" the suit asked.

"Two days, maybe three. I don't know."

"Did you talk to her last night?"

I turned to look at him. My stomach clenched and I went through a dry heave. Both of the cops backed away from me.

They left soon after that.

It wasn't until the next day that I knew exactly what happened. The night before, Martine had heard loud arguing and then a noise that might have been gunfire. For a long time she worried, and then she called upstairs. When there was no answer, she called the police. They broke the door down and found Sasha shot point-blank in the chest with a .22 caliber gun. The assailant, Enoch Bennett, was her brother. The police postulated that he had shot himself in the head after killing Sasha. The police were sure of the murder-suicide theory because Sasha's door was chained from the inside.

After the police had gone, I picked up the phone with no idea about what I was going to do. I entered Jo's number, and she answered on the first ring.

"I knew you'd call right back," she said playfully.

"It's been ten hours at least," I said. "That's hardly right back. I'm sorry I didn't drop by. The night got kinda long."

"Oh hi, L," Jo said. "I was talking to, to August. She was telling me about something and then said she had to get off and I—"

"You remember that woman I told you about upstairs?" I asked.

"The one that slept with her brother?"

"Uh-huh. He came back and killed her last night. At least, that's what I think happened."

"Oh my God," she said, reminding me of the woman in the exhibitionist room of the Wilding Club, which then reminded me again of Sasha's mother. Poor Sasha.

"What happened?" Jo asked.

"She's dead. I think he is too."

"That's terrible."

"Yeah," I said. "But I need you to tell me something, honey."

"What? Oh my God. It's so awful about your neighbor. What did you want to ask, L?"

"Were you ever gonna tell me about Johnny Fry and you?"

The silence lasted a minute, maybe more, and then she hung up.

I cradled my own phone and sat back to figure out my life from that moment on. There were many women to choose from: Linda Chou, Monica Wells, Lucy Carmichael. I had my new profession as a photographers' agent. And I had to consider this thing about Africa. My reasons for starting the charitable organization were selfish and cynical, but I knew for a fact that I could change. I had the power of forgiveness. And if I could forgive Joelle, why not forgive me too?

I went to the foyer and retrieved the paper bag. In it I found my stolen pistol, the box of ammo, and a pink envelope that smelled of patchouli oil. The envelope contained a red capsule and an index card that had a note scrawled on it in unruly cursive.

240

Dear Brother,

Brother. That sounds so wonderful to say. For so many years I wanted to write to Man (that's my old brother's name) but I couldn't. He tried to apologize after what he did to me, but even though I felt sorry for him, I still couldn't trust him. And family has to be people you can trust.

My girlfriends told me to tell the police—I could never do that to my brother. But now it doesn't matter, because after just one night, after all these years of looking, you are my brother and I am your sister. And we will look after each other.

I called Cynthia to thank her for you. She said that she knew we would get along. She's a very wonderful woman, and one day, when you come to stay at my house in Santa Barbara, we'll go to see her and her girlfriend.

Don't lose yourself to an errant lover, Cordell. Don't use this gun to solve your problems. Forgive her. Understand her. Make her understand that she hurt you . . .

I've put all my numbers and my people's numbers on the back of this card. Call me soon. Call me Sister. And never forget that I will love you when everyone else has turned off their lines.

Your sister,

S

p.s. The capsule I enclosed with this letter is one of the designer drugs I use. It will help you if you have a serious problem and need to think it through. Only take it when you have a good long time to consider the alternatives.

I was still thinking about forgiveness when the phone rang.

"Hello."

"How long have you known?"

241

"You remember the day your door was open?" I asked, "and you asked me if I had been there?"

I waited for her to reply, but she didn't.

"I came in and saw you in the living room with him. You were on the couch and, and on the floor."

"You watched that long?" she asked.

"At first I was mesmerized, shocked. And, and then, when I was leaving, I heard you cry out, and I thought something had happened . . ."

"Oh no," she murmured. "No. Why didn't you tell me? Why didn't you try to stop us?"

"I wasn't thinking. I had walked into your house—the only reason I did was because you had told me you would be in New Jersey, and I had to go to the toilet. But I came in on you and Johnny. It wasn't my house. But I wasn't even thinking that. I just wanted to get away. Away."

"And so when we ran into Johnny at the museum, you knew?"

"Yeah."

I was thinking that Sisypha, my adopted sister, was probably crazy. She lived in the shadows of our society. There she made up her own laws and rules of conduct.

"I'm so sorry, L," Joelle said. "I never meant to hurt you like that."

"I know."

"I always made him wear a condom," she said. "I made him get an STD test."

But even though Sisypha was crazy, she was closer to me than I had ever been to Joelle. We, Joelle and I, were like two stones that had rolled up next to each other after an avalanche brought on by an earthquake—we shared a common ground, but that was just about all.

242

But a force as sure as gravity had brought me to Sisypha.

"L?" Jo had been talking.

"Yeah?"

"I asked you what you wanted to do now."

"What's there to do, Jo?"

"I broke up with John that afternoon, after we met at the art museum."

"Because of Bettye?"

In the silence on the line, I thought that there would be hard times with Sisypha. She would ask me for understanding in a world that scared me to death. With her I would use drugs and enter into violence. My sexuality would be called into question every day . . .

"Because of you," Jo said. "Because I want to be with you."

"Why were you with him?" I asked, and then I said, "I want you to understand that I have gone past being mad about this. I want to know why you did it, but I'm not asking so I can have ammunition against you. I only want you to tell me because we should tell each other the truth."

"Are you going to leave me, L?"

"I don't know what we'll do," I said. "For eight years you've been my only friend and family. My mother is lost to me, my siblings feel nothing for me. You have been my only friend.

"But in all that time I barely knew you. Here the most important event in your life was a secret. I don't blame you for not telling me. I don't think you owe me any such thing, but it just throws light on how empty our connection has been."

"You must have secrets," Jo said, defending herself. "You could have had lovers."

"You're right. Of course you are," I said. "But not something like that. My secret was that I was completely oblivious to the

243

emptiness and shallowness of my life. I was living in a hole and calling it a home. The secret I was keeping I kept from myself too."

"There's nothing wrong with you, Cordell," she said. "It's me."

"Yes, I know. It is you. But that doesn't exonerate me. Part of the reason I didn't confront you was because without you, I'd have nothing. My days and nights would have been empty, alone."

"Is that why you had such wild sex with me?" she asked.

"Definitely. And not only you. Since the day I saw you with him, I've had sex with three women in the flesh and one over the phone."

"Who?"

"It doesn't matter who," I said. "What matters is that I'm telling you the truth while you're still lying to me."

Joelle spoke in silences. Her whole life had been one of mum regard. Whenever I got near her truth, she clammed up. I felt bad for her while at the same realizing that whenever she was quiet, my mind went back to Sisypha.

My most precious possession was her desire to be my sister—not whether we ever spoke again, but the wish she gave voice to. It opened up a door inside me. It was the offer that mattered, not her ability to deliver.

"What did I say that was a lie?" Jo asked.

"Not a lie in words," I said. "You did break up with John Fry, but you've spoken to him since then, haven't you?"

Silence.

"Were you really expecting your sister when I called just now? Did you call anybody else before you called me back?"

"Please, L," she pleaded. I could hear the sobs behind her words. "I can't do this all at once."

"Then call me back when you're ready to talk," I said.

"Don't get off."

"You lying to me will never get you what you want, Jo. The only thing it can do is destroy the little we have."

"I won't lie."

"Then answer my questions."

"I, I can't. I can't say something like that to you. All I can say is that you are the centerpiece of my life. Without you I would go out of orbit and crash and die. You being in my life is what holds me in place."

It was my turn to be quiet. I knew that Jo was trying to get out of the sexual tangle she found herself in. I knew that her life might really be threatened. But all I could think about at that moment was Celia: her milk running down my face, her contorted, satisfied look as I licked the air below her breast.

I had always been afraid to find out what my desires were. It was easier to be with a woman like Jo who kept her life in sensible compartments, who had secrets that were ground-shaking but who never wondered how the world shifted in me.

"I don't want you to die, Jo," I said. "But if you can't tell me that you need something from a man that I can't give, then how can we talk?"

"You don't know that," she said angrily.

"Am I wrong? Can you at least tell me that you didn't call Johnny? That you won't see him again? That you don't need to see him?"

This time she only took thirty seconds or so to respond. In that time I wondered what it would be like to see Celia, to know that she was with many men, and probably women, but always came home to me. Was that any different from me with Jo and Johnny?

"I can't tell you but I can show you," she said.

"I don't understand."

"Come over to my place, and I'll show you how I feel."

"I'm a little busy for the next few days," I said.

"With your new girlfriends?" she said, in a derisive tone that I didn't think I deserved.

"No," I said. "Just some people I have to see and, oh yeah, I quit being a translator. Now I'm a photographers' agent. I have a client that I sold to a Midtown gallery. I have to work on that."

"You quit? When?"

"They day I saw you."

"But how will you live?"

"As best I can. I'll come to your place in two days," I said. "In the afternoon. If you need to talk or want to talk before then, all you have to do is call."

It was almost noon when I walked out the front door of my building. I don't know if they were waiting there or if they'd just arrived when I was leaving.

"Cordell Carmel." The big cop that came into my apartment earlier was standing there with two uniforms. One of these was a black man.

"Yes?"

"We're taking you to the station for a talk," he said.

"What's your name?" I asked him, as the black cop put handcuffs on me.

"Detective Jurgens," he said, quite civilly.

When the cop standing behind me went through my pockets, I was relieved that I'd left the pistol upstairs.

They locked me in a room that had a faint odor to it. Actually it was a combination of scents. There was something chemical, acrid, and then there was a stale smell that hovered between vomit and sweat. The final element that bound the stench was sweet like vanilla flavoring. It was this sweetness that fouled the chamber. It reeked of a cover-up; the attempt to hide the truth of that room.

It wasn't a big space, and there were no windows. By that time my feet were also manacled. So I sat in the straight-backed chair behind a table with a heavy black phone on it. Jurgens had read me the story about my rights, and now I was alone.

But I wasn't afraid. I was used to jail cells.

I had been to see my father in jail many a time. He'd get arrested for drunk-and-disorderly and fighting, mainly. He was a brutal man, but my mother loved him as a god incarnate. If he was in the room, her eyes rarely left him. If he was gone, she'd sit in his chair by the phone, waiting for him to get in touch. That's why I was so surprised that they'd never married.

He was always friendliest when they had him chained and behind bars. He'd smile for me and ask about my day. He'd say that he was sorry I had to go through this and ask me to forgive him.

Once, when he was in for thirty days, he told me that I was a bright boy and he wanted to see me in the university. That's the word he used: "university," not college. I was only nine, but from that day on I applied myself to schoolwork, and when I was admitted to UC Berkeley, I went to visit my dad, Carson Carmel, at Soledad Prison, where he'd been sentenced for twelve years for manslaughter.

"What the fuck I care about some school?" he said to me after I proudly told him about my admission. "Did you bring me the fuckin' cigarettes?"

All those years of hard work to make him proud, only to realize that my father hadn't cared past the moment he told me that he wanted to see me in the university.

That was my life, I thought, in that small interrogation room, years of unconscious darkness marked by scattered flickerings of light.

After what seemed like a very long time, Detective Jurgens and a sergeant, Jorge Mannes, came to see me. Sergeant Mannes was slight of build and painstakingly neat. During the thirty-minute interview, he found seven pieces of lint on his dark suit. He removed every one, placing them in a plastic wastebasket that sat in the corner behind him.

"Did you have anything to do with Sasha Bennett's death?" were the first words out of Jurgens's mouth.

"No."

Mannes smiled. He had red-brown skin and a razor-thin mustache.

"Did you know her brother?"

"Last Friday I helped her bring him up to her apartment. He was drunk, and she couldn't manage him."

"Did he say anything?"

"That he loved his sister," I said, thinking that I loved my father. I would have traded places in Soledad with him if I could. I would have taken on the cancer that killed him without a second thought.

"You ever see him again?" Mannes asked.

"He came down to my apartment that night, really in the early morning, about two I think."

"What for?" Jurgens asked. He seemed not to want Mannes to talk.

"He was drunk, more so than before. He was upset."

"About what?" Mannes asked quickly, to be a part of the case.

I hesitated. I didn't owe Sasha anything. But I didn't want her to seem like a bad person. She had been mangled by life like I had, and Jo and Sisypha. She wasn't someone to be blamed.

248

"Speak up," Jurgens said.

"He had had sex with Sasha. I guess they'd been doing that since they were kids, and he didn't know how to stop."

"Except with a pistol," Mannes said with a sly grin.

"If we check her cunt, do we find you or him up in there?" Jurgens asked.

I tried to leap at him, but it was futile. I couldn't even turn my chair over.

"Maybe both," Mannes said, smiling.

They rose together. At the door Jurgens said, "Hang out here for a while until we know what's what."

"Can I make a call?"

Jurgens walked out, but Mannes came back and unlocked my handcuffs.

"Don't worry," he whispered. "He just wants his report to look like he did something. If you were white, he would have left you alone."

As Mannes walked toward the door, he said, "It's only local and toll-free numbers you could call."

He closed the door and left me in the bright light of the dingy room.

My hands felt swollen, but that was only an illusion brought on by the numbness. I relished the feeling as the painful prickles of sensation came back into my fingers. I closed my hands into fists to increase the sensation.

Pain was my friend. He reminded me that I was alive. He came to me when no mother or father or minister would. He was why I loved Sisypha and why I would always refrain from having sex with her.

Jo was a local call, but instead I called Cynthia's main line and entered her name.

"Hello?"

"Hi," I said, exhaling the word heavily.

"How are you, L?" she asked. "Brenda said that you two got very close."

"I'm in jail."

"What for?"

"There was a murder in my building. A murder-suicide, I think, but I had been with the woman a few nights before, the night you told me that I should get out there and experience my desires."

"A husband and wife?"

"Brother, sister."

"Oh," she said. "What can I do for you?"

"Sisypha gave me her numbers, but I don't have them on me. Can you call her and tell her where I am?"

"Sure, Cordell. Anything else?"

"I told Joelle that I knew about her and Johnny Fry."

"How was that?"

"I don't know. I mean, I think deciding to tell her was more important than our talk. She, she's really fucked up about this stuff. We're gonna talk again in a few days. That is, if I can get out of here."

"Tell me where you are exactly," she said.

I gave her what information I could.

"I'll call Bren right now."

When I got off the phone, I realized that Cynthia hadn't asked me if I was guilty. The truth of her omission was like a physical thing in my mind. It was like a compass or a beacon. For Jo, there was something past love that left me behind, but for Cynthia, there was something past innocence, and that was me.

An hour or so later, the door opened. Three men entered. One was Jurgens. He seemed cowed, somehow. With him came a police officer in an ornate uniform with lots of medals and shiny buttons. Next to the uniformed officer was a pudgy little man in a lavender suit.

"Mr. Carmel?" the pudgy man asked.

"Yes."

"Are you all right?"

"I guess I am. My feet are a little numb in these shackles, though."

"You have him chained?" the small man asked the uniform.

"Take 'em off, Mike," the uniform told Detective Jurgens.

Seeing the big cop negotiate with his belly to get down on his knees and unshackle me was funny, but I didn't laugh.

"My name is Dollar, Mr. Carmel, Holland Dollar. I've been retained to get you out of here. Do you wish to press charges against the department for false arrest?"

It must have seemed to Jurgens and his superior that I was considering Dollar's request, but in reality I was thinking that Sisypha had laid out serious money to get me released. Here a lawyer that looked like a fop had gotten Jurgens to get on his knees to set me free. He was there in what must have been record time and got right to me. I remembered a time when it took three days just to get the pass to visit my father in jail.

"My name is Captain Haldeman," the uniform said. "I apologize for any inconvenience you've had, Mr. Carmel."

Mr. Carmel.

Sasha and her brother were dead. I was used as proof that the police didn't take the case lightly. I had been chained and arrested, but in suffering that minor bother, I found that Sisypha would move to save me.

Why?

"Do you wish to press charges?" Dollar asked again.

251

"No, sir. I don't. My neighbor and her brother are the ones who have suffered. Their parents will have to bear this weight. I don't mind if I can just go home now."

"There's a car waiting downstairs."

After my belongings had been returned, I found myself standing with Holland Dollar outside the police station. He handed me a lime-green card.

"Any trouble, any time, all you have to do is call. This number is twenty-four hours."

"Thank you, Mr. Dollar."

"Any time," he said, and then he left me.

Once again Wan let me off in front of my building. While I was climbing out, he was running to get back, to open the door for me, I suppose.

"Good-bye, Mr. Cordell," he said.

"Excuse me, Wan, but can I ask you something?"

"Yes?"

"Are you a driver for hire?"

"No, sir. I work for the company Ms. Landfall owns."

He left me wondering about the porn actress, director, and Internet mogul. She was obviously a millionaire.

In my apartment I called to make a reservation for dinner and then showered. Standing in the prefabricated plastic stall that I had washed in for a dozen years I achieved an erection without intending to. My cock was as hard as it had ever been. The balls were tucked up tight underneath. The water hitting my erection made it jump now and then.

I wanted to masturbate but didn't. I didn't hold back because I expected to be having sex soon; it was because I was enjoying the

252

excitement. I thought about Celia and Lucy and poor Sasha. They were all in that shower with me.

Jo was completely out of my mind.

When I got to the little Italian bistro, Monica was there, waiting at my usual table outside. She was wearing an old-time dress, white with a few big black polka dots here and there. It was a dress that a French model would have worn in the fifties. The full-length skirt flared out, and the bodice was tight around her bosom. She also had on white high heels.

"Am I late?" I asked, coming up to the table and sitting across from her.

"I got off my job at five today," she said. "I just came down here early, is all. I asked them if you had a reservation, and they just put me here an' gave me a glass of wine."

She touched the glass with one finger, and I reached over to touch that finger with mine.

"I'm sorry," I said. "If I'd known, I would have made an earlier reservation."

"I wanted to come early," she said. "I thought you was gonna forget or just not come."

"Why?"

"I just thought that you was flirtin', tryin' t'see if the poor black girl on the train would go out with you. But then when they had your name waitin', I knew you were serious, so I just sat here an' read my French book."

She touched my finger, and the waiter came to leave us menus.

"Damn," Monica said. "This expensive."

"The food's good and I'm paying," I told her.

"But what's this?" she said, pointing to an entry on the typed specials list. "It says a hundred dollars."

"It's a pasta. You know, spaghetti."

"For a hundred dollars?"

"It's made with real French truffles," I said. "They're very expensive."

"Do they taste good?"

"Why don't we split an appetizer of the pasta and then you can order something else for the main course."

Monica loved the truffles. She ate most of that dish. She told me that she knew there was a reason for learning French and now that she'd tasted good French food, she knew what that reason was.

After dinner we went to a movie on Sixth. I don't remember what it was about, because we started kissing the moment the lights went down. They were deep soul kisses that tasted like hunger. I didn't know if it was Monica's longing or mine, but when I was kissing her, there was nothing in my past or my future.

When I moved to touch her breast, she took the hand and moved it.

"I want you to," she whispered, and then tongued my ear until I was squirming in my seat. "But if you make get me excited, the whole place gonna hear it."

Then she put her hand on my erection and squeezed it.

I sat up a little, and she said, "Sit back."

The film was either six hours or ten minutes long. Her hand did not leave my cock the entire time.

When we got on the street, she took my hand, and we walked westward through the dark lanes of brownstones and small apartment buildings. We stopped now and then to kiss. I was breathless whenever we did that.

"I'll put you in a taxi whenever you need to get home," I told her when we got to Hudson Street.

"You live around here?" she asked.

"A little south."

"Let me see your front door and then you can get me a taxi."

We walked slowly, holding hands and stopping to kiss at every intersection. She didn't seem to mind walking in those uncomfortable shoes.

I never wanted that walk to end.

When we got to my door, she looked up and asked, "Which one is yours?"

"Third floor."

"Mmm. You can come on and get me that taxi now."

I took a deep breath and made to walk east with her. But she stopped, pulling on my hand.

"So after you get rid'a me, you gonna go call one'a those girls you been seein'?"

"No."

"You sure?" she asked, with no hint of a smile.

"Yeah. Why?"

"I think you might be a little excited after all that kissin' . . . an' stuff."

I squatted down and wrapped my arm around her thighs. She gasped as I stood up with her hanging over my shoulder.

"What are you doing, Cordell?"

I didn't answer. I just took out my keys and worked them in the locks.

On the way up the stairs, she said, "Put me down or I'ma scream, Cordell." But she never raised her tone, even when I began unlocking the door to my apartment.

I didn't put her down until we got to my sofa. Then I got down in front of her on my knees and raised that French hem.

"Cordell," she complained, but when I pulled her thonged

panties to the side and pressed the flat of my tongue against her enlarged clitoris, she raised her white high heel to nestle against my shoulder, situating her bared pussy so that I could lick it from top to bottom.

"Oh shit, Cordell. Damn, niggah, you know the spot. Shit."

When she came, I wondered if Martine would call the police. I didn't care.

"Stop, stop, stop," Monica cried. "That's too much. Too much."

I moved back six inches, watching the pink insides of her pussy pucker in and out like a hungry mouth chewing on something good.

"Let me up, Cordell," she breathed.

"No," I said, looking up into her eyes.

"Why not?"

"It tastes too good to me, baby. I need more."

"Oh shit," she said, her ass clenching and hot liquid running down from her vagina onto my sofa.

With that, I stuck my tongue up inside her. She reached down and grabbed my head pressing it hard against her flesh. Her thighs sandwiched my ears, and I was trapped by her second orgasm.

When that was over, she asked me again to let her up. Again I refused.

"You know what you taste like?" I asked her, and then flicked my tongue against her clit.

"Oh, oh. No. What?" she said.

"You taste like home," I said, and then I thrilled her some more. "You taste like my dreams in the back room I shared with my brother. You taste like all the love I ever wanted."

I think her last surge of passion was more from me talking to her

256

than what I said or what I was doing. She slid off the sofa and crawled on her back away from me.

I stood up and let my pants fall.

She stared at my erection with the awe of first sight.

I sat down on the sofa and said, "Get up on this thing, Monica."

"But, Cordell, this just our first date."

"Get up here now, girl."

"Cordell . . ."

"Take off those underwear," I said and she did it quickly. "Now come over here and sit on this thing."

She came over slowly, put a knee on either side, but stayed up high so that my cock barely touched her lips.

I put my hands on her generous hips and pressed her down so that she took my whole cock instantly inside her.

She grunted and moaned in my ear and started moving back and forth, saying, "We shouldn't be doin' this, baby. Oh shit yeah. You know we shouldn't."

I hummed a deep bass note in her ear and said, "That's good, Monica. Now I want you to fuck it."

She started going up and down, slapping her big, well-formed ass on my lap.

"Kiss me," I said, and she did. "Don't stop fuckin' me, though, Monica. Kiss me and fuck me at the same time." And she did that too.

It didn't take long for me to get near coming. When I grabbed her waist and started pressing my hips to make her go faster, she cried out, "Don't come inside, baby. Please don't."

I started fucking her faster, harder.

"Please don't," she begged.

"I can if I want to."

She looked at me then, coming down on me as hard as I was

257

coming up into her. She nodded and bowed her head. That's when I moved her to the side and stood straight up. She grabbed on to my cock and I was coming all over the coffee table. I lost my footing but she still held on.

"Damn," she said. "You been savin' it up for me?"

I was on my back by then. She was at my side, kissing my nipple and biting now and then.

"Thank you for not comin' in me," she said. "I know you wanted to. I wanted it too, but I cain't get pregnant right now. I got to make sure Mozelle gotta way to make it first."

"Can you spend the night?" I asked her.

"No, baby. I want to, but I got to get home."

"Okay," I said. It was somewhere around midnight. "I could put you in a taxi, ride with you in a taxi, or walk you over. Whatever you say."

"What did you mean when you said I tasted like home?" she asked.

"When you were a child, did you lie in bed at night thinking about the perfect lover?" I replied.

"Uh-huh. He was a singer and he was real rich and everybody knew him. When he come over, he'd have flowers an' shit. And he had a boat with a glass bottom where we'd make love with fish lookin' at us. What did you dream?"

"About you," I said.

"You didn't even know me," she said slapping my chest. "I wasn't even born way back then."

"I know. But when I was down there on my knees, I remembered all the way back to my dream."

"A little boy, an' he thinkin' about eatin' out some girl?"

"You," I said again, and she kissed me, and we made love again.

We walked arm in arm over to the East Village. We may have kissed for an hour before she went up the stairs to her apartment.

I walked back, thinking about being alive and making love while Sasha was cold in a locker somewhere, killed by her own dark passion.

I ended up in Battery Park, down west of Wall Street.

I sat there on a bench, watching the Hudson River and waiting for the sun at my back. Furtive night figures moved around me: homeless people and other late-night denizens of the city.

No one molested me or even spoke.

As the morning broke, I realized that I was a lost soul, but that wasn't so bad. I had in my pocket all of the pertinent information about Monica's daughter, Mozelle. She had brought the envelope for me to give Marie Tourneau at the French school.

I thought that if I could just get that one child out of one world and into another, my duty in this life would be complete. Then I could wander and fuck until something happened and I died or changed or got put in a cage.

At home I showered and shaved and ate three scrambled eggs. I went to bed but couldn't get to sleep, so I called Ms. Thinnes at the Nightwood Gallery.

"Hello?"

"Ms. Thinnes, it's Cordell Carmel. I have some time this afternoon and I was wondering if I could come by to discuss business today."

"Oh," she said. "Yes, yes, that would be fine. What about two o'clock?"

"Great."

After that, I called Linda Chou and asked her if we could wait two days before our dancing date. When she asked why, I told her

259

about Sasha. She'd read about it in the newspapers and was very concerned about my feelings.

"I just haven't slept in a couple of days," I said. "It's not that I'm aware of feeling upset, it's just that I find myself awake and tired."

"Call me day after tomorrow," Linda said. "I'm looking forward to our dancing and I'm sure it'll take you out of your mood."

I tried to be late for Ms. Thinnes but I was at her gallery door at 2:02. There were a few customers looking at photographs of lichen growing on boulders in different parts of the world. The formations were like maps of alien planets drawn up by astronomers or science fictionists.

"Mr. Carmel," Isabelle Thinnes said. "So nice of you to be on time. Martin, Martin."

A young white man came out of a doorway that must have led to an office or storeroom. He had glasses with thick lenses, and wild, black hair. The ill-fitting suit he wore was the slightest submission to formality. Anywhere but in an art gallery, he would have been seen as an unkempt Bohemian.

"Yes, Isabelle?"

"Will you look after the showroom for a while, dear? I have to do some business with Mr. Carmel."

He nodded with only the hint of a gaunt smile on his hirsute face.

There was a red door at the back of the gallery. This led to a narrow stair, also carpeted in red. The nineteen stairs led to a small office with a round desk the color of ivory, a red velvet love seat, and a hardwood chair. There were paintings and canvases stacked everywhere and a window with the shade pulled down.

The room was homey and more the flavor of Cape Cod than Midtown Manhattan.

Isabelle was wearing a close-fitting gray dress that came down to her ankles and clung to her slim figure. As I said before, she was handsome and had a nice shape. Her sixty-some years hadn't robbed her of all her beauty.

"Have a seat, Mr. Carmel," she said.

When I moved for the chair, she said, "No, on the sofa. You'll be more comfortable there."

I sat where she wanted me to. She took a folder from her desk and handed it to me.

While I went through the papers, she took a seat and watched me.

The folder held documents that were almost exactly the same as the boilerplate contracts that Linda Chou gave me. The cost for each photograph was what I asked for, and the donation to the Lucy Carmichael Foundation was paid for by the customer buying the piece.

I read through them four times and then looked up at the woman, whose eyes were still on me, and nodded.

"Looks good."

"I hold nothing back," she said, a haughty dignity in her mien. "When I want something, I go for it. It's been that way my entire life."

"Can I take these contracts to show to Lucy?"

"Certainly."

I replaced the contracts in the folder and smiled.

"This is a great little office," I said.

"This gallery belonged to my uncle," she said, and then, "Tell me something, Cordell."

"What's that?"

The blue of Isabelle Thinnes's eyes had a lot of gray in it. There was something almost preternatural about them.

261

"You," she said, and then paused, ". . . you aren't a political man, are you?"

At any other moment in my life, I would have felt that the gallery owner was testing me, that she was probing to see what I was made of. I do believe that I was being tested, but not by the woman sitting there before me. In my mind I was brought to that small office to answer for myself, to prove something to the world, to prove that I could speak for myself.

"No," I said. "Not in the least."

"And you're not really interested in art," she said, more as a statement of fact than a question.

"I don't know about that. I don't think you can be a human being and not be concerned with art."

For some reason, this made Isabelle smile.

"I mean, you're not like Martin downstairs," she said. "He went to art school and did a dissertation on Roy Lichtenstein. He lives and breathes for what he believes is transcendent creation."

"No," I said. "It's not that I don't believe in it; it's just that all that kinda thinking is beyond me."

Isabelle Thinnes crossed her left leg tightly over her right. She laced her elegant, aged fingers across the kneecap. Then she took in a deep breath through her nostrils, which flared sensually. It was almost as if she was inhaling me.

"Then how did you get here?" she asked.

I gave up on the $5,000 I'd paid Lucy Carmichael. It was worth it just to consider Isabelle's question. It didn't matter if I got the show. What mattered was that this woman was looking inside me, into my motives. She didn't know what it was that she beheld, and so she asked.

"I . . . I was . . . I don't know. I guess you could say that I got lost, and you and Lucy were people, places, that I stumbled into."

262

The smile on Isabelle's face became a grin.

"It's not that I don't care," I continued. "It's just that I'm not sure."

"Not sure about what?" she asked.

"I can hold a woman in my arms and be transported by her kisses," I said. "That's something I can be sure of. But Lucy's pictures are something that I don't know, not really. I want to know, and so here I am. It's like I'm putting a jigsaw puzzle together having no idea what it will be."

"Do you care about those children?" she asked. "About the art of her photographs?"

"I want to care."

Even after all the sex I'd had, I'd never been so naked. Isabelle seemed content just to sit there looking at me. I believed that she saw more than I could know.

"The photographs are excellent," she assured me, "and the intentions are noble and, more importantly, they're smart. But what about you, dear Cordell? Can anything you've done help you?"

"Maybe," I said. "I don't know."

I wanted to kiss Isabelle. If I had, I think she would have understood that it was because of the deep impact her questions had on me.

"I have to get back to the gallery," she said.

"Yeah. I should go too."

That night I slept for twelve hours. My dreams had nothing to do with the experiences of the past ten days. The images that came to me in sleep were of a carnival my father took me to when I was only five, somewhere near Walnut Creek, California. He wanted me to get on the rides and feed the animals, but I was only interested in the greasy cogs and gears beneath the great machines

263

and the horse dung that was everywhere. I liked the mud and the scuttling beetles that were almost the same color. There were bright red ants sifting through green, green patches of grass.

The cotton candy was nothing compared to the sky.

The elephants looked miserable. I saw them, then and in my dream, as sad kings that had been defeated by the treachery of little men who wanted the kings to suffer because they were jealous of their magnificence.

The next morning, I realized that my house was a mess. I wanted to clean but there was something else I had to do, something much more important.

I hunted up Sisypha's letter and brought out the red capsule she'd enclosed. I swallowed it without hesitation. Sisypha demanded trust; that was my only thought. I had to contemplate everything I'd experienced and that capsule was supposed to help me do it.

I don't know what I expected. Maybe I thought that the moment the chemicals reached my stomach, I would be imbued with omniscience. But nothing happened at first.

Half an hour later, I was still waiting for the drug to take effect. But the only thing I felt was hunger. Actually, I was ravenous. I didn't have anything to eat in my kitchen, but I didn't want to go out, because Sisypha had told me that I needed to concentrate while I was under the influence of her designer narcotic. But soon I couldn't wait. I went outside and down to Dino's diner, where I had last eaten with Sasha.

The same waitress seated me at the same booth I had shared with Sasha. The old couple that had been arguing about a cousin were in the booth that they occupied before; they were still arguing about something.

I ordered steak and eggs with a short stack of pancakes and hot chocolate and coffee too. Before the waitress went away, I asked her for orange juice, a large glass.

I sat there thinking about Sasha's death. She had been so angry about her mother so many years after. The anger and pain in her was worked out on her brother, it seemed, and now he had brought that rage back to her.

I wondered if I was doing something like that with my half-baked plan to kill Johnny Fry. If I had walked into the room and challenged them when I had first seen them, it would have been the right thing to do. Maybe we would have fought, but at least I wouldn't have scurried off like a scared schoolboy.

There was a right way of being, and I had missed it . . . but if I had stood up and faced them, I would never have walked past that video store; I would never have found Sisypha.

I loved Brenda Landfall and she loved me, I knew. She needed my clumsiness and inexperience, my desire to withhold. She wanted someone to recognize the mind behind her rampant sexuality. I needed someone to see my pain and not to turn away out of boredom.

"You were with him," the old man in the adjoining booth said to the woman. "I know that you and Paul Medri went to Hampton Bays together."

"That was almost sixty years ago, Roger," she said. "Why can't you let it go?"

"You went behind me," Roger said. "You and him made me into a fool."

"If you were a fool, you were before we went off. And anyway, I thought that you were having an affair with Cynda MacLeish."

"But I wasn't."

"But I thought you were."

"I hate you, Merle," Roger said. "I hate your guts."

I wondered how I could hear them so clearly, just like they were speaking into an amplifier.

My senses were somehow heightened. Or maybe it was a hallucination. Maybe Roger and Merle were figments of my imagination. Maybe they were there, speaking softly, and I was inventing their words of hatred.

Did I hate Jo? No. Did I hate Johnny Fry? At one time, yes, but no more. Their love, or whatever it was, was separate from me. I couldn't come between them. I had no desire to be him.

"Here you are," the waitress said, placing two plates, two cups, and a juice glass before me.

I ate greedily, rapaciously, devouring the food with such vigor and passionate abandon that people from other tables were glancing at me. One little girl was staring, rapt.

Was this like my brief stint on the small stage of the Wilding Club? Were they seeing something bestial? Was this my sexuality expressing itself in another form?

I gulped down the orange juice and then guzzled the water, crunching the ice cubes after it was gone.

My heart was pounding.

A man behind me asked a woman if she loved him, his voice sounding like mine and a million million million others like me.

The waitress walked up to my table and smiled lasciviously (or maybe it was me smiling like that).

"What's your name?" I asked the brown-skinned Hispanic girl.

"Nina," she said.

"You're beautiful, Nina."

She smiled and turned her head without taking her eyes off of me.

"I have a boyfriend," she said. It was merely a suggestion.

"And still you're beautiful," I replied. "You're the reason I and so many other men come to this little place. It's just so nice to see you and to see your smile."

"You're sweet," she said. "Do you want anything else?"

"Another stack of pancakes and a side of bacon."

"All that?"

"When a man is stripped of love, he turns to food, they say."

"Did your girlfriend break up with you?" she asked.

"No. Not yet. But the love disappeared and became something else. It got lost and turned into, into . . . I don't know."

I looked down at the table, and when I raised my head again, the waitress was gone. The old couple were still arguing, but I could no longer make out—or make up—their words.

It was wrong of me not to confront Joelle and John Fry, but in being wrong I found myself. Using that as the equation to figure out what I should do, I wondered again about killing John Fry. Maybe, even though I was no longer angry, I should shoot him anyway, kill him dead.

He had stolen my lover. He had her all week long when all I got was the weekends. He got the inner nectar when all I had was a few drops of water sprinkled on a dry rag.

If I killed him, shot him dead, then Joelle would feel the meaning of my aching. She would think that I had done it but she wouldn't be sure. There'd be no proof, no gun for them to find. And even if they found it, even if they put me on trial—so what? It would be the perfect statement. My assassin brother would be shocked by me. My addled mother would remember my name. And Johnny Fry, as he lay there dying, would regret every moment he fucked and buggered, pissed on and pimped, slapped and suffered Joelle Petty and her reckless love.

The pancakes and bacon were sitting in front of me. I hadn't even noticed Nina's presence. My cock was hard under the table. It felt like Brad's gun.

I had a hard-on for Johnny Fry. I wanted him to die even though I no longer hated him. The feeling now was one of lust. His blood was singing to me. He needed me to kill him; that was the only way he could be forgiven.

I ate again with gusto. Nina appeared three times to fill my water glass.

I almost told her about my stolen pistol and my rock-hard dick. But I kept my silence. I kept my silence, and it kept me safe.

It was only then that I realized that Sisypha's drug had taken hold. I was thinking in symbols and metaphors. I was concentrating on what was most important to me. This was her thinking drug at work.

As I was walking out of the door, Nina the waitress ran up to me.

"Excuse me," she said.

"Uh-huh?" I turned to look at her, realizing that my eyes had been become intrusive; my mind was in overdrive and I must have looked insane.

"You didn't pay," she told me.

"Oh?" I said trying to look away. "How much do I owe?"

"Twenty-six dollars and forty-one cents."

I handed her two twenties and said, "Keep the change."

"That's too much."

"It's not nearly enough," I told her, approximating sobriety with my tone if not my words. "Not for someone like you."

"Are you okay?" she asked.

I saw in her face real concern for me. I reached out and touched her cheek, noting that she didn't pull away.

"I'm fine," I told her. "Wonderful."

★　　★　　★

268

Back in my apartment, I took out the junkie's gun and put it on the kitchen table in front of me. I opened the box of ammunition, pouring the cartridges across the surface, then I honed my mind in on Johnny Fry.

I thought about him being a white man making my girlfriend his plaything. I wondered if that mattered at all. I hadn't thought much about it before. But now I tried to come to some kind of understanding. Was I the victim of some kind of racism? Did Johnny Fry get off on the fact that he could take a black man's woman and make her cry out his name and to profess passion for him that she felt for no other man?

The idea seemed silly.

Did he deserve to die? Oh yes, he definitely did. And I was the one who should kill him.

Could I do it? Yes again. His blood would bring out hilarity in me. I'd laugh all the way to the graveyard and then I'd climb up and dance on his tomb.

With the gun in my pocket, I took a cab up to the Westside, where I walked some blocks to Jo's apartment building. I stopped at every trash can along the way, making a small deposit in each as I went.

"Go right up, Mr. Carmel," Robert the doorman said when I walked into Jo's building.

The drug had worn off, mostly. I had no thoughts except one as I rode up in the elevator. It seemed to me that the exhibitionist side of Jo's relationship with Johnny Fry would have them fucking in that lift while Robert or any of the other doormen watched. He would hike up her dress and press her against the wall, stick his long thing up in there, while she writhed and moaned, pretending to be shy, pretending not to want it. From the console at the front desk the doormen could turn on the sound so they could hear her begging for more cock while he asked her who was her man?

She answered the front door in the nude. She was naked but not sexual. I thought at the time that she was trying to tell me she would be as honest as she possibly could. That was Sisypha's thinking drug making a slight return.

I kissed her gently, expecting nothing in return, but she surprised me, not for the first time, by returning my kiss with a tender embrace that felt both feathery and strong.

"Come on in, L," she said. "We have three hours."

"Why only three hours?" I asked, though I wondered what we would do with all that time.

"Johnny is coming over after you leave," she told me, looking into my gaze with a crazy kind of certainty. "He's waiting down the street for us to finish. I called him while you were coming up the elevator. He's going to take me in the bathtub and urinate all over me, then fuck me, then sodomize me, and after that, I'll do things to him."

"Why have me come here at all?" I asked. "He seems to be the one that you need."

"I've told you what I will do with him," she said in a monotone. "And I've told him what I plan to show you. He went crazy with jealousy when I laid it out. He cried and said that he wouldn't let it happen, but he needs it as much as I do." Toward the end of this little speech, she was sneering.

"And what do you plan to do with me?" I asked.

"Come in the living room and take off your clothes," she answered.

I did as she said. I didn't feel shy standing there nude in her living room. My penis was completely flaccid. The one thing I was sure was that Joelle and I would never have sex again.

Jo looked down at me and smiled.

"Does my honesty turn you off, L?"

"We've both been through a lot, honey," I said. "And I think we both know that this is over."

"Only if you want it to be," she said.

"What does that mean?" I asked. "You have your lover waiting down the street."

"He's fucked me Monday through Friday for six months and we've still been together," she said.

It was amazing to me that she seemed and sounded like the same woman I had known for years, even though she was saying things I would never imagine coming from her mouth.

"Is that what you want?" I asked.

"Sometimes he'd stay with me until just before you arrived," she replied. "Sometimes, when I'd go for a Sunday run, he'd fuck me in the park while you waited up here."

"I don't get it, Jo. Are you trying to hurt me?"

"Don't you ever get tired of lying, L?" she replied. "Don't you ever want to throw off all the shit you put out twenty-four hours a day?"

I smiled and sat down on the sofa.

"It's funny?" she asked.

"No, not funny, Jo. It's just that you have things to say that you've done. Your uncle. Johnny Fry. The guy with the ties. All I have is the fact that I wasn't raised in San Francisco but in Oakland. It's a lie that doesn't mean anything to anyone but me."

"I have videos of me and Johnny," she said.

That made me think of Sisypha, and the thought of my new sister made me smile.

"He got me talking about you while he fucked my ass," she said.

"I don't want to see your pictures, Jo. They won't do anything for me."

"I got something that will," she said with a sly smile on her lips.

"I'm not taking any pills or anything."

"Bring your heels up on the cushion," she said.

I didn't see any reason to argue. My life with Jo was over. I knew that this would be the last time we got together. I knew that I would be leaving her to Johnny Fry in less than three hours.

She sat down below me and sucked my balls in her mouth. She ran her tongue around them and moaned so that I could feel the vibrations in my sex.

I remember that the feeling was pleasurable, but it didn't excite me at all.

"You have great big balls, L," she said. "I love them. I always have. I used to want to suck on them, but we didn't have that kind of relationship. You were pretty straightforward until you saw me and Johnny."

I almost said something but decided against it.

"Does that feel good?" she asked.

"Yeah," I said noncommittally.

"That night I met Johnny at Brad Mettleman's party, he whispered in my ear that he wanted me to suck his balls," she said. "That's exactly what he said. I thought it was just to shock me, so I told him to come to my place. I said that I'd send you home and suck his balls afterward. I was sure he wouldn't come. But he did. I told him to take his balls out, thinking that that would shut him up. But he took out that great long cock of his and held out those balls like golden apples for me."

The whole time Jo was talking, she was also nuzzling my testicles with her nose, taking them into her mouth now and again and humming low so that I felt it.

"I sucked them really hard, and he told me to do it harder. That's when he had me. That's when I knew that he was going to master me. I just kept on sucking until he said he was going to come. He made me keep on until he came all over my art books and my couch. I laid back on the floor, and he stroked his dick, dripping the last drops on my face."

I could hear the passion in her words and her breathing. I looked at her, and she smiled.

"I didn't let him know how much he had me, though," she said. "I told him that he thought he was so tough. He didn't know what tough was, I said. I went into the closet and took out a belt that my uncle used to make me carry whenever I came to his house. When he wanted to punish me, he'd ask for the belt, and I had to have it, or my family would go for a week without money.

"Johnny laid me across the top of the couch and hit me in ways that even Uncle Rex hadn't known. I begged him to stop, but I didn't mean it, and he didn't stop. He kept on whipping until I was a heap in the corner.

"Then he fucked me and I fucked him. He stayed with me that whole first week."

I didn't want to allow myself to be excited by her story but there was something about the intimacy that I had never known with Jo before. It was one thing to feel close in a friendly way, to be in love. But what she was telling was what should never be said between lovers. She was opening up her insides to me. I could see her beating heart, her blood and skin and bones.

I remembered that she'd claimed to be sick for two weeks after the party. I'd come to her place once, but she stopped me at the door, saying that even the slightest noise set off her migraine.

I thought of him chasing her through the house, flicking that ancient strap and making her scream.

I moaned out loud like a beached walrus.

Despite my resolve, my cock had raised to half-mast.

"Do you feel what I'm telling you, L?" Jo asked.

I groaned again and tried to pull away. It was wrong for me to feel so good about being cuckolded like that. I tried to get away, but she gripped my balls and said, "Stay still, L. You wanted to know and I'm gonna show you."

She wrapped something around my scrotum, above the testicles. It wasn't very tight but cinched close enough that it wouldn't fall off, either.

"Slip down a little bit, baby," she cooed. She was another woman. I was another man.

I scooted down, and she pressed something small into my rectum, something that had a string coming from it.

"I want you to feel how I feel, what I crave," she said. "Not little schoolgirl kisses but knotted up intestines and screams in the darkness."

She took my cock into her mouth and groaned a feral note.

I felt fever overtake me and then shivering cold.

"Sometimes when you'd call me to say good night," she said. "Johnny would come up behind me and shove his cock in while I was talking. You'd be telling me about some translation detail, and I'd be saying about some fabric ad campaign, and Johnny would be driving that dick all the way in and grinding at me. Sometimes I'd ask you to hold on and I'd put the phone on hold and holler and come. Sometimes I'd lick the come off his dick while you read me some paragraph or sentence in French."

I didn't want to, but I began to rock back and forth into her mouth. She screwed up her face while taking me down her throat. Then she'd lean back with a long slick of saliva dripping from her lips.

"I never told him no about anything and I made him degrade me and punish me for all the years I stayed quiet."

274

"Johnny," I called.

He stopped and recognized me. I waved him over, and he came.

"Hello, Cordell," he said. "How are you?"

"I feel like a rat that just swam across a river," I said. "Alive but weak and not sure why I did it."

Johnny sat down next to me.

"She needs me, Cordell," he said.

A spasm went through my spine and I shifted on the stone bench.

"Yeah," I said. "She needs something."

"You're a good guy, Cordell, but Joelle has a really dark side. I don't know what you guys were doing up there, but you haven't seen the half of it. She's a demon on wheels. You're lucky you got somebody like me to take her off your hands."

"So you say," I said. "So you say."

"Are you telling me that you want her when you know everything about us?" he said. "You know, sometimes I was with her from Sunday night to Saturday morning. If you guys had children, they'd all be mine."

"That has nothing to do with me, Mr. Fry." I was enjoying his attempt to turn me from Jo. He was at the disadvantage, and that was fine by me.

"What do you mean?" he asked. "Do you still plan to try and be with her?"

"I have no plans, John. She told me that she was gonna show me something and then you were gonna piss on her and fuck her in the ass."

"You have no right to talk about her like that," he sputtered. "No right. She's got something beautiful in her. She's becoming something wonderful. You have no right to talk about her like that."

"But you have the right to fuck her while she's talking to me on the phone. You have the right to come on her lips while I'm going on like a fool in French or Spanish."

"You don't understand how we feel," he said.

I took out the pistol, holding it in the flat of my hand.

Johnny froze when he realized what I was holding.

"I understand," I said. "I understand what you think. I got this gun to shoot you with. I took it from Brad Mettleman, thinking that you should die because you made me inconsequential . . ."

Johnny grabbed the pistol and pointed it at me.

He jumped to his feet and cried, "You stupid motherfucker! You don't know what it means. I should shoot your fuckin' ass right here in the street. You stupid asshole. You dumb fuck. You don't have any idea what it f-f-feels like to be with her—the real her. You don't know what she is. She's like the sun. She's, she's, she's . . ."

I put my hands up. I wanted to smile, but the depth of Johnny's feelings actually touched me. He was in love even if Jo was not. He was lost in the web of her uncle's abuse more than she was.

"I threw away the bullets, John," I said.

"What?"

"All along the way I threw them into trash cans. I knew I couldn't kill you. I knew I could never have her back."

"Halt!" someone shouted.

Johnny turned quickly and the pointed pistol turned with him. We saw the policemen at the same moment. They opened fire, hitting Johnny Fry seventeen times.

Holland Dollar met me at the police station that evening. They were only questioning me this time.

I told the police most of the truth: that my girlfriend called me over to tell me that she was going to have an open relationship with Fry;

278

that I waited for Johnny to tell him that I knew everything and that I was unhappy about their cheating; that he pulled a gun on me and threatened me but that I didn't think he intended to shoot.

It was mostly true. Mostly.

For some days after that, I sat in my third-floor apartment wondering if I had killed Johnny Fry. I examined my motives and my heart. I can't say that I didn't hate the man—the lessons he taught me were not anything I ever wanted to know. He humiliated me and laughed at my impotence, but in the end I had not planned to take his life.

My pistol was empty, and I didn't expect him to be at Jo's. If she had come out of that bedroom, I was going to give her the pistol as a symbol of how deep my feelings for her ran.

And in the street I didn't expect the police to come or, for that matter, Johnny to grab the gun from my open palm.

I had no idea that he feared my influence on Jo.

In a court of law or just the judgment of common sense, I would be found innocent of having committed any crime.

But there was one moment that I could not explain away. When the first shot hit John Fry, he let out a little grunt of surprise and maybe pain. In that brief instant I felt a moment of satisfaction and hope. There was something inside me that rejoiced at his impending demise. I hadn't called the cops, but neither did I yell out for them to stop. It would have made no difference if I had tried to save Johnny, but the fact that I didn't try meant, in a way, that I *leaned toward* killing him.

Seeing his death in this light, I am guilty for remaining quiet when I could have spoken up. He would have died anyway, I'm sure, but that doesn't exonerate my inaction.

★   ★   ★

279

I haven't spoken to Joelle again. Maybe she hates me, maybe not. She's called, but I never listen to the messages. I erase them as soon as I hear her voice.

I talk to Cynthia about once a week, and Sisypha has been to see me three times in as many months. She really wants to be my sister. And even through all the guilt I'm feeling, she fills me with happiness.

I have been seeing various women—sexually. Linda and Monica, Lucy and Nina too. Lucy's show was a big success. Her foundation made more than $300,000 and funded a home for African children who have been orphaned by endless wars and AIDS.

Monica's daughter, Mozelle, has been accepted to the Lycée Français.

I know that I haven't been a good person in all of this. I have done most things wrong and come out okay anyway. But I try to tell myself that there's always time for redemption and that sometimes even the worst decisions turn out to be just fine.